D1071437

MURDER BY DEFINITION

Also by Con Lehane

Bartender Brian McNulty mysteries

BEWARE THE SOLITARY DRINKER
WHAT GOES AROUND COMES AROUND
DEATH AT THE OLD HOTEL

42nd Street Library mysteries

MURDER AT THE 42ND STREET LIBRARY
MURDER IN THE MANUSCRIPT ROOM
MURDER OFF THE PAGE
MURDER BY DEFINITION *

** available from Severn House*

MURDER BY DEFINITION

Con Lehane

SEVERN
HOUSE

First world edition published in Great Britain and the USA in 2022
by Severn House, an imprint of Canongate Books Ltd,
14 High Street, Edinburgh EH1 1TE.

Trade paperback edition first published in Great Britain and the USA in 2023
by Severn House, an imprint of Canongate Books Ltd.

severnhouse.com

British Library Cataloguing-in-Publication Data
A CIP catalogue record for this title is available from the British Library.

ISBN-13: 978-0-7278-5089-8 (cased)
ISBN-13: 978-1-4483-0815-6 (trade paper)
ISBN-13: 978-1-4483-0814-9 (e-book)

All Severn House titles are printed on acid-free paper.

Typeset by Palimpsest Book Production Ltd.,
Falkirk, Stirlingshire, Scotland.
Printed and bound in Great Britain by
TJ Books, Padstow, Cornwall.

For Dan and Gail Collins

ACKNOWLEDGMENTS

I'd like to first of all thank Severn House – and especially its former publisher Kate Lyall Grant – for continuing the 42nd Street Library mystery series after it was discontinued by its original publisher. I'd also like to thank my pals Ellen Crosby and Jeff Cohen (E.J. Copperman), themselves accomplished mystery writers, for helping me get on board at Severn House.

In addition, I'd like to thank my editor, Rachel Slatter, for her keen insights, helpful suggestions, and encouragement in making *Murder by Definition* a better book when it was finished than when it first got to her. I'd also like to thank Joanne Grant, Severn House's publisher; Piers Tilbury, art director, for the book's stunning cover design; and editorial staff Sara Porter and Mary Karayel for overseeing the careful copy-editing and proofreading.

A special thank you to Marcia Markland, my editor for a number of years at St. Martin's Minotaur, for suggesting some years ago that I take a shot at writing a 42nd Street Library mystery series. My agent since my very first book, Alice Martell, has been unfailingly supportive, amazingly responsive, and always encouraging even during the lean times. Also a shout-out to my friend of more than a half-century, a long-time actor and an early reader of just about everything I've ever written, Carlos Spaulding, for providing the book's title, when I was totally stumped, and to my son Jim, a nurse, for answering my questions about hospitals.

It goes without saying that I, as well as all writers, am indebted to the librarians of the world. But I'll say it anyway because librarians are under attack from too many directions in too many places, specifically this time because of their resistance to attempts by political groups of varying persuasions to ban books whose ideas they find objectionable, and in some cases to silence authors whose personal actions they find repugnant.

Recently, attacks on librarians – not only libraries as institutions but librarians as persons – have proliferated as highly politicized movements opposed to ways of thinking that aren't theirs have sought to pull books from the shelves of libraries, primarily school libraries but in some places public libraries as well. In the process they have threatened with physical harm, loss of livelihood, and public slander, hard-working and dedicated public servants who are simply doing their jobs of providing information to their communities, a service essential to the functioning of a democracy.

In the past in my acknowledgments, I've pointed to the importance of libraries and librarians as founts of knowledge and protectors of liberty. I've also noted the importance to me personally of librarians in schools, colleges, and public libraries (especially the wonderful folks at New York City's 42nd Street Library) who've helped me in so many ways over the years. I'd like to reaffirm my appreciation for and support of all libraries and librarians, and remind everyone of their support of us.

The American Library Association's 'Freedom to Read' statement includes the following tenets: to make available the widest diversity of views and expressions, including those that are unorthodox, unpopular, or considered dangerous by the majority; to contest encroachments upon the freedom to read by individuals or groups seeking to impose their own standards or tastes upon the community at large, and by the government whenever it seeks to reduce or deny public access to public information; and to give full meaning to the 'freedom to read' by providing books that enrich the quality and diversity of thought and expression, demonstrating that the answer to a "bad" book is a good one, and the answer to a "bad" idea is a good one . . .

www.ala.org/advocacy/intfreedom/freedomreadstatement

AUTHOR'S NOTE

The story you are about to read is not true. I made it up. It's not based on actual happenings or actual people. It's not meant to be a portrait of the 42nd Street Library – The New York Public Library Stephen A. Schwarzman Building that houses the library's humanities and social science collections. For one thing, you'll look in vain for a crime fiction collection reading room, or a crime fiction collection for that matter. The story is not meant to be an accurate portrayal of the New York City Police Department or of New York City police officers. The police department and the police officers in this book are fictitious; their only job is to carry out the plot I made up.

Women's Action Against Misogyny, as far as I know, doesn't exist. Nor does The Library Tavern or its bartender. The Wittliff Southwestern Writers Collection at the Albert B. Alkek Library at Texas State University in San Marcos does exist and has a remarkable collection that includes the papers of James Crumely and Rick DeMarinis, to name only two of its authors. But it does not contain the papers of Will Ford because Will Ford does not exist.

A few settings – the Oyster Bar in Grand Central Terminal, Bellevue Hospital, Corlears Hook Park, and others – are actual places in New York City but they're used fictitiously. New York City, of course, exists. But I've rearranged it at will to suit the purposes of the story. That's what this is . . . a story. I hope you enjoy it.

‘I have always imagined that Paradise will be a kind of Library.’

Jorge Luis Borges

PROLOGUE

The man on the other end of the phone spoke with a Southwestern drawl. He wouldn't tell Raymond Ambler his name, instead he asked hypothetical questions about the 42nd Street Library's interest in purchasing the papers of an unnamed crime fiction writer who'd published a half-dozen or so hard-boiled, private-eye books set mostly in the Southwest and the Mountain States – but also a series of three books set in New York. The author had never been a bestseller, the man on the phone said, but his books had won critical acclaim and had influenced a generation of crime fiction writers.

Ambler caught on pretty quickly that he was speaking to the writer himself. As the man bounced between an obsequious friendliness and a truculent argumentativeness, Ambler got the impression he'd been drinking – quite a bit, three sheets to the wind, you might say.

'You guys paid a pretty penny for that hack Nelson Yates; didn't you? You ought to pay more for someone who can actually write.'

Ambler didn't take the bait.

'If you think Yates is a good writer, you don't know who the good writers are.'

'Try me.'

'You tell me.'

Ambler rattled off a couple of names, including Nelson Yates, and paused for a moment. 'Will Ford is another, one of the best hard-boiled writers of his time.'

A long silence at the other end of the phone. 'He's that and more, son . . . but you got pretty good tastes for a Yankee.'

'I guess—'

'Let's talk money.'

'It's not as simple as that—'

Ambler was cut off again. 'Son, it's always simple and it's always the money.'

The smug response was irritating but Ambler was intrigued so he let it go. 'To get anywhere I need to know who we're talking about.'

'I want a hundred grand.'

'I'd like to know to whom I'm speaking.'

'So a hundred grand isn't out of the question?' His eagerness was that of a boy waiting to open a birthday present. 'You know who I am.'

'Not out of the question, Mr Ford, if we had the money.' Ambler wasn't sure he could get approval for the collection if Ford gifted his papers to the library's crime fiction collection, but he didn't say this. Instead, he said the library was interested. He'd need Ford to send a general description of the collection. Once he had that he'd look for funding.

'I thought the library had money.' His tone was petulant. 'You paid for Yates.'

'A donor provided the funding. We don't have an endowment for crime fiction.'

Ford struck Ambler as someone who took counsel only with himself, so it was a waste of time explaining how the library acquired collections. Funding was always difficult. Convincing Special Collections that Ford was worth collecting would be difficult also. He wasn't well known outside of the mystery world and too much of what was known about him was scandalous.

The 42nd Library's directors already looked on the crime fiction collection in the way a prosperous family looks down on its poor relatives. Ford's sordid reputation would make things worse. He'd been married four or five times, fired from more than one university post for lewd behavior; he'd fought his way through notorious barroom brawls, and had been 'thrown into the slammer' more times than he could remember. The project might be more trouble than it was worth. But Will Ford was an important mystery writer; Ambler knew that for sure.

After the phone call, he went to find his friend Adele Morgan at the information desk in the main reading room. He didn't want to talk to Harry, his boss, until he had a convincing argument for acquiring the papers of a disgraced writer who hadn't published anything in a decade.

'Why would you want to?' Adele asked when he told her what he wanted to do. 'A drunk, a drug-abuser, a womanizer, a misogynist, a deadbeat. Who knows what else? Good Lord, Raymond.' She gave him a look you might give to someone kicking a dog and went back to the information desk.

Ford sent the materials Ambler had asked for sooner than he expected, so over the next couple of weeks as the New York City winter worked its way slowly and soggily into spring, he put together a portfolio of Ford's reviews and awards, including testimonials from a half-dozen well-known writers who considered Ford an important influence.

The collection Ford offered were his papers from the mid-1980s through the early 1990s when he lived in New York and published three books and some short stories set in the city featuring a ne'er-do-well private eye named Francisco 'Cisco' Garcia. Garcia had left Texas a disgraced cop and set up shop in the city, working the shady side of the law. The first novel in the series won an Edgar Award from the Mystery Writers of America.

With an assist from an unlikely ally – Lisa Young, a member of the library's board of trustees and his grandson's maternal grandmother – he raised enough funding to satisfy Ford and, despite the misgivings of the Manuscript and Archives director Harry Larkin, the 42nd Street Library's crime fiction collection acquired the Will Ford papers (1986–1991, five boxes). The rest of his papers Ford had donated to Texas State University.

ONE

Ambler finished reading the short story 'The Unrepentant Killer' for the second time, more troubled than he'd been the first time he'd read it. It was vintage Ford – sadistic cruelty, graphic violence, borderline depravity, ending with a bloodbath, the victims a street thug who ran a gaming room in the basement apartment of a brownstone and his mistress who ran a brothel upstairs – the kind of folks the city forgets a couple of days after their deaths.

The killer, a corrupt plainclothes cop, walked away from the murders – after a standoff with Cisco Garcia – in the company of a beautiful young prostitute Cisco was in love with.

A note at the bottom of the last page of the manuscript, written in the same cramped handwriting as Ford's editorial notes in the margins, read, 'Dear Reader: The story you just read is based on an actual incident. I've changed a few names and details to protect the innocent . . . and the guilty . . . but the story you read is no more fictional than the newspaper accounts of the actual murders.'

The story had never been published. Ambler found that curious, more so when he came across a letter from Ford to the publisher of a small avant-garde press that was publishing a collection of his stories. The tone of the letter was apologetic. Ford asked that 'The Unrepentant Killer' be pulled before publication. 'The story, which I like very much, is too close to the truth despite the changes I made,' he wrote, 'and because of this might cause irreparable harm – like getting me killed. I think it best I tuck it away for a while until the coast is clear.'

Intrigued by the author's note and the letter to the publisher, Ambler spent a couple of hours in the library's periodicals reading room going through back issues of the city's papers. Ford's short story took place in the winter of 1990 in what was then a crime-ridden and drug-infested neighborhood on the city's Upper West Side. He'd thought it would be easy to find the murders Ford's story was based on. But 1990 was the middle of the crack-cocaine era when the city averaged six murders a day. It was also a banner year for corrupt cops, as the city found out a few years later from the Mollen Commission.

Ambler had stayed away from murder investigations for going on two years and wasn't interested in a new one. But when he found the news stories on the killing of a hero undercover cop in a shoot-out on Manhattan Avenue in the winter of 1990, he was pretty sure he'd found the incident Ford's story was based on. He printed out copies of the stories and called his friend Mike Cosgrove, a veteran NYPD homicide detective, and invited him for a drink at the Oyster Bar after work that evening.

A couple of hours later, they shared a platter of oysters and a bottle of Sancerre while the detective read Will Ford's story. Ambler could tell by Mike's expression as he read that he didn't think much of it.

'So?' Mike dropped the manuscript on the small table in front of them. 'Sex and drugs, blood and guts, dishonor and betrayal, murder and mayhem, life in Fun City in the good old days. Back then, they had a poster on the bulletin board in the seven-five that said, "Give us twenty-two minutes and we'll give you a homicide." He contemplated an oyster for a moment before meeting Ambler's gaze. 'I don't even try to tell new guys what it was like . . . Why bring this shit up now? Bad enough to go through it the first time.'

Ambler handed him the news stories he'd made copies of. The actual events differed from Ford's fictional portrayal in significant ways. But two of the victims, a brothel madam and a street thug who ran a craps table and a blackjack game, were the same as in Ford's story. What was different was the cop and the prostitute left standing in Ford's story were killed in the actual incident and the cop in the news stories was a hero not a crook.

'Did you read the author's note at the bottom of the last page of the story?'

'It's a story. Writers find something in a newspaper and use it as a starting point. They make up the rest. You told me that.'

'Not with a note that the story is true.'

Mike's eyebrows spiked and stayed spiked. 'You're fucking with me, right? The story in the newspaper is fiction?' He snorted.

Ambler took a breath. Mike might have a thousand gripes about the police department and once in a while might complain to Ambler. But any criticism from the outside, he circled the wagons. Ambler treaded softly. 'Did everyone die at the scene? Was anyone charged with any of those murders?'

Mike stiffened. He threw a shell onto the tray. His face reddened. His cheeks bulged. Whatever he said next would bounce off the Oyster Bar's terracotta-tiled walls and probably crack a couple of the tiny light bulbs in the ceiling. Like most cops, Mike believed his job was misunderstood by citizens and maligned by the press. 'This guy's story says a dirty cop killed a couple of people – in cold blood. The newspapers say the cop died a hero in a shoot-out. If we believe the writer's note, neither is the truth. Writers like him make cops look bad; it sells books.'

'Take it easy,' Ambler said. 'I'm asking; that's all.'

Mike wasn't going to take it easy. 'We got hundreds, maybe thousands, of homicides from those days still open. I can look up the case. But why should I? No matter what I find, it won't tell you anything. Ask the writer to tell you about any murderers he thinks we missed.'

'We'll get a chance,' Ambler said. 'He'll be in town in a couple of weeks when we open his collection to the public.'

Mike's glare at the few remaining oysters probably cooked them. He grabbed his wineglass with both hands like he would choke it instead of choking Ambler. 'You ruined a nice after-work snack; fresh oysters . . . a good wine. Now I got indigestion. You wanna talk about some wild-assed story, next time do it over a cup of coffee at a greasy spoon.' He glowered for a moment longer.

The next morning, Harry Larkin knocked on the doorframe of the crime fiction reading room. The door was open, and

Ambler warily watched him walk in. A visit from Harry never boded well. And trouble it was. A reporter from *The Herald* had asked the library president for a comment about the women's groups who were up in arms about the library honoring Will Ford.

'They're going to picket the opening ceremony,' Harry said. 'Arthur was apoplectic. He's never heard of Will Ford and didn't know we'd acquired his papers. He doesn't know why the hell we ever created a crime fiction collection to begin with and wanted to know if you still worked here. He said the newspaper stories about you and that other murder gave the library a black eye.'

'I didn't ask them to do the story.' Ambler didn't like that he sounded defensive. 'The reporter asked me questions, so I answered them. She didn't tell me the story would be about me.'

'I think she's the one who called the president.'

Ambler knew what was coming. 'Don't even ask. We're not going to drop the Ford collection or cancel the event. We can't let protestors bully the library.'

Harry spoke softly. 'Mistreatment of women is on everybody's minds these days.' He hated controversy. He wanted everything about the library and especially everything about Manuscripts and Archives to be beyond reproach. He devoted himself to smoothing feathers.

For his part, Ambler didn't like crowd-think and had no problem with controversy. 'So now we're only going to take collections from writers on the approved list?'

'The library has a reputation, Ray. There's the board of trustees. The donors.'

'If we give into bullying, we might as well appoint a library censor.'

'All well and good.' Harry's voice rose. 'Tell Arthur and the board of trustees we don't care about the library's reputation.' His voice softened. 'Before you do that, you can call Doris Wellington. Arthur gave me her number.'

'Who?'

'She's the president of Women's Action Against Misogyny.'

* * *

Adele sat in the corner of Ambler's couch, her legs folded beneath her, a glass of white wine on the end table beside her, the manuscript she'd finished reading in her lap. 'It does stop you in your tracks, doesn't it? You'd rather not know people do such depraved and cruel things. But they do. So, OK, it's a powerful story, although I could have done without the grisly details. Not a lot of people want to read about folks who're rotten to the core. I'm not surprised it wasn't published.'

Ambler, sitting in his armchair in the corner of his small living room, sipping a glass of wine, had watched her face while she read the story. She was so sensitive and her face so expressive, he could tell which part of the story she was reading by the way her face changed. 'He didn't want it published; he pulled the story from a collection.'

Adele unfolded her legs and repositioned herself on the couch. When he glanced up from watching her cross her pretty legs, she smiled, so he realized she'd watched him watching her. 'I don't like censorship any more than you do. And I'll admit Will Ford's work is not "without redeeming social value". Still, only a sick mind could come up with that sleazy character who's supposed to be the hero and how he treats women.' She eyed Ambler. He didn't know if it was a rebuke or a warning. 'You're going to have a tough time convincing that women's group his work has any value.'

Ambler liked to look at Adele – sometimes he'd watch her from the next room when she was in her kitchen making a sandwich for his grandson, or from a distance at the library when she was helping a patron at the information desk. Or like now, he watched her and wondered if she knew what he was thinking. She did sometimes read his mind.

They'd known each other since she first came to work at the library not so many years before. Young women, even young pretty women as Adele was, had come and gone over the years he'd been at the library without him paying any of them much mind. Adele was different. She fascinated him – and this was the unfathomable part – she'd latched on to him from almost the first moment they met, as if she'd been sent by destiny to be part of his life.

From the beginning, even as a probationary employee, she

risked her own good standing with the library management to defend him against the not infrequent fallout from his proclivity to take on quixotic battles for truth and justice that most other folks were willing to let slide.

Later, when Johnny came into his life, Adele took his grandson under her wing, too. The boy quickly grew to love her . . . and Ambler came to understand that he loved her, too – was in love with her, couldn't stop thinking of her in ways you didn't think about just a friend.

He'd fought against the attraction that in her mercurial way Adele both encouraged and fought against, too. There were the times she did come into his arms; there were the very few times they'd kissed – passionately – and came within a breath of going beyond but had stopped and the moments had passed. They were like young lovers, filled with passion, but afraid to let go, not sure – except that she was young and he was not.

Having once more read his mind – he hoped not all of it – she interrupted his reverie. 'You want me to go with you when you talk to Doris Wellington,' she said. 'I doubt it will do any good, but OK. I'll read up on the group – WAAM – and perhaps wear my combat boots.'

He looked at her curiously. 'You're joking?'

She laughed. 'I'm joking.'

They met Ms Wellington in the basement apartment of a brownstone on 94th Street a half-block east of Broadway that had been made into an office. She sat at an old-fashioned wooden desk in the front room. The place was austere, as was she. A dozen or more posters from women's marches over the years bedecked the walls – some of them from back in the '70s – along with photographs of groups of women demanding equal pay or equal rights or for the government to keep its hands off their bodies.

Adele hadn't worn combat boots but she did dress in jeans and a parka and wore running shoes, which was along the lines of the attire of the few other women in the office including Ms Wellington, whose feet remained under her desk, so there was no telling if she wore boots.

They exchanged introductions, the air around them crackling

with tension as if the cramped office knew they would disagree. Which was what they did. Ambler told Ms Wellington that the crime fiction collection was an insignificant part of the library's overall collection. He could rarely acquire bestselling or popular authors because other libraries with large endowments would outbid him. 'Not every author sees the advantage in being included in a collection dedicated exclusively to crime fiction writing.'

'You managed to find quite a collection of he-man writers,' Ms Wellington – call me Doris – said in a tone that left little room for disagreement. Otherwise, when she spoke, she came across as more bemused than severe, as he'd expected her to be. She wore her long brown hair, going grey in places, in a tightly wound braid that pulled her face taut and her eyelids back from her eyes which gave her the severe look.

'That's who wrote most crime fiction for a long time,' Adele said. 'Raymond has an advisory panel to help him increase writers from underrepresented groups in the collection—'

Doris interrupted her. She had a point – that she was prepared to drive home with a hammer. In truth even to Ambler, Adele sounded like an apologist for him. 'Who was the last woman author you added to your collection?'

Ambler named a couple of recent acquisitions, including one that had led to a murder investigation and the newspaper article the library president had complained about.

Ms Wellington wasn't impressed and moved on to Will Ford. 'Did you know his reputation when you decided to honor him?'

Ambler fought back the urge to tell her she was wrong and being unfair; he tried to be placating instead. 'We're not honoring him. We thought his work was important enough that scholars would want access to his papers . . . It might be a scholar who would write a critique of his work that told the truth about him – including his horrible treatment of women in his work and in his life.'

Placating Doris Wellington was like trying to calm a junkyard dog. They went round and round for another half-hour. In the end, she was less hostile to Ambler and downright friendly with Adele. But she hadn't changed her mind about Will Ford.

'We're asking women whom he's abused to speak publicly. If they do, we'll publicize the allegations. I believe in free speech. I admire that the library stands up for the right of those they disagree with to be heard. I also think too much crime fiction by men makes light of violence against women.'

Doris Wellington had done her homework in tracking down women who'd accused Ford of abusing them. She showed Ambler and Adele a clipping from the *Daily News* from around the time of the murders Ford's short story was based on.

The *News* story was about a domestic dispute that spilled over into the halls of ivy, specifically a hallway in a classroom building at Columbia University, where Will Ford was spending a semester as a visiting professor in the creative writing program. A woman – a spurned lover, according to the *News* – attacked Ford and stabbed him as he was leaving his night-time fiction-writing workshop.

The wound was superficial. Ford was treated at a nearby hospital and released. The woman was arrested – but not prosecuted because Ford didn't press charges. Despite his magnanimity, the woman, Tiffany Belle Smith, told the *News* he was a two-timing, abusive weasel and she wished she'd cut his heart out.

No doubt if Ms Smith was the type to hold a grudge – which indications were she was – she'd be a prime candidate to pillory Ford at the rally WAAM was planning. For Ford's sake – and somewhat for his own sake – Ambler hoped Doris Wellington wouldn't find the woman.

Three days later, imaginary hat in hand, Ambler met with the library president, Arthur Ledyard, Lisa Young, the chairman of the library's board of trustees, and Harry. True to her word, Doris Wellington and WAAM held a press conference on the library steps at which two haggard, middle-aged women, both of whom gave the impression they suffered from depression, read prepared statements in which they charged Will Ford with sexual assault.

Ambler had been moved as he listened to the women speak. Their anger came through clearly enough, but with it an under-tone of bewilderment as well, as if they'd been swindled;

someone supposed to be on their side hadn't been. They weren't only angry; they were disappointed; they'd been taken advantage of. Ambler understood their feeling of betrayal better than he'd thought he would, so it was fine with him if they dragged Ford's name through the mud. He deserved that and more.

'Has anybody read anything this man has written?' Arthur Ledyard looked at Ambler.

Ambler of course had read Ford and he'd given Lisa Young two of his books which she had read. Harry admitted he'd read one book by Ford and found it well written and surprisingly compassionate, despite its graphic violence.

Ambler began naming the critics who'd praised Ford's work and the writers who'd been influenced by him, but Ledyard lost interest after about thirty seconds. Bent over his desk, he watched everyone in the room from under his eyebrows, which were thick enough to brush the floor with. He cut Ambler off. 'He's pretty awful, isn't he . . . an embarrassment to have him associated with the library?'

No one responded. The trustees' chairman acted as though he were there as a spectator. He deferred to Lisa Young, as did Ledyard. Descended from generations of New York high society, married to a partner in one of Wall Street's powerful law firms, she was highly confident of her own judgment and accustomed to deference.

Ambler hadn't always deferred to her – they'd had a number of battles over custody of Johnny, their grandson – but on this he was happy to defer. She was, at least for the moment, on his side.

'No one came here to vouch for Mr Ford's character,' she said. 'We're not building a statue to him. No one objected when we acquired the Nelson Yates papers. Yates's past is at least as sordid as Ford's. I imagine we'd find a lot more mistreatment of women if we looked into the private lives of many of the literary luminaries we have housed here.'

Ledyard's expression was pained. His eyebrows drooped lower toward his eyes. 'The allegations are serious, Lisa. Criticism is mounting—'

'I don't expect you to hide under the bed every time there's criticism, Arthur. I'm not swayed by it. I'm sure the board isn't.' She glanced at the board chairman, whose eyes popped open like he'd been called on in class when he was daydreaming.

'Absolutely,' he said.

The tide was turning. With Lisa Young and the board chairman on his side, he was going to win hands down. But Harry wouldn't leave well enough alone. He proposed a compromise to save face for Ledyard. The library would keep the Will Ford collection and open it to researchers without fanfare the following Saturday. The public event commemorating the opening would be cancelled. Ambler could hold a small private reception at the library for a limited number of invited guests with no publicity.

TWO

When Mike Cosgrove left his pal Ray Ambler at the Oyster Bar, he was out of sorts for a bunch of reasons, not the least of which was that he knew more about the 1990 Manhattan Avenue murders Ford's short story was based on than he'd revealed to Ray. A memory was rattling around in his head. He'd had a rotten feeling more than once in his career about homicide cases that weren't handled right.

He called a friend who'd worked at the two-seven precinct. Chris Jackson, now a lieutenant in the nine-nine, had been his partner and protégé in the early '90s when Jackson first made detective. He didn't think his former partner had ever been a dirty cop, yet Chris, who'd moved to the two-seven and a street crimes unit after his time with Cosgrove, landed in one of the dirtiest precincts in the city. He'd been called in by the Mollen Commission and testified. But he came out clean. And that was that, as he worked his way up the ladder in the department.

Chris didn't want to hear about the Manhattan Avenue murders. 'Forget it,' he said when Cosgrove asked. 'I don't know what went down. I doubt I ever knew, and if I did, I've forgotten.'

They talked for a few minutes more about their families. Both were divorced, Jackson married again, with two sets of kids, two from his first marriage, two from the second. Cosgrove had one daughter, who was more than he could handle through her teen years.

'You trying to repopulate the city with Jacksons?' he asked.

Chris laughed and Cosgrove remembered how much he'd liked his partner's hearty laugh. It cheered you up in spite of yourself. 'My second wife Claudine took all the kids under her wing. She's a woman of faith and got them toeing the line. Me, too.'

As he was about to hang up, Cosgrove realized something. Chris most likely remembered the case and didn't want to talk about it on the phone. 'I'm gonna be on the Upper West Side tomorrow. How about I buy you lunch. It's my turn.'

Chris bellowed his hearty laugh again. 'How do you know that? The last time we had lunch was nearly thirty years ago.'

'I remember all my lunches.'

Chris roared again. 'Your ass . . . That diner by the river. 125th Street, across from the market. 1:30.'

The next morning, before lunch with Jackson, Cosgrove visited another former partner, Sal Ippolito, now a detective in the Manhattan cold-case squad. This time he went in person, so he talked to Sal at his desk in the cold-case office in the bowels of One Police Plaza. He hadn't seen Sal in years either.

'Still at it,' Ippolito said. 'I put in my papers a couple of times. Every time, I took them back. What am I gonna do if I retire? Security for some big company? Who needs it? Let 'em pay their fucking taxes like they're supposed to, so we could have a real police department and they wouldn't need their own security.' Ippolito went on about corporations not paying taxes, cuts to the city budget, and lousy cops' salaries. He was on to cops' pensions when Cosgrove steered him toward the reason he was there.

'Jeez, Mike. We got thousands of cases from back in them days. I mean thousands. You remember what it was like? We'd go out sometimes on one homicide and find the victim you were standing over wasn't the one you went out for. The one you wanted was across the street.

'I don't remember the case you're asking about . . . and you think I would when it was a cop who bought it.' Ippolito got started again, this time on the crack epidemic. Cosgrove remembered that he was like that when they worked together. He'd start yacking the moment he got in the patrol car, stop when they got to a crime scene or went to interview a suspect, start right back up again when he was back in the car, never lost his place.

Sal did finally haul himself out of his chair to go look for the file on the Manhattan Avenue case. He was bulkier than

Cosgrove remembered, moving like it was something he didn't do much of any more, spending too much time at a desk, too many deli sandwiches, too many donuts. Newer cops tried to stay in shape, worked out, ate healthier. Sal was like him, stuck with bad habits they picked up when they were young.

He'd brought along the newspaper clipping Ray gave him so he had the date and location of the murder for Sal. The guy was gone for some time, longer than Cosgrove would expect even for an understaffed and underfunded office. When he came back, he was shaking his head.

'Can't find it,' he said. 'You sure it wasn't closed back in the day? It coulda been weeks later and everyone forgot about it. I mean it could have been closed a year later or two. Still, when a cop was killed you'd think they wouldn't of forgot about it. Still, it coulda been the perp bought it himself.' Sal lowered his voice. 'Or they hung it on some creep that was goin' away for ever for somethin' else.' He glanced at Cosgrove out of the corner of his eye.

Cosgrove knew it had been done. They'd get a guy who wasn't playing with a full deck and use him to clear up some cases for them. The dummy wasn't getting out anyway. What difference did it make?

'We never got the case here,' Sal said. 'That's why I don't remember it.'

Cosgrove left One PP shaking his head. It wasn't the first head-shaker he'd had in his career, but this one was a doozy. You'd think Ray'd know enough to look for a follow-up story when he found the first newspaper story, a friggin' librarian no less. He tried to call him on his way uptown to meet Chris Jackson but didn't get an answer. Actually, Chris could tell him if the case was cleared.

His former partner hadn't put on weight, as slim and straight as when Cosgrove first knew him, straighter and stiffer now that he was a lieutenant. He wore an expensive pressed suit – not the baggy sack of mismatched sport jacket and slacks or off-the-rack suit that Cosgrove and most detectives wore. He hadn't lost his intimidating manner either. Back in the day Cosgrove compared him to Robert Parish, the guy who played center for the Celtics; 'the Chief' they called him. He was known for his game face, unsmiling, a hard stare that dared you to mess with him.

Cosgrove understood Parish's game face and he understood Chris Jackson's game face, too. Chris knew what the guys who smiled to his face said behind his back. If you were Black, you needed a steel spine and ice water in your veins to make it up the ranks in the NYPD. Every promotion you got, a thousand white guys told each other you made detective, or you made sergeant or lieutenant because you were Black. Affirmative action pushed you along and left them behind.

He and Chris got along; they made a good team. Cosgrove never doubted his partner deserved his promotions. They'd gone through tense moments together when Chris could have hung Cosgrove, the only white guy in the room, out to dry. But he made clear he and Cosgrove would go down together if it came to that.

Out of habit, Cosgrove cased the diner before he sat down. Despite both he and Chris being in plain clothes, everyone in the joint knew they were cops. Back in the day, the place would've emptied out by the time they got their menus.

'So, what's with the I-never-heard-of-the-case?' he said before he looked at the menu. 'You were working in the two-seven when it happened. How would you not know?'

Chris held his menu in front of his face for a moment before he spoke. 'You wearing a wire?'

Cosgrove was so dumbfounded he didn't answer, just stared at the menu in front of Chris's face until he lowered it. Finally, he asked, 'Are you being investigated?' When he didn't get an answer, he said, 'Do you remember who I am? We can go to the men's room if you want.'

Chris shook his head. 'You caught me by surprise. I had a flashback.' The menu shook in his hands. 'I didn't sleep without nightmares for years after my time in the two-seven. It was a rats' nest. You remember Serpico? I expected that to happen to me, even though I didn't do what he did.'

'You testified before the Mollen Commission.'

'That was later. I was out of there by then and the whole thing had blown wide open anyway.'

'The two-seven was bad.'

'Damn right, it was. You're gonna bring back my nightmares.' He took a deep breath. 'Worse than anyone knew. How many homicide cases did you work at a time?'

Cosgrove didn't like the memories either. 'Getting back to the case I asked about . . .'

Chris put down the menu. 'I didn't know why you were asking. We haven't talked in years and you drop that on me out of nowhere.'

'Was there a collar?'

He took a long moment before he answered. 'A couple of weeks later a creep they got on a different homicide copped to that one and the Manhattan Avenue case.'

'A cop got killed. What kind of investigation was it? Who handled the case?'

Chris didn't say anything for a long moment. When they worked together, he'd do that to make a suspect he was talking to nervous. Use his silence to control the situation. You didn't know if you said something wrong and he was going to explode or if he knew something you didn't know that was going to make you look like a fool. It was part of how he intimidated people. This time was different. He was the uneasy one. He licked his lips, his expression pained, his gaze unsteady.

'I don't remember. It was a long time ago. I wasn't in homicide. I was working street crimes.' He shifted uncomfortably in his seat. 'What's going on, Mike? Why are you coming to me with a murder from almost thirty years ago?'

Cosgrove didn't get why his old partner thought he was out to get him, but he let it go and told him about Ray finding Will Ford's short story. 'He asked me about it. So I'm asking you. I didn't expect I'd kicked over a hornets' nest.'

Chris looked stunned and then let out his raucous laugh. 'This is about some book?'

'Not a book. Something Ray found in some papers in the library.'

'What the hell does that have to do with anything?' Chris stopped. 'Your friend the librarian . . . Atkins?'

'Ambler. Ray Ambler.'

'He was part of that run-in you had with the Intelligence

Bureau a couple of years ago. You don't know how many cages you rattled with that one.' He lowered his voice and leaned forward on the table. 'Forget I'm telling you this. I got called in by a deputy commish. Lunch like you and I are having, except with a white tablecloth and a glass of wine. He wanted to know if you were a rat. Someone with a lot of cred told the commissioner you were out to get the department.'

'Nice to know the commissioner thinks about a small-potatoes guy like me. What'd you tell him?'

'That I was lucky to have had you for a partner. You did things the right way. You made me a good cop.'

Cosgrove was stumped for a moment, surprised by a feeling he realized was pride that welled up in his chest. He lowered his gaze.

Chris let out his hearty laugh. 'I don't know if that cleared you or made me suspect.'

Despite Chris's cheerfulness, Cosgrove felt irritation prickling at the back of his neck. 'For what it's worth, some reporter got Ray to say some things he might have been better off not saying. I never talked to the reporter.'

'I didn't figure you did . . . I'm not telling you what to do, Mike. You've been around longer than I have. But this guy . . . Adams . . . is a loose cannon—'

'Ambler.'

'Ambler?'

'His name is Ambler. Ray Ambler.'

'He likes to make the cops look bad.'

Cosgrove didn't say anything.

Chris's expression was mournful. 'Maybe the librarian found something we missed back in the day. I don't think so. But it's possible. A lot of crazy shit went down. What good does it do anybody to shine a light on it now and make the department look bad all over again?'

Cosgrove got irritated. 'No one's trying to make the department look bad. Ray came across something. He asked me. I asked you. You told me. That's it. Case closed. What am I missing?'

'Nothing.' Chris leaned back in the booth, relaxed. 'That's what I was saying, Case closed.'

'Except you're talking like you got something you'd like to keep buried.'

Chris stiffened. His game face came back. '*You're* talking like you're looking for trouble. We both know what went on back then. If this was tied to a case you're working on, OK. I'd say go ahead. I know you. You go where the case takes you. Consequences be damned. That's one reason I admired you.'

He spoke earnestly. 'We've all looked the other way on . . . looked the other way when we shouldn't have, when we didn't want to. Maybe you less than most cops. Me, I saw more than my share, enough to make me disgusted with myself for not blowing the whistle. There was a time I got fed up. I was ready to quit and drive a bus. Really, I'd put in the application and had an interview. But I got talked out of it. Someone with rank told me stuff about being Black and being a role model. He said he'd have my back.' He laughed, not so hearty this time. 'I may have sold my soul.' He looked out the window for a moment and then turned his attention to the menu.

Cosgrove looked at the menu, too. Nothing appealed to him. He ordered a grilled cheese sandwich. After they ordered, they sat in an uncomfortable silence. Cosgrove asked a couple of questions about the cop who was killed. Chris mumbled half-hearted answers, said he didn't know the guy. That didn't ring true. But it was possible.

Chris didn't pull rank but he let Cosgrove know about the gulf between a detective third grade and a lieutenant. He'd decide how much he'd say about the two-seven. If he didn't want to go into detail, he wouldn't. Cosgrove knew not to push him.

They talked some about when they worked together. But the tone was different, distant. They were like two guys thrown together after a period of time who didn't have much interest in one another, forced to make small talk.

After another silence, Chris said, 'Still homicide after all these years. I guess it was your calling . . . Sometimes, I miss it, working a case.'

An echo in his words asked without asking about Cosgrove's career track. Chris did what ambitious cops did; he went back into uniform to take the sergeant's test and then the lieutenant's. You pretty much needed a rabbi to move up as a detective. You'd need a rabbi to work up past lieutenant, too.

Chris acted like he was relaxed; but he wasn't; he was up to something. 'You ain't so old. You should still be in line for a Detective Two. Beef up your pension for a couple of years before you retire. Working a cold case won't help that. They don't count. Your boss, his bosses up the ladder, won't care if you close a cold case.'

Cosgrove was hardly listening as he tried to digest what he'd heard. Did Chris just hint at a promotion if he laid off the case? He knew closing a cold case didn't count toward the Comstats. He didn't care and had no interest in the ass-kissing that moved you up in rank. His former partner should know that.

Cosgrove was OK that it had been different for Chris. He came out of the two-seven unscathed – no rumors about him – and he had someone above him, a rabbi, watching over him. If he still did, he might be in line for captain.

'I don't know why you're wasting your time with it.' Chris tried to sound casual. They stood outside the diner for a moment. The day was overcast and chilly, a cold wind blew in from the river. The traffic rattled the West Side Highway roadway above them.

Cosgrove laughed. 'I don't know why either. I did a favor for a friend. I'm on the job and not working a case. You could give me a reprimand.'

'Go back to work, Mike. It was good seeing you. All I see these days is a computer screen. It's good to catch up with a real cop doing real work.'

As Chris started to walk away, Cosgrove asked, 'Any chance the cop who was killed was dirty?'

Chris turned and glared at him long and hard. 'No.'

THREE

Lisa Young helped Ambler put together the Will Ford reception and arranged to hold it in the Wachenheim Trustees Room, the oak paneling, tapestries, tuxedo-clad servers providing an incongruously elegant setting for the scruffy group of well-wishers who attended. Ambler had asked Ford for a list of fellow writers and friends he'd like invited to the small reception, a suggestion he realized was a mistake when the assemblage began to gather.

The dozen or so cronies who showed up were Ford's ne'er-do-well drinking buddies from beer joints and gin mills of the East Village and the Upper West Side in the old days. Where they hailed from now that gentrification had pushed out the sacred gin mills he had no idea. But this night the crew found its way to 42nd Street and Fifth Avenue and the free drinks.

Ford himself was half-lit when he arrived with a couple of pals who looked like they'd ridden in on Harleys. Ford was charming enough, dressed in jeans and a cowboy shirt and wearing a Stetson hat that went with the outfit. The only alarming aspect of his attire was a plastic cup he picked up from the bar and used to spit chewing tobacco juice into.

He took a shine to Lisa Young and surprisingly she reciprocated, taking him by the arm through the sparsely populated room, introducing him to a few of her friends from the Social Register and the library board of trustees who'd chosen to attend, all of whom kept a closer eye than usual on their watches, jewelry, and wallets.

Quite a few of the library staff also showed up for free drinks and hors d'oeuvres. They tended to band together, huddling against a wall like teenage boys at a school dance. Ambler huddled with them and was holding a glass of red wine in one hand and a canapé in the other when Adele with her glass of white wine crossed the room to stand beside him.

'Quite a gathering.' She gestured with her wineglass. 'I'm

betting there'll be at least one fistfight. Where's McNulty. We may need a bouncer.'

'I invited him.' Ambler glanced at the rowdies gathered near the portable bar. 'He probably knows some of these guys since he knows most of the reprobates in the city.'

McNulty showed up a few minutes later. He wore a white dress shirt, open at the collar, and black slacks, basically what he wore behind the bar of the Library Tavern. He cased the room, picked up a glass of wine, and sauntered over to Ambler and Adele.

'Quite the soirée,' he said. 'It looks like everyone's gone to a neutral corner. Like the weddings I worked where the groom was Irish and the bride Italian, or vice versa.'

He was right. The librarians were grouped together against one wall, Ford's cronies occupied the bar area near one of the windows, the society folks and board members gathered across from the windows near the door to the hallway, possibly to be near the escape route.

Ambler would have to make a short speech, not something he looked forward to. Harry Larkin as director of manuscripts and archives usually handled the ceremonial stuff, but he'd sat this one out. Arthur Ledyard, the library president, provided remarks when the acquisition was important enough. This one he wouldn't touch with a ten-foot pole. That left Ambler.

When the time came, Lisa Young spoke for a couple of minutes about the library's collections and the importance of libraries as institutions that were free and open to everyone. She kept the pitch for donations short.

Ambler talked about the crime fiction collection and about Will Ford's contribution to the mystery genre. He said the library was pleased to add Ford's papers to the collection and he hoped readers and scholars would make use of the collection once it was opened to researchers. He mentioned a few of Ford's books and quoted from a couple of favorable reviews from *The New York Times*, *Saturday Review*, and other publications, a few that no longer existed. He didn't mention that Ford's last book came out more than a decade ago.

No one was much interested in what he had to say, not even him, so he didn't speak long. He thanked everyone for coming and hoped the party would wind down quickly after that. McNulty left to go to work. Ambler told him he and Adele would stop by later. Folks started to straggle out, the society contingent leading the way. The library staff wasn't far behind.

The aging bon vivants hung on as long as they could, waiting as the servers cleared the bus stations and the bartenders closed up the bar. Ambler gathered that they waited for direction from Ford, who didn't look to be in any hurry to leave. In an annoying stroke of fate, one of the winos who'd been talking with McNulty remembered the Library Tavern, so the reprobate crew decided they'd head over for another round for the road.

'Poor McNulty,' Adele said as the gang shuffled out.

'Do we dare go?' Ambler asked.

Adele said it wouldn't be fair to sic Ford and his pals on McNulty without lending support. It took some time to get everything squared away at the library, so Ambler expected they'd find another party in full swing when they got there.

What they found was a commotion in front of the bar. Ford's entourage was gathered around a couple of figures on the sidewalk, like boys cheering on a schoolyard fight. McNulty was one of the figures on the ground. It took a moment to see who the other figure was because his face was mashed into the pavement, McNulty holding him down with his knee on his back and keeping him still by holding his arm twisted above his head.

Adele peered past a couple of the hangers on and grabbed Ambler's arm with both hands. 'Is that Will Ford underneath McNulty?'

'I should have known,' Ambler mumbled, more to himself than to Adele.

The hold McNulty had on Ford didn't require a tremendous amount of effort on his part, probably because, somewhat strangely, Ford was negotiating with the bartender rather than struggling to get free. From his perch atop the author, McNulty glanced about until his gaze landed on Ambler. 'I can give him to you or give him to the cops. Up to you.'

A couple of patrol cars, lights flashing, pulled to the curb, causing about half the onlookers to head at a brisk clip down Madison Avenue. The first cop on the scene knew McNulty and asked him what was up without more than a cursory glance at Ford. McNulty heaved himself off Ford and stood up. 'I'm getting too old for this kind of crap,' he said.

'Pickpocket?' the cop asked.

'He put his hands on the waitress,' McNulty said.

Ford tried working himself to his feet, having first to roll over to his hands and knees and try to push himself up from there. The cop, joined by the cop from the other cruiser, stood a few steps back alongside McNulty watching, none of them inclined to give Ford a hand. He didn't look like he was going to make it, so Ambler offered his hand.

Ford ignored it but after a couple more fruitless efforts realized he wasn't going to make it up on his own, so he stuck out his paw. Ambler watched it for a moment before he took hold and pulled the grunting author to his feet. Ford shuffled a bit uncertainly and scowled at his surroundings.

'I didn't mean to offend the young woman. I meant to compliment her. My intentions were honorable.'

'Bullshit,' McNulty said. 'Maybe you get away with that shit where you come from. But you don't do it in my bar. You're lucky she didn't slug you . . . You're lucky I didn't slug you.'

Ford peeked out from under his eyebrows at the small group around him, the realization dawning on him that he faced a hostile audience. 'I'm a stupid man,' he said, speaking not humbly as you might expect, but matter-of-factly. 'I've embarrassed myself and caused distress to a young woman whom I should not have bothered.' He watched those watching him like a conman watches his marks. 'Can I make amends by buying drinks for the house – including the staff?'

McNulty turned to Ambler. 'If you ask me to put up with this jerk, I will. He wants to make amends, I'll make sure he does. Is he good for the tab?'

Ambler studied the writer for a moment. He didn't come across as contrite, but he'd lost his truculent edge. 'I'll make sure.'

He went up to Ford. 'If you don't go to jail, it's on my say so. I don't want to be wrong.'

Ford looked at the top of Ambler's head and then down at

his feet. When he met Ambler's gaze, his expression was almost contrite. 'I'm not a complete jerk. I've got a credit card and twenty grand in a bank account in Texas. I'm celebrating. No more trouble. I got enough enemies. I want to make friends.'

The cops left and the remaining hangers-on plus a few of McNulty's regulars filed back into the bar. Ambler and Adele followed. After an hour or so, close to what would be the normal closing time, McNulty lowered the lights and locked the front door. He ordered a bunch of appetizers and a variety of sliders on Ford's tab, and when they came poured drinks for the kitchen workers and the waitstaff.

'I'll give him a break on the tab.' McNulty set a brandy snifter down on the bar across from Adele and Ambler. 'But he's buying me Cordon Bleu.'

'I think you've partially civilized him,' Adele said.

They watched Ford, who was talking with two men about his own age, the three of them drinking bourbon and water like it was water. Which McNulty admitted it mostly was. 'When you've had as many as they've had, you can't taste the whiskey any more. I put in enough for color and charge him for every third round. His hangover won't be as bad.'

Ambler, who'd been watching Ford and the men he talked with, said, 'I think that's Ted Lowell, one of the second-generation Beat poets.'

McNulty and Adele turned toward the group. 'I didn't know there was a second generation of Beat poets,' Adele said. Her tone softened. 'He looks like he's had a difficult life.'

He sure did. Ambler had noticed that, too. If you ran across him on the street, you'd think he was a wino. And you might be right. 'There wasn't actually a second generation, just some poets who came along too late. He did publish a couple of chapbooks, and poems in good literary journals like the *Village Review*, and he might have made a career. But he got caught up in the Sixties life, drugs, and flower children.'

McNulty, who'd been listening, said, 'I've known a hundred guys like him. You played around and played around. One day you looked up and you were over the hill.'

'That's what he looks like,' Adele said. 'Like he's in his fifties or sixties and never grew up.'

McNulty smacked his lips after sipping some cognac. 'I've had a tough time getting a start in life myself.'

Ambler picked up his beer mug and walked over to where Ford and the two other men were talking. He asked the man with Ford if he was Ted Lowell.

Lowell raised his heavy-lidded, red-rimmed, rheumy eyes. His cheeks were hollow and his scruffy grey beard was rusted near his mouth. His teeth were discolored, some missing. He nodded solemnly. He was one of the confessional poets, whom Ambler discovered in grad school. He told Lowell that and that he still had a couple of his chapbooks.

Lowell nodded again and said thank you so softly there was no sound, only the movement of his lips.

Ford kept his eyes on Ambler and Lowell, his expression alert despite all he'd had to drink. 'I told him he's a better poet than he thinks he is. Just because the publishing world forgets you, you don't lose your talent.'

Ambler wondered if Ford was talking about himself.

The man next to Lowell was a one-time Village Voice writer who'd drunk himself out of a career. After a moment, Ambler had the strange thought that he was standing among the ruins of a bygone era. Talent, and the sensitivity that came with it, didn't always fulfill its promise nor win success or lead to happiness.

He stood for a few moments and listened to the conversation, but had a hard time following what they were saying because their conversation was disjointed, each of them talking about something different. The journalist repeated what he must have said earlier about his former wife's infidelity, which Ambler gathered took place many years before though he railed about it as if it were yesterday. Ford talked about a one-night stand with a cop's wife in Dallas that almost ended badly. Lowell didn't have a story to tell. He held his rocks glass with both hands and stared into it.

Ambler, who'd thought telling the all-but-forgotten poet someone still remembered him would create some good fellowship and good cheer, instead watched a cloud of sadness settle over the man. He turned without saying anything else and walked back to Adele.

'You look unhappy,' she said, her eyes round with worry. 'What happened?'

'I'm glad you're here,' he rested his hand on her shoulder. 'I started to feel lonely. I missed Johnny, I think.'

Adele hugged his arm. 'You missed me. You just don't know it.'

After McNulty gave last call and the bar began to clear out, he poured himself another cognac and set it down in front of Ambler and Adele. 'Your cop friend didn't come by. You told me he wanted to meet the distinguished writer.' He rolled his eyes in the direction of Ford.

'I invited him. I thought he would,' Ambler said. 'I'm surprised he didn't. But it's probably just as well or Ford might have wound up in jail.'

Ambler and Adele stood together for a moment outside the Library Tavern waiting for a cab. As they waited, she slipped her arm through his and leaned against him. Her face had a kind of glow from the wine and her eyes a devilish glint. She pulled herself tighter against him, her breasts pressed against his chest. A spark went off between them that hadn't been there for some time. She lifted her face to him and he kissed her. The kiss lasted until a cab pulled to the curb in front of them.

Ambler – feeling a glow from the wine himself, not to mention the glow from the kiss – whispered, 'Johnny's at his grandmother's . . .' and was about to ask her to come home with him when she put her hands on his chest and gently pushed herself back from him.

'We need to talk,' she said before getting into the cab.

He was still watching the empty space where the cab had been when he heard McNulty lock the door and felt him sidle up beside him. 'You let her get away again.'

Ambler watched the almost empty street.

'When are you going to tell her you're in love with her?' McNulty's tone was gentler than it usually was. 'You're not getting any younger.'

'That's the problem,' Ambler said after a long moment.

FOUR

The next morning at 11:00, as planned, Will Ford found his way to the crime fiction reading room. The door was open and Ford was standing in the doorway watching him when Ambler glanced up from his computer. Ford's expression was pensive, as if he'd been studying Ambler.

'You fit your surroundings,' Ford said as he walked into the reading room and took a seat across the library table from Ambler. 'Like the bartender last night fit his surroundings, like a mallard in a marsh, like a bear in the woods.' He laughed.

Ambler was taken aback; Ford was so different from the night before. Not only because he spoke lyrically but his manner was unassuming, almost shy.

'I'm delighted my papers found such an illustrious resting place,' he said quietly. 'I owe you a large thank you for bringing this about.' He gestured at the oak wall and book-lined shelves around them. 'When I called you, I wasn't sure you'd know who I was. I didn't think anyone remembered me.'

'Your work deserves to be remembered,' Ambler said. That he said 'your work' wasn't lost on Ford.

'You're right. The work is what's important not the man. I've never thought I deserved to be honored.'

Ambler didn't know if what Ford said was genuine or a self-serving diffidence so he didn't have to defend his behavior last night. It sounded practiced. But it created an opening.

'I came across an unpublished story of yours when I was assessing the collection.'

Ford's eyes opened wider. This didn't look practiced.

'"The Unrepentant Killer".'

Ford sat perfectly still. His eyebrows returned to normal, and his face became a mask.

'I was especially interested in the author's note.'

Ford spoke without altering his expression. 'I wrote a lot of stories.'

'You don't remember this one?'

'I don't remember everything. If I wrote that note, I don't remember it.'

Ambler thought it peculiar he didn't ask what was in the note. He gave Ford a bare-bone summary of the story and quoted the author's note. 'The story is true . . .'

Ford sat back and crossed one leg over the other, appearing nonchalant. But his gaze was as intense as an eagle's. 'I thought I buried that one. Not one of my favorites. I didn't want it published.'

Ambler pressed him. 'I found some newspaper stories on the murders I think the story was based on, the newspaper stories you said were fiction.' He showed Ford the clippings.

Ford glanced at them but didn't read them. He didn't say anything for a moment and then cleared his throat. 'I get what you're up to . . . I remember now you're a detective . . . an amateur sleuth. Conan Doyle and Poe thought they could solve real-life murder mysteries, too. "The Mystery of Marie Roget" was Poe's attempt to solve the real-life murder of a New York cigar girl. Conan Doyle helped free a man wrongly convicted of murder. You're part of a grand tradition.'

'I don't write mysteries,' Ambler said.

'You collect them. Same difference to my point, which is that unlike you I'm not a writer who attempts to solve real-life crimes.'

'Why the author's note?'

'I don't remember. Maybe it was a joke.'

'Do you remember the newspaper articles?'

'I read the papers. I probably read those stories. At the time, you could read about murders every day of the week. Take your pick.'

Ambler asked Ford again why he hadn't wanted the story published.

Ford chuckled. 'I guess I didn't need the money at the time.'

'You told the editor publishing the story might get you killed.'

He chuckled again. 'I make enemies. A lot of people wanted to kill me back in the day, most of them women.' He shook his head. 'You're like a fucking bulldog . . . Maybe *you'll* get me killed.' He glowered at Ambler for a second and then laughed, more heartily than before. 'I should've burned the fucking thing. For now, what I want is to pull the story from the papers I gave you. I have a file back in the library in Texas of papers that are embargoed until I'm dead. You know what that means?'

Ambler said he did.

'This one will go in there. I wanted to write the story because of one of the characters, a young woman. Then the story took on a life of its own and got too ambitious. I realized I might have stepped on some toes. No big deal.'

Ambler wasn't satisfied with Ford's answers. But at the moment, he couldn't do anything about it. He didn't like that Ford would pull the short story from the collection. But he couldn't do anything about that either. Still, he knew more now than he did before he confronted the writer. Sometimes a person answers a question by the way in which they don't answer it.

Ambler went over the deed of gift with Ford and gave him the check for the collection, which was the purpose of his visit to the library. It wasn't a hundred thousand but it was substantial. Ford thanked Ambler again for being supportive of his work. He might have been a bit sheepish about dodging Ambler's questions but that didn't stop him from waving off Ambler's last-minute attempt to ask again about the Dear Reader note at the end of 'The Unrepentant Killer'.

'We'll have a drink one night before I leave town, and I'll tell you about the real-life model for Cisco Garcia,' he said.

Later, over lunch at the Szechuan restaurant on 39th Street, Ambler told Adele about his visit with Ford.

'He was evasive and wouldn't talk about the note he wrote.'

Adele was more interested in the diced fish and potatoes than she was in Ford. 'Even if he lied to you and did know about a murder a quarter of a century ago, what difference would it make now?' She waited a moment. 'The only good outcome would be if you found out he was the murderer and they put him in jail and let him rot.'

Ambler didn't fully share Adele's hostility. But he wasn't going to argue with her. 'The smart thing for me to do would be to forget about that story,' he said.

'The smart thing would have been to not pay any attention to something written by a man with the morals of an alley cat.' She poked at her plate with her chopsticks. 'Let's not talk about him. It makes me sad and angry. I hope he leaves town and we can forget about him.' She brightened. 'Is Johnny staying with you this weekend?'

This time Ambler poked at his plate. 'No. He's going to be in Palm Beach with the Youngs. It's his spring vacation.'

'He's spending a lot more time with his grandmother these days . . . I guess that's good. They have a lot to offer.' Sensing Ambler's irritation, she corrected herself quickly. 'Not more than you have to offer. You're everything to him. What they offer is different.'

'Yeh. What money can buy.' He heard the bitterness in his tone and tried to soften it but didn't do much better. 'When Arthur Young got to know Johnny and discovered what an extraordinary kid he is, he decided to let him into the family despite his unseemly origins.' Ambler knew he was being disagreeable and tried to compensate. 'It's good of him to make Johnny part of his family when the boy's not his actual grandson, and it's good for Johnny to know both sides of his family.'

Ambler had something else to be appreciative for as well. Young, a Wall Street lawyer with a network of social and political connections in the city, had told Johnny he'd look into getting his father a new trial and a reduced sentence, something Ambler had been unable to do ever since his son, Johnny's father, was sentenced.

Adele loved Johnny as much as Ambler did. In the best of worlds she might have taken over mothering him. That wasn't how things turned out. Lisa Young and Ambler discovered they had a grandson at the same time, and both wanted their grandson in their lives. So they shared custody of a grandson that neither of them knew existed until he turned up, a boy of eight, under tragic circumstances not many years ago.

'It's all new to him,' Adele said. 'For a boy who had so

little to now have so much has to make his head spin. He's not going to want to be away from you for very long.

In the middle of the afternoon, when he returned to the crime fiction reading room from a staff meeting, Ambler saw a message on his cell phone that Mike Cosgrove had called.

'I thought you'd come by last night to meet the author of the story I showed you,' he said when he called back.

'Something came up,' Mike said. 'I still want to meet him. By the way, I looked into those murders you asked me about.' Ambler could tell from Mike's tone that he'd found out something that would annoy Ambler. 'The case was closed with a collar not long after it happened.'

As Mike described his conversation with Chris Jackson, Ambler could read between the lines that his friend didn't completely buy what Jackson told him.

'Were you satisfied?'

'Satisfied with what?'

'That they got the right guy?'

Mike started a quick retort. 'Why would . . .' and then stopped. 'Interesting you should ask that question. You think someone cops to a murder they didn't commit?'

'He confessed. Who was he? What was the motive?'

Mike paused for longer than usual. 'Good questions. You're learning . . . Let's have a drink tonight. I want to hear more about your writer friend.'

They met at the Library Tavern for a beer. It was Friday so the library closed early and they arrived in the middle of cocktail hour. McNulty indicated two barstools that would soon be available, something he did for Ambler and Adele regularly.

'Greetings, officer.' McNulty made a show of carefully wiping the bar in front of Cosgrove.

'Not officer. I'm a detective. Mike is fine, unless you insist on formality.'

McNulty nodded. 'What can I get you, officer?'

'A beer would be fine . . . Mr McNulty.'

Cosgrove went over what Chris Jackson had told him. 'Chris

was working in the precinct where the murders took place, assigned to an anti-crime task force. That precinct was one of the worst in the city for corruption. He said he wasn't part of the corruption, and I believe him . . . Chris didn't like reliving those times. He was embarrassed. I don't blame him for that either.

'It was tough. Punks broke the law in broad daylight and laughed at the patrol cops trying to do their job. Then the cops doing their job found out other cops were as likely to be robbing drug-dealers as arresting them. So the punks on the street thought cops were just like them, running a hustle. . . . Chris knew what happened. Like I said, he didn't like talking about it.'

Ambler waited a couple of beats. 'He was being evasive. So you're being evasive.'

Cosgrove took a long drink of his beer and watched the glass for a moment. 'If that's how it comes across, I can't help it. I'm not holding back anything he told me.'

'But you're not satisfied.'

'I gave you the answer to the question you asked me. The case was closed with a collar. You could have found that out yourself if you'd dug a little deeper. What did your friend the author say about it?'

Ambler took a slug of his beer before he answered. 'He was evasive, too.'

Cosgrove reacted quickly. 'So are you . . . Did he say a cop got away with murder?'

Ambler picked up his bar napkin, folded it in half and then in half again and again in half one more time. 'He said he wasn't a writer who tried to solve real-life crimes.'

They drank in silence for a moment watching McNulty behind the bar, like watching a dancer. He didn't walk, he glided from the service bar to a customer at the front bar who needed a refill, next to clear and wipe down a space along the bar that had been vacated, and then to place a bar napkin in front of a new arrival, back to the service bar to make a few drinks, squeezing lemons or limes, spooning bar sugar, pouring with both hands, sometimes stirring a drink, sometimes shaking two at a time, one in each hand.

They'd just about finished their beers and Ambler expected Cosgrove had enough of their chat and would call for the check and make ready to leave. Instead, he signaled to McNulty for two more. 'I'm going to level with you,' he said as they watched the bartender draw the beers. 'Chris asked me not to look into this.'

Ambler waited a moment before he said, 'And so?'

As Cosgrove picked up the glass of beer McNulty placed in front of him, the bartender said, 'My patrons start out speaking softly about the important things they're discussing and stop speaking when I'm in earshot. This works for the first drink, and maybe halfway through the second drink. Then, they forget I'm there. I become the invisible man and when I care to I can listen to everything they say.

'Usually, I don't listen. They may think what they're talking about is interesting or important; I don't.' He paused to survey his domain. No one in need of anything, he said, 'With you guys, it's different. I've got an instinct, a finely tuned awareness when talk turns to crime.

'Over the years, in some joints I worked, when my antennae went up it was guys talking about where or when or how to do the crime. Or where or when or how they did the crime. In those cases, I never let those guys know they'd been overheard. What I heard I kept to myself. One takes up the stick deaf and leaves the bar dumb.'

Mike listened with interest to McNulty's soliloquy. Ambler had heard it before, so he paid as much attention to Cosgrove as he did to McNulty. 'So you were listening to us now?' Mike asked.

'I let you two in on this habit we bartenders have because what you're talking about is how to solve a crime.' He glanced at the tipplers on either side of Ambler and Mike to make sure they weren't listening and addressed himself to Mike. 'Ray has taken me into his confidence before when, as I understand it, he was helping you with a case you were working on that got too complicated for you.'

Ambler watched Mike's cheeks bulge and his face redden. McNulty caught this, too, and placed his hand on top of Mike's wrist where it rested on the bar. 'What I'm saying is all three of us know where we stand on things. We don't need to bullshit one another.'

'So you were eavesdropping,' Mike said.

The bartender leaned closer. 'You were talking about the distinguished writer who, like too many people, becomes an asshole when he drinks. You were talking about the murders that story he wrote that Ray showed me and my guess would be showed you, too, was based on and wondering what truth there might be to the story.'

When McNulty went to the service bar again and then got involved in some bantering while freshening up a few drinks for some of his regulars, Mike asked Ambler, 'Why'd he just tell us that?'

'I think he has something to tell us about Will Ford.' Ambler's guess was McNulty had eavesdropped on Ford's conversations the night before. But Ford wouldn't have talked about the short story or the murders. Ambler didn't ask him about the story until the next day.

McNulty worked his way back and leaned on the bar in front of them again. 'Last night the distinguished writer was bragging about his wild oats days in the city. His stomping grounds in those days were neighborhoods I'm familiar with, including my own. He mentioned a couple of joints, gone now, that I knew well – one of them we used to call Hanrahan's Bucket of Blood, on Amsterdam a few blocks above 96th Street.

'Two things about that bar. Hanrahan himself is long gone. God rest his soul . . . if he had one, which many doubted. But Joe Dunne, who began tending bar there when he was a child – you could work the stick at eighteen in those days – stayed until they tore the place down a few years ago. These days, he tends bar up in the Bronx near Yonkers.'

Mike's eyes opened wider.

'The other thing you'd want to know,' McNulty said, 'is in those days Hanrahan's was a cops' bar.'

Ambler now understood Mike's interest. 'You knew that?'

'There were a few bars like that in every borough,' Mike said. 'Still are. Places where a cop can feel comfortable, know he won't be bothered by someone with a hair up his ass for cops.'

'A very chilly place for the uninitiated,' McNulty said. 'On most nights, if you happened to wander in, you'd catch on pretty quick you weren't wanted and leave. Some nights they had a guy on the door. Very careful who they let in. Very few altar boys.'

'Drugs?' Ambler asked.

'Drugs were everywhere in those days,' McNulty said. 'Coke in every bar that had a bolt lock on the men's room door.'

Mike watched McNulty head back to the service bar. 'Sometimes, I think if it weren't for cab drivers, bartenders, and doormen, cops wouldn't solve half the cases they do.'

FIVE

Mike Cosgrove slept fitfully that night. First, his daughter was out on a date and he never truly went to sleep until she got home. He didn't talk to her when she came in; he'd learned not to ask questions. When he heard the front door open, close, and the lock click, he closed his eyes. This night he heard the lock click shortly after midnight. Denise had started college that fall. She was almost through her first year at Hunter – and had become amazingly responsible. Still, a cop with a kid, he worried; he imagined horrors tripping on the heels of horrors whenever she was out.

He'd also gotten an interesting phone call earlier that evening. A woman he'd known since childhood – a childhood sweetheart in fact, Anne Gannon – called to tell him she'd left her husband and was suing for a divorce. Something she should have done years ago. Her husband Gary was a fellow cop, also someone he'd grown up with. He'd never liked Gannon and Gannon didn't like him. Anne's call was to tell him Gary was angry about the divorce and blamed Mike.

'I don't think he'd do anything about it,' she said. 'But I thought you should know. He swears you and I have been having an affair for years. And since your divorce, he thinks my leaving him is part of a plan. He's too self-centered to believe I'm leaving because he's been such an asshole to me since I married him. I've known for twenty years I'd leave him once Kate was out of the house. She's in her second year at college now in Pittsburgh and she swears she's never coming back.'

'I'd like to see you,' Cosgrove said.

'I'd like that, too,' Anne said softly, and after a pause, 'It would be better to wait until the divorce is final and things have calmed down. I'm getting a restraining order against Gary and that will really drive him up the wall. You should stay away from him, too.'

Cosgrove held the phone for a few minutes after Anne had hung up, looking at it and feeling a strange glow, wondering what it would be like to see an unmarried Anne again after all these years. His talk with Ray was on his mind also. More worrisome, Chris Jackson's unexpected reaction to his questions ran through his mind like a news video on a loop. He wouldn't say it out loud, definitely not to Ray, but something didn't smell right.

Cosgrove realized he'd been wide awake for a while staring into the darkness, so he got out of bed and made some notes: 'Check for DD5s for the Manhattan Avenue killings to see who did the original homicide investigation.' Chris wasn't going to like him doing this but might not find out about it.

If the detectives who caught the case were still on the job, talking to them would be tricky. They'd want to know why he was nosing around in an old case. And what would he tell them? He couldn't get authorization to look into the case without giving his boss the reasons. And he couldn't do that without bringing Chris into it. Once that happened, the case would get squashed before he got started.

With luck, the cops would be retired if they were still alive, and they'd probably be old-school guys who wouldn't have much truck with the new managers at One PP. If it turned out the original homicide cops were in on the cover-up, he'd know that as soon as he talked to one of them. And that would be a dead end. On the other hand, someone might talk to him.

If he was asked why he was doing this, he'd have to call it curiosity. He might also call it instinct. For almost thirty years he'd heard about investigations that sounded plausible enough but for one or two things that didn't add up. When that happened, when he believed the story he heard was missing something, he needed to follow it up to find out if he was right.

That was his job – not something he'd say out loud either – to find what was true. That's what kept him going – he'd stopped believing a long time ago that what he did had much to do with justice. He had a place to start. He'd do some snooping on his own. If he found anything, he'd go to his boss and let the fur fly. Having come up with a plan of sorts, he slept like a baby.

In the morning, he called in and took a vacation day. He then called a civilian clerk he knew at the Central Records Division at One PP. He'd been to the records division countless times over the years and had learned to bring a box of donuts each time, so he was thought of as one of the good guys.

Being thought a good guy by the civilian employees made a difference in whether someone helped you find what you were looking for or you were sent to look for it yourself. What Cosgrove wanted to know – and what he was told a couple of hours later – were the names of the detectives who investigated the homicides he'd asked Chris about. Getting the files that contained the DD5s would take longer. But his friend Sally Esterbrook at Central Records thought she could find them.

In the meanwhile, he called the Detectives Endowment Association and asked about the two detectives whose names he'd gotten from Sally. The first one, Tim O'Hanlon, had retired in 2004 and died of a heart attack in 2005. The other detective, George Lawrence, retired in 2010 and lived in Suffern, New York. Cosgrove called him, had a nice chat about the precincts they'd worked in and cops they knew in common, and made an appointment to visit him that afternoon.

The drive to Suffern in the middle of the day took a little over an hour up the New York Thruway. Lawrence lived in a small house near what there was of a downtown Suffern. Rockland County grew up in the '60s and '70s as an extension of the Bronx as Long Island became an extension of Brooklyn. The whole county, as much as Cosgrove knew of it, was spread out across what used to be apple orchards, a bunch of towns with names and shopping centers but not much in the way of downtowns. Suffern – officially the village of Suffern – at least took a stab at building a downtown, with a railroad station, a movie theater, a strip of more or less useful kinds of stores, and bars and restaurants.

On the drive up, Cosgrove realized he hadn't been out of the city in a couple of years, not since a case he worked on took him to Greenwich, Connecticut. He told himself he should get out of the city, spend more time in the country, maybe retire to Rockland County like George Lawrence.

The day was warmer than the recent days had been. The sun was bright in an almost cloudless sky. Lawrence sat on the porch of a small wooden frame house that squatted on its neatly trimmed little plot of land on a quiet street lined with tall well-established trees leafless in the early spring. He was surprised Lawrence was African-American. Usually, he could tell from a man's voice. But Lawrence didn't have much of an accent. He was quite a bit older than Cosgrove, or at least he looked it. His face was thin and wrinkled and his skin on the lighter side. His shoulders were broad; he was a big man; but he hadn't gone to fat, still looked to be in pretty good shape. He must have been one of the early Black guys to make detective, getting his gold shield during the first affirmative-action push in the '70s.

Cosgrove wondered if Lawrence knew Chris Jackson. Chris's name hadn't come up when they talked on the phone and he wondered if it would make a difference when his name did come up. Lawrence waved to him as soon as he was out of the car. No one else was in sight. Nothing moved on the street. The quiet felt ominous to Cosgrove after the constant noise of the city.

He plunked himself down into an Adirondack chair, the same worn green color as the one Lawrence sat in, and told him upfront about the case that brought him there.

'I know it's out of the ordinary,' Cosgrove said. 'You probably think I'm nuts. Someone told me about it. I asked someone about it. What he told me didn't add up, so I got to wondering . . . and it kept eating at me.' He watched Lawrence out of the corner of his eye, trying to gauge how the retired cop took what he said. Watching his face was like looking at the face on a statue.

'You from cold case?'

Cosgrove started to explain but Lawrence cut him off.

'Internal Affairs?'

That gave Cosgrove a start. 'No. I told you—'

'How'd you know it was my case?'

Cosgrove told him.

'Who'd you talk to about it?'

Here goes, Cosgrove told himself. 'Lieutenant Jackson. Do you know him?'

Lawrence watched the empty street for a moment. 'I knew him before he got to be high and mighty . . . Not an easy man to get to know. Kept everything close. Probably was on me but I didn't trust him.' He laughed. 'You know what they say, "Don't trust a man who doesn't drink." I don't know if he drank or not. But he never let his guard down.'

Lawrence spread out his large hands on his thighs. 'I thought that case might come back to bite somebody. Years went by; when it didn't, I'd almost forgotten about it.' He paused. 'There were other ones I thought might come back, too. They didn't come back neither.'

He lifted his hands from his lap and looked at them. 'You're old enough to remember. Those days, even if you didn't want to be sloppy, you couldn't help it. The cases kept comin' at you. Files piled on your desk; the phone ringing every other minute. Some weeks I never went home. We had cots in one of the empty offices. No problem getting overtime.'

'Cops on the take?'

Lawrence stared into the empty street in front of him. 'We had some. You know that. Too easy not to. The young guys in particular, the ones hired after the layoffs. They didn't know nothing. But they figured out pretty quick, "you can't beat 'em, join 'em." You reported another cop for shaking down a dealer, nothing happened to him. You watch a guy frisk a punk, find a wad of dough in his pocket. He took the dough and let the punk go. What were you gonna do?'

Cosgrove listened. He'd let the old cop get to the Manhattan Avenue case in his own good time. After a few minutes, Lawrence stopped speaking as if he waited for something. Cosgrove didn't know what he waited for, so he waited too.

'I caught the case because I was a few blocks away. I was finishing up with a stickup on Amsterdam and I guess I was the closest detective. My bad luck. It was a slaughterhouse. Blood everywhere. Four victims. Multiple gunshot wounds. I got there after the patrol officers. They'd cordoned off the building. A brownstone. Three stories. The upper floors was a whorehouse. The basement apartment was a gambling operation, blackjack and craps. I knew the place. I'd helped bust it a year or so before. I guess they started paying off because we never went back.

'The sergeant from the street unit – they called it an anti-crime task force – had taken over. Chris Jackson might have been one of the plainclothes guys. I couldn't say for sure now. I may think that because you said his name. He was on that anti-crime task force at the time. There were maybe a half-dozen uniforms and the crime scene unit. The sergeant told me to hang tight. The brass was coming down. An undercover cop had been killed. I did what I was told.'

Cosgrove wanted to press Lawrence on whether Chris Jackson was at the scene of the crime. If he was, that meant he lied about what he knew. Lawrence though wasn't going to remember any better under pressure, so he let it go. He could check on it later.

'A captain from Manhattan North showed up and he and the anti-crime squad sergeant ran things. They treated me like I was the batboy. It was still my case, the sergeant told me. But they'd handle the initial investigation because of the UC.' Lawrence took a deep breath. 'Do you think I cared? I had a foot-high stack of open cases on my desk. I was glad to turn it over to them.

'They told me to open a file and they'd send me a DD5 when they got things straightened out. They didn't want me hanging around the crime scene, but my partner, Tim O'Hanlon, an old warhorse, wouldn't leave. He hated the new managers who took over after the Knapp Commission. Anybody above sergeant could kiss his ass.

'Before I ever saw a DD5, that captain held a press conference. He said an undercover NYPD officer who'd infiltrated a criminal enterprise had been exposed and killed in a shoot-out, along with the gangster he'd had under surveillance and two other suspects.

'That wasn't the scene O'Hanlon and I saw. When I read the DD5, I thought someone had mixed up the cases . . . I called the Chief of Detectives' office and talked to the captain who was at the crime scene. He said everything was as it should be. He'd have the sergeant, whose name was Kowalski, go over it with me and O'Hanlon.

'I knew about Kowalski. He had a rep for tuning up the dope-slingers and gangbangers. He'd won a bunch of citations, one of them came from a shoot-out with a roomful of Colombian traffickers. He and his partner working undercover up in Washington Heights got exposed. His partner and two of the Colombians got killed. Kowalski was hit twice, almost lost his leg. He had enough of a limp he could've done a disability retirement. He wanted to be a hero instead and went back to working undercover. For that, he got to head up a street crimes unit, the anti-crime task force.

'Then he got detective. He had an uncle, one of the suits at One PP. Still, Kowalski was an OK guy, at least when he talked to us. He said things were confused at the crime scene. It took a lot to sort through it. What he said without saying is they reworked the crime scene to make something right. He said they had a good reason.

'O'Hanlon bought what he said, so I did, too. At the time, O'Hanlon and I were working a child murder, so we had enough on our minds.'

'What was the reason they needed to rework the crime scene?'

'He didn't say. We didn't ask. We trusted if he said they had a reason, they did.'

When Cosgrove got back to the city, he did some checking. Kowalski was still on the job, a deputy inspector now. His uncle retired years ago as a deputy chief. The street crimes unit Kowalski headed was closed down after the Manhattan Avenue murders. He testified in a closed-door session with the Mollen Commission but came out clean, despite a dozen or more excessive-force complaints, none of them substantiated, although the city settled some lawsuits he was named in for big dollars.

Cosgrove had been around long enough to know nobody in the department would lose any sleep over an excessive-force complaint. Kowalski wasn't so different than a lot of cops who went to war on the streets in those days. You needed to show the punks the cops were in charge; sometimes the only thing that persuaded them was being more brutal than they were.

SIX

Ambler took the train – the Number 1, Broadway Local – with McNulty to the next to last stop at 231st and Broadway in the Bronx. With all the jerking about and the stops every few blocks, it felt like the trip took the entire afternoon. They were meeting Joe Dunne at a Dominican restaurant on Broadway where he ate his dinner each night before starting work at the Plow and the Stars, one of the few remaining Irish bars in Kingsbridge. McNulty told him there once were dozens.

Dunne was a husky man with a ruddy complexion, red hair going to gray, and lively blue eyes. He had a gruff manner but in a hearty, friendly, charming way. They found him at a booth in front of a plate piled high with chicken and rice.

'Sorry to be chowing down while we talk, fellas. But I'll need to be getting to work.' He waved his fork. 'Brian, it's great to see you. You're handling your age well.'

'Back at you, Joe,' McNulty said. 'I'm surprised you're still working. I thought you'd have stolen enough to retire to Florida by now.'

Dunne glanced at Ambler and gave McNulty a warning look.

'Don't worry about him,' McNulty said. 'He's a librarian.'

Somehow this was reassuring to Dunne. Ambler had no idea why. He sipped his café con leche and let McNulty ask the questions, thinking he'd only get in the way of two journeymen bartenders talking.

'It was a good job, Hanrahan's,' Dunne said between mouthfuls. 'For one thing, you didn't worry you were goin' to get robbed . . . which was something to worry about those days if you were open to four o'clock like we were. It was neutral territory. Cops drank there . . . and Hanrahan's goombas drank there. The boss was connected. The cops never so much as looked sideways at the hoods and vice versa. If a dustup started, it got shut down before it began. I never had to worry about straightening anybody out.'

'The guy I'm interested in,' McNulty said, 'is a writer. His name is Will Ford. He's maybe a few years older than me, the kind of guy who'd get himself into a dustup, not because he's a tough guy, because he doesn't watch his mouth when he drinks. He used to frequent your joint back in the day.'

Ambler showed Dunne a copy of a book jacket photo he'd taken from the library.

Dunne took a hard look at it and then worked on his chicken and rice for a moment. 'He drank Appleton's on ice. A good many of them over the course of a night. After a few, he got an attitude, pissed people off. You'd think he did it on purpose. He was teaching at Columbia. A guest lecturer. We called him the professor. He taught one class in the afternoon and another one the same night two times a week. He'd go to the West End between classes, teach his night class half-sloshed, and come here afterward to finish the job.

'He took to the nightlife and went to other joints too, after-hours places deeper into Harlem, the kind of joints they frisked you at the door and had a locker for your piece.' He engaged McNulty. 'You were working over on Broadway at the time. I'm surprised you didn't run into him.'

'I might have,' McNulty said. 'I don't remember everyone.'

'You'd remember him. He was the kind of guy you'd watch from the minute he came through the door. His picture should be in the asshole hall of fame.'

McNulty took a slug of his beer. Dunne tended to his chicken and rice, so Ambler asked, 'Do you remember one night a number of people were shot dead in a brownstone gambling parlor on Manhattan Avenue? I think it was the winter of 1990.'

Dunne stopped eating and faced Ambler with a peculiar, pained, expression. 'So that's what this is about?' He turned to McNulty and nodded toward Ambler. 'You say he's a librarian?'

'I know he's a librarian.' McNulty filled Dunne in on why they were there and what Ambler was looking for. By the time he got through, Dunne had finished his dinner and needed to get to work, so they followed him to the Plow and the Stars. Ambler thought it should properly be Plough. But he kept this to himself.

The bar Dunne stood behind like the captain on the prow of his ship was an old-time, battle-scarred, massive mahogany structure. He served mostly shots and beers with an occasional whiskey and ginger ale or scotch and soda. The patrons were slow steady drinkers who didn't demand much attention, so he had time to talk.

'The cop who got killed, Billy Donovan, was a regular,' he said. 'A street crimes cop. They wore regular clothes and drove in beat-up cars. You weren't supposed to know they were cops but everyone knew. They were a special unit that was supposed to get guns and drugs off the streets. They went after the Dominican and Puerto Rican kids on the street selling dope, mugging drunks. Billy wasn't supposed to be in the bar drinking when he was on duty. He didn't care. No one cared. None of the other cops would say anything. He was crazy. Chip on his shoulder. Nothing scared him.' Dunne paused. 'God forgive me for speaking ill of the dead.

'The task force was three or four cops and the sergeant. They'd all stop in once in a while, Billy all the time. He was the kind of guy who took up more room than anyone else. He's the one I remember best.' Dunne was thoughtful for a moment. 'Maybe I remember him best because he got killed. It was a shock. You thought nothing could touch him. He killed a guy who shot at him in the projects over on Columbus Avenue. Everybody knew about it. He was like the gunslinger everyone hid from when he rode into town.

'I remember the sergeant, too. I can't think of his name now. A Polack. A tough guy, too, but not crazy like Billy. Quieter. You watched him for five minutes you knew he was in charge. Even Billy, who fucked with everyone, wouldn't fuck with him. The sergeant spoke, everyone listened. The Mob guys ignored most of the cops. This sergeant they gave respect.

'Billy liked to mess with the writer guy you asked about, Ford. Yank his chain. He'd tell him tales – lies probably; some of them you hoped were lies. He wanted the guy to write a book about him – the cowboy cop who ruled the streets of Manhattan Valley and the Upper West Side.

'Everybody was busted up when Billy got killed. The cops more than anybody. They go nuts when one of their own gets killed anyway. They wanted revenge. Hanrahan convinced the cops it wasn't the Mob that done it. That wasn't how the Mob did things. In those days they didn't kill cops. Still the Mob guys stayed away from Hanrahan's for a couple of weeks. That's how bad it was.

'The cops took it out on the streets. Anyone in or around a crack house, anyone out at night in the projects, anyone on a drug corner when the cops got there, they just waled on everybody they saw. Did sweeps through the projects. Busted into a drug house and clobbered everyone in it – nightsticks, glove saps, gun butts. The Emergency Room at St Luke's had stretchers lined up out the door.

'They emptied the streets of punks for a couple of weeks. You could walk down Amsterdam or Columbus at three in the morning and not worry. After a while, everything calmed down. Everything went back to normal. It was coming on Christmas. The goombas came back. The cops gave out free turkeys and the junkies they gave them to sold them on the street. Hanrahan played Christmas carols and Irish-wake music on the jukebox; everybody was crying in his beer.

'I don't remember seeing the writer much after that. The semester ended and he told me Columbia didn't invite him back for the next one. He was drunk teaching his class, for one thing. For another thing, he got stabbed by a crazy woman student he was having an affair with. He didn't get hurt bad. But the college didn't like the publicity, so they got rid of him. He went back to wherever he came from.'

'Texas,' Ambler said.

'No kidding,' Dunne said. 'Texas, huh? . . . After Billy was killed, the sergeant and the street cops crew stopped coming in. They disappeared. I figured the higher ups moved them to a different precinct so they wouldn't be reminded about Billy and beating up everyone.'

* * *

Ambler had enough of the Number 1 train, so he and McNulty grabbed a car service cab on Broadway. On the way downtown, McNulty was quiet for a while, and then he said, 'I knew some of those street crimes cops back then. That's what they did. Street crimes. Not all of them. Not most of them. A few of them. They busted up drug houses and stole the drugs. They robbed the kids selling dope on the street. You wanna know why kids from the projects hate cops? That's why. What Joe said. The cops would wale on them. Not just when a cop was killed. Whenever they felt like it. The cops were a gang with badges. And what were the kids gonna do when they got beat up, when they got robbed? Call the cops?'

'So everyone's corrupt,' Ambler said. 'Even the bartenders. What was the joke about Dunne stealing enough to retire?'

McNulty harrumphed and answered with a scowl. 'It's different. You tip big; the bartender swings you a couple of drinks. You tip the usher big, you sit in box seats that aren't being used that day at the Stadium. It's the city; everybody's got a hustle. In the old days, the cops had their reasons, too. Everybody's corrupt right up to City Hall, so why shouldn't they get theirs? A cop comes into your place and has dinner, the owner picks up the tab. That's one thing. The cops come looking for a payment; that's something else. They're shaking you down. That's what the Mob does.

'You run a dope pad, a gambling parlor; that's one thing. You pay the cops; you pay the Mob; you're paying for protection. It's a cost of doing business. You run a cigar store, a pizza slice place, shoe repair, it's not right to pay protection for that. The Mob maybe you can't help paying if they control something like the garbage trucks – which they did. But you shouldn't have to pay the cops for protection.'

'The cop Joe Dunne talked about, you think he was one of those corrupt cops?'

McNulty spoke softly. 'I didn't say that. I don't know what he was. What Joe said got me to thinking. I know cops like that were around then.'

Ambler had a good deal to think about himself on the way home. McNulty wanted to stop off and visit a crony of his at a bar in Inwood, so Ambler dropped him at 207th Street and headed home. He wanted to call Mike Cosgrove but decided not to from the cab because you never knew who was listening. Plainclothes cops sometimes drove livery cabs.

He had no reason to hurry. Johnny was in Florida with his other grandparents, and the dog walker had taken Lola out. He thought he might see if Adele wanted to have dinner, but it was late and he felt tired and out of sorts, and he was nervous seeing her after last night. Instead, he called Mike when he got out of the cab.

'Maybe it's time we compared notes,' Mike said after Ambler told him about Joe Dunne. 'I'm off the reservation on this one as it is, so what do I have to lose? Meet me in a half-hour at Fitzgerald's. I'm in the mood for bangers and mash.'

Cosgrove was something of a gourmand and had a map of the city's restaurants in his head that told him where to eat what. In Ambler's neighborhood it might be Fitzgerald's for bangers and mash, but it would be someplace else for shepherd's pie, Norma's on Third Avenue for arancini, a small French restaurant on Madison for the prix fixe dinner.

Ambler got to Fitzgerald's before Mike and found a booth in a quiet corner away from the dart-throwers. While he waited, he thought about what Mike said about being off the reservation. Mike had come on the job not long before the crack epidemic began and the whole city went nuts. He'd been on the streets and then a detective during those times. He might easily have known and worked with the kinds of cops McNulty talked about.

Those days were before Ambler knew him and they'd never talked about them. The out-of-control cops who terrorized the streets with their nightsticks, saps, and guns worked mostly in the dangerous, crime-ridden precincts in Brooklyn, the South Bronx, Northern Manhattan. Mike might not have known about the police corruption at the time. But like everybody else in the city he knew about the crime wave and afterward like everyone else learned about the police corruption. Mike had never talked about that or a lot of things about his work. He'd never talked about gunfights or said he'd killed anyone, though Ambler knew he had. Like with other cops, most of what happened stayed behind the blue wall.

Mike had once busted a former cop for murder. Ambler knew about that because he'd helped him do it while they were trying to free a man charged with a murder he didn't commit. And Mike paid a price for doing it. It wasn't as bad as it might have been because the cop he collared had been a high-ranking officer, not one of his fellow cops, and had left the force by then. Still some cops saw him as a rat. That wasn't easy for him to take. Mike was a cop down to his toes.

When he arrived, they ordered bangers and mash and pints of Guinness.

'I told you on the phone Ford knew Billy Donovan, the cop who was killed in that bloodbath on Manhattan Avenue,' Ambler said. 'A plain clothes, anti-crime, or whatever they called street crimes cops at the time.'

Mike nodded.

'Do you know anything about him?'

'How about you tell me what you know?'

Ambler told him what he'd learned from Joe Dunne.

Mike listened without interrupting and what he heard, Ambler thought, made him sad.

'Joe Dunne didn't tell me this.' Ambler didn't want to bring McNulty's take on crooked cops into the conversation. 'But his description of Donovan led me to suspect he might have been a dirty cop.'

Mike hesitated, his fork halfway between his mouth and the plate, and then continued eating before he said, 'That's a big leap. There's a difference between using a little extra force at times and being dirty. I talked to a couple of people and found out a few things, too. I told you the case was cleared.'

'What's that mean?'

'What I'm told is Donovan was undercover on a job and got exposed. The investigation wasn't handled in the usual way. Sometimes that happens. It might be a CI, a confidential informant, is at risk. It might be the incident overlapped with a larger investigation. Whatever the reason, the brass handled the investigation. And they closed it.'

Mike talked a bit more about what George Lawrence told him. But what struck Ambler was the way Mike recounted what he'd learned. He hardly looked at Ambler; he spoke barely above a whisper. He sounded like a man awkwardly making a false confession.

Ambler let him squirm for a moment before he said, 'So that's what you heard. What do you think about it?'

Mike finished up what was left of his sausage and potatoes. 'When we wrap up a case, get the loose ends tied up, the i's dotted and the t's crossed, we let it rest. We have the next murder to solve.'

'That's your answer?'

A weariness came over Mike magnifying the sadness that had been there since he'd arrived. 'I talked to another former partner before I talked to Chris. We talked about retirement. The more I think about it, the better it looks. A guy I know retired a few years ago. He runs a hot-dog cart on a beach down on the Jersey Shore in the summer and spends his winters in Florida. He makes enough in the summer he doesn't need to sell hot dogs in the winter. I could do something like that . . . maybe a gourmet burger cart.'

Ambler was surprised. Shocked was more like it. Not so much because Mike had avoided answering his question. Not because he looked so down in the dumps. But because he couldn't imagine Mike not being a cop. He couldn't picture him as a child nor as an old man. He could only see him as if God had plunked him down on the earth fully formed as a cop and he'd stay that way until he was summoned home.

'I don't expect you to understand, Ray. It's not like all cops are the same or we think the same or agree about everything or agree about anything. I've had partners I'd no more in common with than if I'd spent my shift with a kangaroo.

'But in one way we're the same. We're in this thing together and no one else is in it with us. It's like when you're in the army and you go into battle. All you have is the guys going in with you. You gotta be able to depend on them. And they gotta be able to depend on you. One misfit, one guy out of step, and you all go down the drain.

'Those murders were a police matter. And the police took care of it. And they cleared it. It wasn't my case and who am I to say they did it wrong? The process might not have been perfect. Rules might have gotten bent. Someone might not have used the right procedure in the heat of the moment. It's possible someone got hurt who shouldn't get hurt, though I don't see that. But the case is cleared. The fat lady has sung.'

Ambler smiled. He understood the kind of stress cops felt, he knew the toll the job took on Mike who was a lot more sensitive than he let on. He remembered having dinner with him one night a few years ago when Mike couldn't eat the German dinner he ordered. He'd come from a crime scene where he arrested a fifteen-year-old boy for shooting and killing his brother by accident.

Mike knew something was wrong with the Manhattan Avenue murder case. Justice had not been served. But he wanted to let it go. Ambler wasn't sure what he thought about that.

SEVEN

Mike Cosgrove was unhappy with himself. He was holding back a lot of things from Ray and it made him angry at Ray, at himself, at the world. In the past, he'd withheld information because it was his job; he followed department policy. That never bothered him. This time, department policy had nothing to do with it. He wasn't on the job. So what he told Ray or didn't tell him was up to him.

He told Ray – or at least let him believe – that as far as he was concerned the Manhattan Avenue case was closed. All things considered, it might be he should let it go. And it might be that he would, except he didn't like being played with. Chris Jackson would most likely retire a captain or possibly a deputy inspector because he knew how to play the game. Cosgrove knew how things worked also.

It wasn't smart to do this investigation without someone above him authorizing it, without anyone on the job even knowing about it. You needed someone to cover you and on this he didn't have any cover. He hadn't even let Ray in on everything he was doing or everything he found out. That might change. He'd wait for Sally Esterbrook to find the DD5s and see what those told him about the guy who copped to the Billy Donovan murder.

That part of his plan turned out to be the easiest. Felix Hernandez was serving a life sentence currently at the Greenpoint Correctional Facility in Dutchess County. If Cosgrove was to play by the rules, he'd need approval from the department to talk with the guy, which would involve a mile or two of red tape and take who knows how long, and then he'd need to get the guy's lawyer to go along with it. He decided to skip the department and try the guy's attorney, probably a legal-aid lawyer.

The lawyer, a one-time legal-aid lawyer now in private practice, turned out to be someone he knew. His name was

Levinson and he'd represented McNulty, the pain-in-the-ass bartender friend of Ray's, when the pain in the ass was charged with murder a couple of years back.

The lawyer wanted to know if Hernandez could be charged with any additional crimes if Cosgrove talked to him.

'I'm interested in something he may not have done, not anything he did do,' Cosgrove said.

This satisfied the lawyer, so he made the call to set up the visit. Cosgrove drove up to the prison that afternoon and interviewed Hernandez. It didn't take long to find out what he was afraid he might find out.

Hernandez had gotten religion in prison, he told Cosgrove, which led him to feel a need to make amends, so he wanted to confess and tell the truth. He tried hard to make Cosgrove believe he was a reformed man. Cosgrove had heard it all before and took it with a grain of salt.

Most of what Hernandez told him Cosgrove would keep to himself for now because he wasn't sure he believed him and would need to confirm what he'd been told. But one thing the guy told him he wanted to tell Ray. He called on his way back to the city.

'Here's something you can talk to your buddy about,' Cosgrove said. 'I'm on my way back from a prison upstate where I interviewed a con named Felix Hernandez, who confessed to manslaughter in two of the murders in that Manhattan Avenue case.'

Ray tried to interrupt him with a question but Cosgrove stopped him. 'He had some things to say about the murders I'm not going to tell you about right now. What I will tell you is he knew our friend Mr Ford back in the day. Ford was romantically involved with the hooker who was killed and buddies with the other two victims, Gilberto Sanchez, the guy who was killed, and the madam of the brothel. He knew all of the people murdered in that apartment that night. We might have a chat with him now that we know more about what he knows. Can you set that up?'

Ray called back that evening and said Will Ford would be in the crime fiction reading room the following afternoon at two. Cosgrove debated with himself for an hour or so but at around nine thirty he called Chris Jackson and told him about the next day's confab. 'I'd like you to sit in on the interview.'

There was no sound from the other end of the phone for a long moment, and then an un-Chris Jackson-like whine. 'Why do you want to do this, Mike? . . . Are you crazy?'

'Some information came to light about the author of that story I think we should look into.'

After another silence, Chris said he'd be there.

The atmosphere in the crime fiction reading room the next afternoon was almost comical. Ford and Jackson circled each other like two ill-disposed dogs, tails high, ears pricked, hackles raised. Neither Chris nor Ford wanted to be there; that was for sure. Ray stayed in the background pretending he was doing something on his computer – like the guy in the old mystery movies who had his ear pressed against the door and fell into the room when the inspector yanked it open.

Interviewing two suspects together was the opposite of what the book said. You didn't want them to hear one another's story because you wanted to get one guy's story before he knew what the other one was going to say.

Cosgrove brought Ford and Chris together because he didn't want to confront Chris with what Hernandez told him unless he had to. He had no idea what Ford was going to say. With luck Ford would blow holes in Chris's story and that would force the lieutenant to come clean. Ford was certainly going to get knocked off his game.

He introduced Ford to Chris. Eyes focused on the floor, they shuffled toward one another and reluctantly shook hands like two boys told to make up after a fistfight in the schoolyard. Ford's expression when he saw Chris gave Cosgrove pause. He was surprised. Maybe the writer was surprised to see a well-dressed Black man in the room. It might also have been the surprise of recognition.

'Mr Ford,' Cosgrove began, 'Lieutenant Jackson and I want to ask you some questions about a story you wrote that we think was based on a multiple homicide some years ago.'

Chris watched him carefully as he spoke, casting a quick glance at Ford but concentrating on Cosgrove.

Ford acted confident, smug you might say, sitting back in his wooden armchair, one leg crossed over the other. 'That's the story Mr Ambler discovered in my files, I'm guessing. I told him I wish I'd burned it. It wasn't much of a story to begin with. I never got it quite right, so I never published it.'

Cosgrove waited a couple of beats. 'The name Gilberto Sanchez mean anything to you? How about Felix Hernandez?'

The color drained from Ford's face. He uncrossed his legs and put both feet on the floor, leaning forward like he might spring up and run for it. Instead he sank back in his chair. Some color came back into his face but it had a greenish tint.

'How about a cop named Billy Donovan?'

Ford turned to Ambler as if to ask for mercy. When he turned to Chris Jackson, their eyes locked and held. Cosgrove thought for a moment a message went between them – perhaps a warning from Chris.

'Let's put our cards on the table,' Cosgrove said. 'You told Ray you didn't know anything about the murders your short story was based on. Now, I'm going to ask you what you know.'

When Ford made a motion as if he might say something, Cosgrove held up his hand. 'I don't want you to embarrass yourself by getting tied up in lies, so we're going to let you in on what we know.' Out of the corner of his eye, he watched Chris intently watching Ford.

'I don't know if you were involved in criminal behavior and that's why you lied. We have witnesses who say you were friends with or at least spent some time with Gil Sanchez and the two women who were killed along with him. We're also told you knew the officer who was killed, Officer Donovan.

'I can't promise nothing you say will be used against you. But unless you were directly involved in the murders, you're not going to be charged with anything. Ray and I spoke with a couple of different people who knew you in the old days. Ray can give your memory a little boost.'

Ray told Ford what he'd learned from the bartender Joe Dunne. Ford looked kind of sickly as he listened. Ray matter-of-factly repeated what Dunne had told him. Ford didn't deny anything. Chris listened without any change of expression, so no way to tell if it was news to him or something he already knew.

When Ray finished, Cosgrove said, 'Now that we've refreshed your memory, how about taking another stab at answering some questions. You knew the people who were killed. Maybe you could tell us how you came to know them.'

Ford snuck a glance at Chris. Chris had his game face on. Ford was making up his mind what he should tell and what he shouldn't tell; you'd wonder why he looked at Chris for help.

'I don't have to answer any questions, do I?'

'Why wouldn't you?' Cosgrove had interrogated suspects he had dead to rights who were more comfortable being questioned than Ford was.

Ford's response was brusque. 'I'm not asking you. I'm asking the lieutenant. I figure he'll follow the rules.'

Chris grimaced but gathered his wits pretty quickly. He'd always been good on his feet. 'You're not under arrest. Anything you say is voluntary. You being here is voluntary. I don't know what Detective Cosgrove is up to. But it's his show.'

Ford thought that over for a moment. 'Not much reason not to tell you. Nothing earth-shattering. It was a long time ago. I don't know why you're digging it up now.' He sat back for a moment and looked to the ceiling, probably arranging the events of the story he was about to tell.

'I knew the unfortunates who were murdered. I ran into them at an off-the-beaten-track bar off Amsterdam Avenue across from Columbia University. I was teaching there for a semester in the fiction-writing program, and I'd stop in some nights when I finished my workshop. It was the kind of bar I liked, the kind of place Charles Bukowski might fit in. No frills. No pretense.

'You could get a drink, place a bet, on occasion find a woman who might go with you if you were flush with cocaine. Whatever your vice, you were welcome there. No questions asked. If you were stupid enough to ask any, they didn't get answered.

'If you're familiar with my work' – he glanced about him – 'which you're probably not, you'd know that the characters who populate my novels and stories are folks like that, from – as an editor once described it – "the city's underbelly." Folks like these interested me as a writer . . . and as people.

'I liked their company. I prefer the authenticity of such folks to the hypocrisy of the suit-and-tie, home-in-the-suburbs types, or worse, the pampered Columbia professors. The man you mentioned, Gil Sanchez, I based a character in that story on him. I didn't know him well. I like to base characters on people I don't know well, so most of what I attribute to the character I can make up. I knew Gil ran a gambling parlor and that someone more dangerous than him bankrolled him.

'His wife, mistress, girlfriend, whatever she was, Annabelle Lee, ran what she considered an upscale whorehouse she referred to as a brothel. The place was kept up, walls painted, rugs on the floors, nice furniture in the sitting room, pleasant bedrooms; decent liquor. The girls were clean, well dressed, capable of a conversation, and used condoms.

'I took a shine to one of the whores – Dominique, the girl who was murdered. She was sweet and in a strange way innocent. You'd take her for a kindergarten teacher before you'd think she was a hooker. The girls who worked for Annabelle Lee, including Dominique, were strung out on heroin. She kept them in line and semi-respectable with maintenance doses.

'What struck me about Gil and Annabelle Lee – and Dominique, too, I guess, though I didn't know it then – why I cared about them, why I wrote about them, was because they were doomed.

'Gil had been a street hustler – policy slips, loan-sharking, wholesaling bootleg cigarettes or knock-off watches. When he hooked up with Annabelle Lee, he got lucky. Someone she knew bankrolled him, so he opened a blackjack game and a craps table at that building on Manhattan Avenue downstairs from Annabelle Lee's "brothel" where he was killed. He paid protection to the cops, gave a cut to whoever bankrolled him.

'He thought he was slick; he thought he was tough. He wasn't either of those things, and everyone knew it except him. He skimmed from whoever was backing him. He shortchanged the gamblers when he thought he could get away with it. Annabelle Lee bailed him out when he fucked with the wrong guy. But you knew one day something would catch up with him.'

'Do you know who murdered him?' Cosgrove knew Ford wasn't going to answer. But sometimes an unexpected question throws a suspect off course.

Ford said no.

'You must have thought something at the time.'

Ford clasped his hands in front of his chest. 'I thought the chickens had come home to roost.'

Cosgrove tried another tack, trying to connect two things the writer hadn't connected. 'How well did you know the officer who was killed, Officer Donovan?'

'I knew Billy from another bar I went to, as Mr Ambler told us.'

'It's interesting you knew all of the people who were murdered. Did they know one another?'

Chris came halfway out of his chair before Ford could answer.

Ford watched him for a moment before he turned back to Cosgrove. 'I don't know. I knew what I read in the newspaper that it was an undercover sting that went wrong.'

Chris, who'd been chomping at the bit, stood again and turned his focus to Ford. 'Detective Cosgrove wants to know why you didn't tell him or Mr Ambler you knew the victims of a murder. Why would you hold back on something like that . . . unless you have something to hide? Did you tell the police at the time?'

Ford's eyes opened wider and he appeared to back away from Chris although he didn't move. Cosgrove knew how Ford felt; he'd seen Chris lean on a suspect before. 'I didn't have anything to tell them.' Ford shifted uneasily. 'I knew the victims but that was all I knew.'

Jackson bent toward Ford. His voice grew stern. 'Could it be that you – acquainted with Officer Donovan and acquainted with the criminal element as well, whose company you preferred to that of law-abiding citizens – kept what you knew about the crime to yourself at the time and continued to keep that knowledge to yourself because you were in fact a direct cause of Billy Donovan's murder?'

Ford stared at Chris like Chris had pulled a gun on him. His mouth moved but no words came out.

'Did you tell Gilbert Sanchez that a man he thought was a gambler was in fact a New York City police officer working undercover?'

Ford stared at Chris. Ray appeared as bewildered as Ford. Cosgrove enjoyed watching Chris cast his spell. He'd been doing it since he was a rookie cop; he could intimidate anyone.

'I wasn't crazy enough to do something like that,' Ford said. 'Even if I did what you said – which I didn't – how could you possibly know? How could anyone prove it?'

After a long pause, Chris said, 'The fact that you may have caused a man's death through carelessness, stupidity . . . or because you were showing off to your hoodlum friend is something you hoped never to have to answer for. A cop was dead. It was your fault and you were scared to death so you skipped town, went back to the hole you crawled out of.'

Chris sat down. No one said anything. After a moment, he said, 'It's a good thing you kept your mouth shut and ran. As despicable an act as that was, it's not actionable now, if it ever was. We'd need to prove intent, and I don't see how we could.'

Chris turned to Cosgrove and then to Ray to include him. 'You were right. Mr Ford knew more about the Manhattan Avenue murders than he admitted to. I don't know why he's still lying. But it doesn't change anything. What happened, happened. We don't know for sure he outed Billy. My take on it is as good as anyone's. I don't need a confession to confirm that.'

Cosgrove watched Ford. He didn't show the indignation a man who was wrongly accused would show. He looked bewildered. Cosgrove had a thought he often had when he interviewed a suspect: the guy was guilty of something; that was for sure. But it wasn't for sure what he was being accused of.

EIGHT

Ambler watched Mike and Lieutenant Jackson walk out together. Tight-lipped, grim expressions, they didn't look like two pals going out for a beer. It had been a strange encounter. He wasn't sure what he'd witnessed except that everyone in the room but him knew something about the Manhattan Avenue murders. It might be each knew something that the other two didn't know, or it might be they all knew the same thing. Whatever it was, each for their own reason didn't want to tell him.

The weirdest thing was what went on between Jackson and Ford. Ford seemed to look to Jackson for permission before he said certain things or approval after he said certain things. Mike also had cards up his sleeve he didn't play. His off-hand manner – the assuredness of a poker player with an unbeatable hand – meant he was a couple of steps in front of everyone else in the room.

After a couple of moments, while he and Ford sat together each with his own thoughts, Ford said, 'I need a drink.' He drilled Ambler with a hard stare that softened before he said, 'You opened a hell of a can of worms.' A tiny smile, more chagrin than amusement, made him look almost kindly. He stood and made an elaborate gesture with his arm, as if they were old friends. 'C'mon, I'll buy you one. Maybe you can tell me how to get out of this mess you got me into.'

Ambler was prepared to say no. It was a couple of hours until the library closed and he was behind on a number of things including writing the finding notes for Ford's papers. Instead, he sent an email to Harry taking the rest of the afternoon off and another email to Adele inviting her to meet him and Will Ford at the Library Tavern.

The familiar watering hole was mostly empty; a late afternoon somnolence had settled over the place – a man and woman left over from a late lunch, seated across from one another at a booth, talked quietly, two men in suits at the bar, ties loosened, early arrivals for cocktail hour, relished their first ones of the day. Ambler took his usual seat at the short end of the bar nearest the door and after greeting McNulty ordered a beer. Ford ordered a double shot of Appleton's straight.

McNulty free-poured the rum – a generous pour – in front of Ford. 'That's because you didn't say, "neat".'

Ford laughed. 'I began drinking these before the term "neat" came into vogue.' He held the glass in front of his eyes. 'This was Billy Donovan's drink at Hanrahan's. I have one now and again as a tribute of sorts. A strange duck, Donovan. I've seen a redneck batter a man's face into the barroom floor and not stop beating him until his face was pulp. He had nothing on Billy Donovan when it came to beating a man.

'Billy commanded the street – the cop, judge, jury, and executioner – and hated anyone who crossed him.' Ford poured a few drops from his glass onto the floor before taking a genteel sip. 'I was sad to see him go, but relieved for society at large.

'One night, he rescued me from a mugger. A skinny, fidgety kid with a steak knife. I might have taken him myself. Billy collared him, pushed him into an alley, and slapped him until he cried. He finished up by breaking three of the kid's fingers one at a time while the kid wailed.'

Ambler didn't like Ford's story. It was sadistic and sounded too much like hero-worship, so he watched McNulty cutting up fruit and kept quiet. He'd come with Ford hoping a couple of drinks would loosen him up and he'd talk more than he otherwise might about what he knew but wouldn't say about the murders the story he wrote was based on.

'The sound of the fingers snapping and the kid's screams made me sick,' Ford said. 'When Billy left me at the bar, I went back, found the kid, and called an ambulance. He was still sobbing. I gave him a few bucks.

'A couple of nights later, Billy spent half the night telling me why what he'd done was the right thing to do. "They gotta respect you," he said. "You gotta be tough or they eat you alive." I don't think he knew it but he was trying to convince himself what he did was right.' Ford watched his rocks glass, talking to it as much as to Ambler. 'He wanted me to say it was okay to maim that kid. I told him it was criminal. Some part of him knew that was true but he couldn't admit that to himself.

'I understood him.' Ford took some time sipping his drink and admiring the glass after each sip. 'The drug-dealers, the numbers runners, the muggers, the winos, the punks who made their living on the street, Billy treated them all like that.' Ford shot a sharp glance at Ambler. 'They weren't choirboys, you know. They'd gash your head with a bottle or stick a knife in your gut if they thought you had coke or money on you. Billy wasn't any more brutal than the streets he worked on.

'He went out and got a couple of my books. That surprised me. He was unpredictable like that; he'd do things you wouldn't expect of him, a *sui generis.* In one of the books, I had a character, an ex-Confederate soldier who became a sheriff in a small Texas town. He ran the town, terrorizing everyone except the banker he was in cahoots with who owned everything worthwhile in town. Everyone worked for the banker or borrowed from him. The sheriff took care of anyone who got in the banker's way.

'Billy loved the sheriff.' Ford glanced at Ambler from under his eyebrows. 'You read the book?'

Ambler said he had.

'Don't like to give away the ending if you hadn't.' Ford ordered another double. McNulty eyed him carefully and poured a lighter drink this time. Ford watched him and scrutinized the glass.

McNulty got to him before he could complain. 'You're a lousy drunk,' he said by way of explanation.

Ford ignored the rebuke and didn't miss a beat with his story. 'The sheriff wasn't an admirable character. Even I didn't think him admirable. Billy liked the book. But he said the sheriff should have done things differently to overcome his tragic flaw. If you remember, the sheriff was betrayed by a woman – as most men are sooner or later.' Ford watched Ambler to see how this bit of wisdom sat with him. Ambler didn't bite.

'"He should've killed the bitch," Billy told me. 'In a twisted way, he got the point of the story. That was the tragic flaw. The sheriff was a tiny bit human – capable of love. Not evil enough, not so entirely lacking in humanity he could kill the girl. So that tiny bit of humanity got him killed.'

Ford paused to take a drink. 'Billy would have killed the girl he loved. He told me when he was a kid he wanted to be a cop when he grew up so he could shoot people.'

Ambler thought about that for a moment. 'Maybe he was joking.'

'Maybe.' Ford smiled. 'He had notches on one of his guns. Three of them. He showed them to me.'

Ford made a dismissive gesture as if he knew what Ambler was thinking. 'He wasn't completely wrong in his thinking. Some people should be killed. In those days, like he said, cops got no respect unless the punks knew the cop was crazy enough to beat them or shoot them legally or not so legally. That was Billy's reputation. The lowlifes hated him; but they feared him. He got the respect he wanted.'

Ambler wondered how much of what Ford said was true and how much made up. Then again, it might be he didn't make any of it up. Sections of the city in those years were outlaw territory. Everyone he knew, including him, had their apartments broken into. It wasn't unusual for someone to come into work and tell you they were mugged on a subway platform the night before. The jails and courts were revolving doors. The cops on the street adapted – some overcompensated.

'How did you get to know Donovan? Cops aren't usually that friendly to civilians.'

Ford didn't answer right away. After a few moments, he said. 'Billy liked that I was a writer and he liked to brag. He wanted me to write a book about a hero cop on the streets of Northern Manhattan. He'd be the model for the cop and my expert source. It would be a book no one else could write. He'd tell me how things really worked, things no civilian would know about. The book would be the biggest exposé ever of how cops really fought crime.

'So he started telling me stories. He didn't understand I couldn't write his stories. I might use material from him.

But the stories would be mine, filtered through my imagination. Still, he told me a lot of incriminating stuff. Things, it turns out now, I'd have been better off not knowing.' Ford waited a moment, swirling the rum in his glass. 'The story based on those Manhattan Avenue murders was my story. Not Billy's. From my imagination; I'm a novelist not a journalist.'

Ambler could buy most of what Ford told him but not all of it. 'Do you know why Donovan was in that gambling room the night he was killed?'

'How would I know?'

'The lieutenant said you told Gil Sanchez Donovan was a cop. Did you?'

Ford started to say something, hesitated, and then shrugged. 'Sanchez knew he was a cop. Billy was on a team of plain-clothes anti-crime cops. They knew Gil and Gil knew them. They knew about the brothel and the gambling, like everyone else in the neighborhood who walked the mean streets knew about it.'

Ambler sat back. A whole new kettle of fish. 'Why didn't you tell the lieutenant Sanchez knew Donovan was a cop and you didn't blow his cover?'

Ford consulted with his glass of rum before he said quietly, 'I didn't know why he said that. I didn't know what he was after.' He turned to face Ambler again. 'I wasn't going to argue with him. What do I care what he says happened?'

'If Gil Sanchez knew Billy Donovan was a cop, the story about Donovan being an undercover cop whose cover was blown falls apart. If he wasn't undercover, what was he doing there?'

Ford flashed an exasperated look at Ambler. 'I'll walk you through this one more time. You don't know what happened that night. Neither do I. If the cops say that's what happened, that's their business.' He watched Ambler slyly. 'I made up a story. Why can't they make up a story if they want?'

'That's what your endnote to your story said. The story the newspapers told was made up.'

'Billy told me things cops did – maybe thinly disguised things he did – bad things including murder. What he told me gave me raw material for a story . . . You got that? I made up a story.' Ford's expression was defiant.

Ambler didn't believe him. He knew more about the murders than he'd say. But for now they'd gone as far down that road as they were going to go. It looked like the police lied about what happened that night on Manhattan Avenue. Or it could be Ford was lying. The question remained. Did Ford know what really happened? Ambler also wanted to know why he didn't clear things up when Chris Jackson accused him of revealing Donovan's identity. It was as if Jackson said to Ford, 'Here you are. This is the story we're going with.' And Ford agreed.

So many lies were flying around it was hard to keep track of them, much less figure out what the truth was. For the moment, he'd let what Ford said stand unchallenged. Later, he'd talk to Mike. Maybe Jackson came clean to him about the bullshit that went on that afternoon when Mike questioned Ford. Meanwhile, there was something else he wanted to ask Ford.

'What about Gilberto Sanchez? Did he want to be a hero in your books, too?'

Ford relaxed. He appeared to like the question. The rum had some effect. He liked to hear himself talk. 'Gil couldn't care less that I was a writer. I don't know that he ever read a book. He stopped going to school when he was nine and ran the streets until he was sent to reform school.

'He had no idea he was helping me write a book. He liked to brag, too, and he wanted to impress me. Most people will tell you a lot about themselves if you take the time to listen.'

Ambler wondered when Ford would catch on that this was what he was doing. Ford, despite his bluster, was both insecure and vain like many writers. He clung to his Norman Mailer-type bad-boy reputation because, buried in some dark place near his heart, a large and ornery doubt whispered that his work wasn't as good as everyone once told him it was. His early success was illusory and he was now an all-but-forgotten, down-on-his-heels, has-been writer.

That insecurity, self-doubt, whatever you called it, was written in the lines of his face. Like Gil Sanchez, he needed to brag. The irony was Ambler admired his writing. Ford was one of those writers who revealed truth in their storytelling without being fully aware of the truth they revealed – who told a story without knowing fully what the story was.

When Ford went to the men's room, McNulty sauntered over and told Ambler Ford's current drink would be the last one McNulty served him today.

'I'm trying to get him to talk,' Ambler said. 'Could you hold on for another drink?'

McNulty frowned. 'The problem is he gets ugly. I can see it coming on. He gets ugly with you and you're OK with that, fine. If he bothers anyone else, I'll have to put him out of here. I've gotten rid of the drunks like him over the years. It don't take much. One or two episodes like the other night and people start to talk. The joint gets the wrong kind of reputation.'

'If he bothers someone, I'll take him out myself.'

'Lucky you,' McNulty said and headed for the service bar.

'You were telling me about Gilberto Sanchez,' Ambler said when Ford returned from the men's room.

'Was I? . . . He thought he was a big tough gangster. The real gangsters, the real tough guys laughed at him.'

'The character in your story was convincing.'

Ford looked at him with the kind of blank stupid expression drunks take on when they're angry and can't formulate what they're angry about. Ambler was struck by how much Ford changed between the time he left to go to the men's room and the time he came back. His voice was a growl and his expression mean.

He finished what was in his glass and gestured with it toward McNulty. The movement was imperious, not so obvious that anyone would notice but McNulty and Ambler. In all the time Ambler had frequented the Library Tavern, he'd never seen McNulty miss an empty glass. If he was occupied with something else, he let the impatient tippler know by word or gesture, usually with his eyebrows, he'd get to him shortly.

He did this now with Ford. And the gesture he made with his eyes held a warning. Ambler had seen that before, too, though infrequently. It was like a parent telling a child to mind his manners but doing this in a way only the child would see and would not be embarrassed by being called out.

Ford got the message and put his glass down. He turned to Ambler. 'Gil Sanchez wasn't the character; I created the character. As I told you, I make things up.'

McNulty replenished Ford's drink and drew Ambler another beer. He didn't say anything to either of them while he did this.

'The real gangster was a great character also,' Ambler said.

Ford nodded.

'His viciousness was hard to take.'

Ford eyed him. 'If you'd run across the real guy, you'd know I went easy on him.'

Ambler decided to keep quiet and hope Ford would say more. He gave the bar a quick rap with his knuckles. Knock on wood.

'Big Nick. Nicholas Pappas. You never heard of him. No one did. He ran a crime empire. He might still be running it. He's killed as many people as might die in a short but bloody war. Never left a fingerprint on anything.' Ford muttered something to himself. To Ambler, he said, 'I can tell you his name because it won't mean anything. The cops know his name. They know what I just told you. They can't touch him.

'He could have you killed tomorrow—' Ford chuckled, a laugh at Ambler's expense. 'I could tell the cops he did it . . . and nothing would happen. He runs a liquor-distribution business that covers the Bronx and Upper Manhattan and he lives in Yonkers. To everyone, he's a successful businessman.'

'Did Big Nick bankroll Sanchez's gambling parlor?'

Ford raised his eyebrows. 'You catch on quicker than I thought you would. Do you think anyone would know if he did?'

'Sanchez would know. I'm wondering if you know.'

Ford gave a half-laugh, more of a grunt. 'No he wouldn't. He dealt with one of Nick's goons; he had no idea the goon worked for Nick.'

'Did you know this Big Nick?'

Ford gestured with his glass toward McNulty. 'You're going to need to read my memoirs to find out about Big Nick . . .

although if he finds out about this half-assed investigation you and your cop buddy are attempting, you might not be around to read my memoirs. Worse for your cop buddy. There's a long trail of dead cops who thought they'd put a collar on Mr Pappas.'

Ford smiled when he saw McNulty headed their way with the rum bottle in his hand.

'This one's on me,' he said after pouring Ford a normal-sized shot and topping off Ambler's beer. 'I expect you'll be paying up and moving along after this.'

Ford took a slug from his drink and didn't say anything for a while, shifting his gaze between the rows of bottles on the back bar and his glass of rum. McNulty's regulars had been drifting in, singly, in pairs, in small groups. Ambler was happy to see Adele coming in behind a small group of office workers out for some sort of office celebration. Not regulars; amateurs, McNulty called them.

Adele's face was faintly flushed; she had a worried, expectant look as if she might be late or have missed something. Ford caught a glimpse of her arriving in the mirror behind the bottles and made an elaborate motion of climbing off his barstool and moving to the next one over so she would sit between him and Ambler.

There wasn't a stool on Ambler's opposite side so nothing much he could do. He thought about sliding down to the stool Ford vacated and giving her the one he was on so he'd be between her and Ford. In retrospect it would have been a good idea. But the moment passed too quickly. She gave him an exasperated look, thanked Ford without enthusiasm, and sat down on the barstool he offered.

'I'm glad you came,' Ambler said.

Her you're-going-to-owe-me-for-this glance was more meaningful than words.

Ford tried for gallantry, asking what she'd like to drink, suggesting a daiquiri, whiskey sour, gin gimlet, but he'd drunk too much to pull it off. He leered at her and slurred his words, coming on to her in a way that would turn off any woman.

She told him McNulty knew what she drank and would bring her a beer, and turned toward Ambler.

Ford wouldn't quit. He told her she looked lovely this afternoon. She pointedly kept her back to him, and said to Ambler, 'I expect you'll be taking me to dinner.'

Ford's gallantry was the patronizing manner of a barroom Casanova left over from another era, wasted on Adele.

McNulty brought her a mug of beer. Placing a coaster and then the mug of beer in front of her, he said, 'Ah, Adele. Those beautiful brown eyes; I'll never love blue eyes again.'

She blushed and smiled. 'What do you say to green-eyed women, McNulty?'

The bartender laughed.

Adele's smile widened. 'My mother warned me to beware of bartenders.'

'As well she should have.' McNulty headed off to the service bar.

Ford watched the exchange with the bewildered, can't-quite-think-of-it expression of the intoxicated, looked for a moment as if he might say something but didn't.

'Mr Ford was telling me about some friends of his.'

Ford gave Ambler a sour look and spoke with an edge to his voice. 'Friends call me Will. But I don't guess we're friends. I don't like men who think they're better than me trying to con me with fake formality.' What had been a conversational tone for most of the afternoon turned nasty. He turned to Adele.

'Years ago when I was young and naive, I fell in with some small-time criminals. Thanks to your boyfriend here and an over-eager cop, repercussions of those associations are coming back at me in ways that are more threatening to me than either of the two idiots I just mentioned understand.'

Ambler could feel the fear behind Ford's belligerent tone. 'Why?'

Ford hadn't taken his eyes off of Adele. 'Bodies don't stay buried.'

When Adele started to speak, Ambler touched her shoulder as a warning not to engage Ford, but her sympathetic nature got the better of her common sense. She spoke softly. 'If something Raymond did put you in danger, that's not what he intended. And if you feel threatened, you should tell Detective

Cosgrove. He wouldn't put you in danger if he knew he was doing that. Neither would Raymond.'

Ford gave her an elaborate condescending smile. 'Father forgive them for they know not what they do.'

'I'm sorry you don't trust us,' she said.

Ford's smile, meant to be seductive, came off as lewd. 'I could find a way to trust you.' His tone, which he meant to be rakish, was smarmy. 'How about you ditch your boring boyfriend and we go somewhere and talk about it?' His gaze traveled up and down her body and stopped at her eyes. 'I'll give you a night you'll never forget.'

Ambler bristled, but he knew it was best to let Adele handle her own difficult situations, including difficult men, unless she asked for his help.

Her tone was chilling. 'It would be a night I wouldn't forget, but not for the reasons you think. You have no right to talk to me or any woman like that. Only an asshole would find your bullshit appealing.'

It was hard to tell if Ford was embarrassed. He watched her with a lecherous smile. 'I like feisty women. I like to make them whimper and moan. You'd be surprised. Women don't know what they want until they get it from the right man.'

Ambler moved his barstool a foot or so to his left so Adele could move farther away from Ford, who had inched his way into her space and was leaning too close to her.

She wore a plaid knee-length skirt and brown boots and the skirt slid up her thigh a few inches when she uncrossed her legs to step down from her barstool. When she noticed Ford eyeing her thighs, she started to turn her legs away from him. But he reached out and ran his hand along her thigh.

She jumped off the barstool and turned on him, squeezing the handle of her beer mug. 'I'm two seconds away from throwing this beer in your face.'

He sat back. 'It won't be the first time.' His expression was smug. 'And you won't be the first bitch I knock on her ass.'

Ambler moved quickly between them. 'If you touch her again, you'll be sorry.' He took a deep breath and sank into a bow posture, the basic tai chi fighting stance, an automatic reaction for him.

Ford recognized there was a method to what Ambler was doing. 'What are you, some kind of kung fu fighter?' He tried for a mocking tone but the mocking was tempered with uneasiness and more than a trace of alarm. He was off his stool with his back to the bar and didn't notice, as Ambler did, that McNulty was behind him with a leather sap in his hand.

After a few seconds, Ford realized the fix he'd gotten himself into. Like the night of his reception, the fight went out of him. He went from belligerent to an attempt at ingratiating submissiveness. 'I'm sorry. I didn't mean to offend the lady. Sometimes, I get carried away.'

'You need to leave,' Ambler said.

'Or what?' Ford said mildly.

'I'll have you arrested,' Adele said. She was shaking, her mouth moving before any words came out. Ambler knew it was anger, not fear. 'If you don't leave right now, I'm going to smash you in the face with this beer mug.' She yanked the mug from the bar and swung it in front of her, her hand shaking, beer sloshing over the rim.

My God, she's going to swing, Ambler realized. He touched her arm and put his hand on the beer mug. 'If you hit him, you'll be going to jail with him,' he said quietly and watched the fury in her eyes subside.

She hesitated. 'Just one whack?'

Ambler smiled.

She put the mug on the bar and her arm through Ambler's.

As they left, he glanced back at McNulty who, still holding the sap, had come from behind the bar and stood beside Ford as the writer fumbled through his pockets for the cash to pay the tab. McNulty rolled his eyes. 'I got it.'

NINE

A couple of hours later, after a wonderful dinner at an intimate and romantic French restaurant on a quiet street off Second Avenue, they were at Raymond's apartment. Adele had practiced what she'd say any number of times. She'd almost gotten up her nerve to tell him her plan two or three times but something always got in the way. Now, when she didn't expect it, she'd found the perfect time. Johnny was away for the entire week. They'd run the gamut of emotions already that evening – the horrible scene with that awful man and then a romantic dinner. Afterward, Raymond had kept his arm around her as they walked to his apartment. She could feel his excitement like a wave of electricity when he touched her.

They'd come close to making love more than once in the past. They both knew they would one day when the stars were aligned right. She'd already told him part of the plan. The rest shouldn't be so hard. She knew how she'd begin. 'Raymond, I want to tell you about my biological clock . . .' So she told him. 'We do love each other,' she said. 'I know that.' He didn't interrupt her. 'I want to have a baby. I've known since I was a little girl that I'd have a baby. And I want you to be the father.'

She knew what he'd say because he'd said it before, so she said it for him. 'You already have a son almost as old as I am, and you have a grandson, and you think you're too old to be a proper father to a baby.'

His expression was pained. 'You're the most wonderful woman I've ever known,' he said. 'You should be a mother. Your baby will be the luckiest kid in the world. I'm just not the right . . .' The lines of pain on his face etched deeper. She put her finger to his lips.

'I've thought this through, Raymond, in every possible way. It was very stupid of me, but I've fallen in love with you, and I don't want to find someone else to have a baby with.'

Now his expression was blank. It wasn't blank so much as uncomprehending. If she were to be perfectly honest, he might be taken for the village idiot – an adorable village idiot – so she kissed him.

She hadn't planned for it to be this night. That didn't mean she hadn't planned. She'd planned for a long time and was one hundred percent sure. The only question had been when. And this night after all that had happened she was smitten by him – and it was the right time on the clock, on the calendar. This was the night.

He was surprised when she said she didn't want to go home. She wanted to watch the baseball game with him. She kept giggling because he looked befuddled. He knew she was up to something; he'd never in a million years have guessed what.

She asked for another glass of wine, and then feeling ridiculous told him she wanted to take a shower and borrow a pair of his pajamas. When she finished, she talked him into taking a shower and putting on the pajamas she'd given him for Christmas. She said she wanted to curl up on the couch with him in their pajamas and watch the game. The Yankees were playing someone. It was spring training but Raymond was a big fan and watched the games almost every night they were on anyway.

When she cuddled against him on the couch after his shower, she felt his reaction when he discovered she wasn't wearing anything under the pajama top. He jumped when he touched her breast and snatched his hand back. She took his hand, kissed it, and put it back on her breast, nestling into him before he knew what was happening. The crowd at the baseball game was screaming about something in the background, but she'd gotten his full attention. Kissing him was lovely. They'd kissed before and it had always been good. But they'd never gone beyond that. This time her head was in a whirl.

When she came around again, it was the ninth inning. She was naked; Raymond's pajama bottoms were around his ankles. With his dazed expression and angelic smile, he watched her with a kind of tenderness she'd never seen. 'Wow,' he said. 'I'm seeing stars.'

She took his hand in hers. 'I think the Yankees are losing.'

'How did that happen?' He squeezed her hand.

'Watch the game,' she said.

They slept together that night but didn't make love again. Something about how perfect their lovemaking had felt told her it had worked.

In the morning, over eggs and bacon and toast that he made for them, she told him, 'We might have made a baby.'

Not much shook his tranquility. But this did. He stopped eating and stared at her speechless.

'You could have said no. You know how babies are made. You could have asked if I used protection. You could have offered to wear a condom.'

He cocked his head like his dumb dog Lola did when she heard something she didn't understand. The dog had slept on the floor next to the TV during their lovemaking, and alongside the bed with them afterward.

'I wanted to make love with you last night,' she said. 'No deception there. You swept me off my feet. I'm guessing you wanted to make love with me. We waited a long time and it was wonderful and I'm really, really happy we waited and really happy we didn't wait any longer. If a baby happens, I'll be especially happy. If not, we can try again.' She laughed.

When Ambler thought about it afterward, when he remembered every second of that evening, every word they'd spoken, every tender touch, every not so tender kiss, Adele's abandon, his rhapsodic reverie, he saw that Adele had seduced him. She'd taken charge – of what they did, when they did it, and why.

'You're too old fashioned to understand this fully,' she'd told him that morning. 'But I'll tell you anyway. Women's lives are different today than you could have imagined when you first learned about love and marriage. Families are different. The nuclear family is fine but no longer necessary. Choosing to raise a child as a single woman is a viable choice. You'd be surprised how many women think it's a better choice.

'I looked into in-vitro fertilization; but I wanted having a baby to be more personal than that. I thought about asking you to be a sperm donor; I thought if I did and had a son he might be like you. And then I thought: why couldn't we be lovers and have a baby the old-fashioned, more fun, way? The things that complicate our lives – that make it difficult or maybe impossible for us to be together – are circumstances that don't have to do with whether we love each other.'

Ambler hadn't quite caught up with what she said. 'If you do get pregnant and want to keep the baby,' he told her, 'I would feel that I should marry you.'

She turned on him like a dog ready to bite. 'You knock up your girlfriend, so you have to marry her . . .? You really are a relic of the fifties.' She watched him for a long moment, her eyes darkening. 'You'd marry me if I was pregnant because it was your gentlemanly obligation. You wouldn't marry me because you love me.'

His thoughts lay in his mind tangled up in knots. Adele had misunderstood what he'd said, or understood it in a different way than he'd meant. Yet he didn't know how to undo what he'd said. 'You don't understand. What I said . . .' he tried but stopped. 'I don't think *I* understand what I said.'

She laughed. 'It's because you're an anachronism. Fortunately, you don't have to understand. I'll take care of everything. If I get pregnant, I want you to be happy for me because I'll be happy. The question of love and marriage is an entirely different question. When you've thought about this for a while, you'll understand.'

Ambler thought about it a long while. What he understood was Adele wanted to have a baby and so she would. What he didn't understand was whether he'd have a baby.

TEN

As they'd walked out of the 42nd Street Library down the steep granite steps, past streams of tourists headed up and down the stairs, Cosgrove wondered if Chris would clue him in as to why he put on the dog and pony show with Will Ford. At the bottom of the steps, Chris didn't say anything, only shook his hand and beat a hasty retreat, not asking which way he was headed, not offering him a ride in the chauffeured squad car waiting at the curb.

So he was surprised when Chris called him the next morning and said to meet him at Corlears Hook Park near the softball fields at 10:30. That was all he said. The park was on the Lower East Side on the East River, a few blocks below the Williamsburg Bridge and the Fire Boat House, not far from Chinatown and the Vlasdek Houses, and not so far from One PP. Because the park was next to the river, it was a kind of secluded place to meet.

He found a parking space on Jackson Street, put the NYPD permit in the windshield, and walked a couple of blocks to the park. The sky was blue, the sun shining, small kids screeching and shouting ran around the playground while their moms or nannies, more moms than nannies in this neighborhood, watched them. A tugboat pushed a barge up the river and a cargo ship with a red hull headed down the river.

The view uptown toward the Williamsburg Bridge and downtown toward the Manhattan Bridge was peaceful. A few dogs meandered around the dog run while their owners leaned on the fence and watched. Some of the park's trees had developed springtime pinkish buds and he thought they might be cherry trees. Parks in the city were a good thing, he decided.

You came into one off the teeming city streets your mind buzzing with all the things you had to do and everything going too fast in your life, and the space, the trees, and little kids playing, and trees budding, and birds whistling, and you came to a stop, your mind stopped buzzing, you watched the boats on the river, or the river flowing, and you felt a kind of peace for a change.

He hadn't thought much on the way over about what Chris might want to talk about. But he knew the idea wasn't for them to have a few peaceful moments in the park. Chris didn't want to be overheard, for one thing. It was also likely he didn't want anyone to see them together. He might want to explain his strange questioning of Ford. Or he might want to read him the riot act for sticking with the case when he'd been told to drop it.

The ballfield was empty but two men in windbreakers sat together in the first row of the bleachers. When he got closer, he saw one was Black and one was white. He didn't have to guess. Chris brought reinforcements. He took a guess as to who the second man was.

They both stood as he got closer. Deputy Inspector George Kowalski was a bit shorter than Chris with broader shoulders and a chest like fifty-five-gallon drum. He wore glasses and had a mustache, not bushy but not a thin line either, and he had dimples when he smiled, which was sort of disarming. His gaze through his glasses was direct and challenging but not unfriendly. You thought him unimposing until you watched him for a moment. The dimples threw you off.

Chris introduced them and they shook hands. You'd almost say Kowalski was beaming with good nature. 'Good to meet you, Mike. I've heard from Chris here for twenty years or so you do a good job.' He frowned. 'I bet you didn't get any awards for that. Do things the right way, the best you can hope for is they leave you alone.' He shrugged and smiled, a self-deprecating gesture. 'I guess I mean "us" not "they" since I'm one of them.'

Kowalski went on like that for a while, as if they'd run into one another in a bar or at a PBA picnic. He came across as easy-going and down-to-earth, a one-of-the-guys manner that felt sincere. When he asked Cosgrove something or Cosgrove said something, he listened with interest. Cosgrove knew when someone paid attention or only waited until he could get on to saying what he was going to say next. Still, there was an officer-to-enlisted-man air about Kowalski. He didn't forget he was the boss; neither did Cosgrove. But when he finally got around to it, he laid his cards on the table, no apologies, no tiptoeing about. He spoke man to man, cop to cop.

'I was Billy's sergeant. He was a handful . . . headstrong. Always right. A pain in the ass. But you never wondered where he was when you were in trouble. You never asked who'd go in first if Billy was there. In some ways, what happened was my fault. I trusted my guys. You been around long enough. You remember what it was like. When it came to dishing out street justice, if that's what they needed to do, I didn't call them on it.'

At first, Cosgrove wasn't sure what he was being told. But he caught on quickly. Chris had talked to Kowalski and they'd decided that Cosgrove should hear the truth about the Manhattan Avenue murders. So he wasn't surprised when Kowalski looked him in the eye and said, 'I'm telling you the truth. Chris says you're a good cop.' Kowalski let this sink in. Cosgrove thought he probably should say something, but he didn't know what, so he kept quiet.

Kowalski didn't seem to mind. 'Maybe I should have called them on it, put a stop to it. When I look back, I can see where I might have been wrong. I wish some things that happened didn't happen. I wouldn't let anyone get away with that kind of crap now.'

He watched the ballfield for a moment and seemed to reconsider his regrets. 'That was then and that's how things were. We worked the streets, plain clothes. We did a lot of good. Took guns and drugs off the street. Put the fear of God into muggers. Showed the punks we were in charge. The system was rotten. You'd lock somebody up and two days later he'd be sniggering at you from some doorway. If we didn't mete out justice, no one would. Someone filed a complaint about a nightstick poke in the ribs, a knot on the head from a sap glove, the complaints got lost before they got anywhere. It wasn't like it is now.'

Kowalski smoked cigarettes and took one out now and lit it with a lighter. Every once in a while as he spoke, he'd glance at Chris. They'd look at each other for a moment and then

Chris would look at Cosgrove, meeting his gaze, as if to back up what Kowalski said. This happened a few times, so it felt like Chris was part of the conversation even though he didn't say anything.

'I'm telling you things you already know because I want you to understand.' They sat alongside one another on the front row of the bleachers, so it took some effort for one of them to meet the gaze of one of the others. Despite the effort, Kowalski had no trouble locking on to Cosgrove when he wanted to. 'You got interested in this case, the case where Billy bought it. You saw something wasn't right. I don't fault you for looking into it.' He shot a sharp glance at Cosgrove that contained a warning. 'Other cops might.'

What Kowalski told him confirmed what Cosgrove had discovered or guessed so far on his own. He'd also figured out a couple of things Kowalski hadn't gotten to yet. Knowing he probably wouldn't get to those things made Cosgrove uncomfortable.

'Billy got carried away,' Kowalski said. 'He got cocky, drank on the job, started doing coke . . .' Kowalski took a deep breath, a long sigh. 'He was doin' doors.'

Cosgrove got the message. 'Doin' doors' was cop talk for busting into drug locations and instead of arresting the dealers beating them up and stealing the money or the drugs or both. Cosgrove had suspected this and was inclined to believe Kowalski was being straight with him.

'I let him get away with too much. He came to think he didn't need to answer to anybody. The other guys on the team knew where to draw the line. Billy didn't.' Kowalski didn't like having to say what he was saying, so it sparked something in him. His face muscles tightened. The expression in his eyes hardened. He got mad at himself . . . but directed it at Cosgrove.

'This guy he went after, Sanchez, was a scumbag. What Billy did was bad. But Sanchez deserved what he got. He was connected so he thought he could do what he wanted. He thought he could push cops around, embarrass them, tell them to fuck off. He tried that with Billy. Billy didn't shake down mom and pop bodegas or the shoemaker or a pizza joint. He went after scum like Sanchez.'

Cosgrove wanted to help Kowalski get on with his story before he talked himself out of telling it. 'So Donovan busted the gambling operation on his own.'

Kowalski glared at him for a moment to tell him he'd overstepped his place. It wasn't a reprimand or pulling rank. It was the reaction of a man who didn't back down when another man challenged him, a *mano a mano* thing. Kowalski would have reacted the same way if it were the commissioner, the mayor, the president, or Al Capone who challenged him.

In that glance, he let Cosgrove know he was ready for whatever Cosgrove would bring his way. For his part, Cosgrove had no interest in taking him on and with his glance let him know that, so the moment passed.

'Billy went in after the joint closed when he thought Sanchez would be the only one there. He judged it wrong, got into a firefight. Everyone was killed except one of Sanchez's lowlife cronies. It was him who shot Billy, and we got him later.

'What we did after that is on me. That's why Chris didn't tell you about it. If it was only him, he would've.' He exchanged glances with Chris. 'We fixed the crime scene so it looked like Billy had been undercover and his cover got blown.' Kowalski's expression softened. Again, he didn't pull rank. He made his case: You're a cop. I'm a cop. Do the right thing.

'Billy had a wife and two kids. You know what would've happened if the real story got out. The brass would've thrown him to the wolves – dirty cop, disgraced his uniform – nothing about the good he did, the ordinary people he helped, the creeps he put away, the times he put his life on the line for a fellow officer. None of that meant anything.

'After his being a good cop and making a bad mistake, his wife would end up on welfare with two kids because she doesn't get his line-of-duty death benefits. What we did was make sure his widow got the benefits. That's the story. That's the cover-up.'

No one said anything else for a few minutes. They sat alongside one another on the bottom row of the bleacher seats staring at the empty field as they might if they watched a ballgame. Kowalski and Chris waited for him to come around. Cosgrove felt the uneasiness you feel when you know something you wish you didn't know that puts a hole in the story someone told you that you'd rather believe than disbelieve.

'I talked to Hernandez,' Cosgrove said, figuring he'd give Kowalski a chance to cover a base he skipped. Because he watched carefully, he noticed the flinch.

Kowalski looked Cosgrove over for a moment, like a teacher might look at a student who doesn't know an answer he's supposed to know. 'That asshole. If he ever told the truth about anything in his life, it was by accident. I'm surprised he told you his right name. We gave him a break . . . manslaughter on two charges. Either one could have been murder one.'

'He got religion.'

Kowalski lit another cigarette. 'Let me guess what he told you . . . He didn't do it.'

The skepticism was to be expected. Cops heard all the time, 'I didn't do it,' from perps as guilty as sin. He hadn't made a judgment himself as to whether he believed Hernandez. 'I told you I talked to him. It's out there. I'm not the only one who's going to hear it.'

'Yeh, it's out there because you put it out there.' Kowalski's voice shook with anger. 'That's what happens when you go digging up bones. Chris told you to drop the investigation. You should've listened. Now you rattled this douchebag's cage – these guys ain't dumb; they're smart like weasels – so he gets that someone's maybe opening up the investigation. He knows what's gonna happen – a dirty-cop story and a cover-up.

'Everything the dirty cop touched is tainted. He starts bellowing he was framed by the cops who did the cover-up. The judge throws out the conviction. If he's lucky, he gets off on the other murder, too, because that investigation is tainted by association. Two murder ones and he walks, gets back on the street so he can kill someone else.'

Cosgrove judged the look Kowalski gave him to be the kind of disgusted look one gives to a pile of dog shit you've stepped in. But Kowalski walked it back. He finished one cigarette and lit another. 'So you talked to him. You're not hiding it. You're telling us. You did the right thing. What he has to say don't mean shit if you don't buy it. I went off on you because punks like him playing the system makes me mad. They get away with it too much.'

Cosgrove had to step carefully. Kowalski could bring the department down on his head if he wanted to. 'You know, I didn't go looking for this,' he said. 'I stumbled into it. I wish I hadn't. Someone tells you two plus two makes five, you wonder why. One thing leads to another. I didn't fall off the turnip truck a couple of days ago. I've been on the job goin' on thirty years.'

Chris spoke for the first time. His voice cracked like a schoolboy on a stage. 'No one's questioning you on that, Mike. You came across something that didn't seem right so you looked into it. To be honest, what happened bothered me when it was happening. A lot of people would say it wasn't the right thing to do. The thing was, there wasn't a right thing to do. What good would it have done for Billy to go to his grave a disgraced cop?'

Chris glanced at Kowalski, who dragged on his cigarette and followed what he was saying with as much interest as Cosgrove. 'George knows it was hard for me to go along. The choice was to follow the book. Or do something else. Billy's kids lost their father. Wasn't that enough? Did we have to rub their noses in dirt?'

Sweat beaded on Chris's forehead. He looked to the sky; he looked at his feet. He reminded Cosgrove of a suspect making a confession who really did feel remorse. 'I'm not going to apologize for Billy. I didn't like him and he didn't like me.'

His expression was pleading. It was as if his life was on the line. And in a way it was. If what they did – covered up for a fellow cop who committed murder – got out, he and Kowalski would go down as disgraced cops along with Donovan. The possibility of ruining his friend's life hadn't caught up with Cosgrove until now.

'I didn't like how Billy did things. He knew I didn't so he never trusted me. He thought I might be a rat.' He glanced at Kowalski. 'If it wasn't for George, he and the other guys in the unit would have set me up or pushed me out.'

Chris let out his breath, a whoosh, as if he'd been holding

it for a long time. 'George told me something that in a crazy way made sense to me. Billy didn't do those robberies because he was a crook. He saw it as how to do his job. The system didn't punish these dirtbags, so he punished them. That didn't make it right. But it made a difference.'

Cosgrove let out a sigh himself. Chris was being straight; he believed that. He remembered the crack-cocaine epidemic, going out on two or three homicides a night, sleeping on a cot in the locker room, overwhelmed by the magnitude of what he and the other cops faced each day. Watching the patrol cops in uniform get heckled and humiliated by the same folks who called them and hid behind their doors when a maniac was menacing their block with a machete.

He found a way to smile. 'Makes you wonder why anyone with a half a brain would want to do this job, doesn't it?'

Chris and Kowalski stared at him for a moment and then they laughed, harder than they might under normal circumstances, a release of tension for all of them.

Kowalski threw away his cigarette butt and folded his arms across his chest. 'I told you what happened because Chris said you'd keep digging until you found out anyway. You know enough to hang us. I didn't even check you for a wire. I believe Chris when he says you're a good cop.' He paused for a long time, glancing this way and that, every now and again drilling Cosgrove with a hard stare. His scrutiny told Cosgrove he had something to answer for. Kowalski lit another cigarette. Cosgrove felt a rush of adrenaline like a blow to the gut. He knew what was coming.

'You made enemies with that Intelligence Division brouhaha, more than maybe you know. It takes a lot for a cop to turn on another cop. Not something you expect from a seasoned vet. But sometimes a guy has reasons.' His gaze drilled into Cosgrove. 'The thing is, what it'll look like if this gets out is you're making a habit of it.'

Cosgrove didn't flinch. If Kowalski expected mea culpas, promises, and oaths of allegiance, he was shit out of luck. They both knew he could have Cosgrove walking a beat in Staten Island or doing night duty in the Douglass Houses. Instead he did this man-to-man, cop-to-cop, do-the-right-thing

. . . until now. One time, Cosgrove hadn't looked away when some cops thought he should have. The stupid ones. Cops who knew him knew who he was. More important, he knew who he was.

After a moment, without letting go of the eye lock, Kowalski said, 'I got a meeting I got to be at. You wanna know more, Chris will fill you in on whatever you need.' He paused, his eyes still on Cosgrove. 'You're OK. Chris is a good judge of people.'

Watching him walk away with a decided limp, Cosgrove remembered that Kowalski had been shot early in his career and his partner killed. The guy had paid his dues. Still when he left, the tension that had been there went with him. The park was an oasis again, the river flowed gently; in the distance a ship's horn moaned. He looked at Chris and almost smiled. The poor guy looked like he'd wrestled an alligator.

ELEVEN

Ambler spent a distracted day at the library. He didn't see Adele except in his imagination where he couldn't stop seeing her – standing in front of the couch in his unbuttoned pajama top. It wasn't her day off but she'd called in.

'It was a peculiar call,' Harry said, peculiar enough for Harry to come to the crime fiction reading room to tell him about it. 'I don't know why she called me. She never has before. I don't keep her schedule. I told her I was sorry she wasn't feeling well. She laughed and said she'd never felt better. I didn't ask her anything after that.' His brow wrinkled and he got that owlish expression he got when he was worried. 'Did you notice anything unusual about her lately?'

A picture of her in that pajama top flashed through Ambler's mind's eye again and he felt himself blush. 'No. She's fine . . . I'm sure she's fine.' He realized he was smiling, a kind of goofy smile.

When Harry left, Ambler stared blankly at the rows of books in front of him. He wondered if Adele felt the same sort of giddiness that he felt. Something remarkable had happened to them the night before, beyond the joy of lovemaking; it was the bringing to the light of day the possibility . . . the chance . . . the likelihood they were in love. Like Adele, he could have laughed and told Harry he never felt better – like the guy in the song who hopped and jumped so merrily over the water pumps.

She wanted to have a baby. Of course she wanted to have a baby. She should have a baby. The question was should he have a baby. Anyone with sense would say: Of course not. What a wonderful thing and at the same time what an insurmountable problem. First, you had almost a twenty-year difference in age between him and Adele. Then you had what would be a thirtysomething-year age difference between his older son and his younger child, with a grandson who would be ten years older than the young child, who'd be his brother? nephew? uncle? Who the hell knew? It didn't seem like it should be possible to have a son or daughter younger than your grandson.

He was sitting in the crime fiction reading room, his head spinning, laughing out loud, his mind racing through the improbable probabilities of his family relations, when his phone rang. It was his son's lawyer, David Levinson.

John was in prison on a murder conviction. Some years before, he'd killed a man he shared an apartment with in a fight fueled by alcohol and cocaine. John killed him with the gun the other man had pulled on him; it went off as they wrestled for it. John had been a drinker, a pot-smoker, a traveling musician living the nightlife – not a solid citizen but not a criminal.

His son had taken a man's life and deserved to be punished. He should have been charged with involuntary manslaughter but because of a botched defense, an aggressive prosecutor, and a tough-on-crime judge, he was convicted of second-degree murder and sentenced to serve a minimum of fifteen years.

David had won a new trial for John and had been negotiating for a plea deal with the District Attorney's Office. The phone call was to tell Ambler the ADA would agree to a reduced charge of manslaughter if John would plead to it. The problem was the DA's office wouldn't agree to time served. John would have to go through a parole hearing.

Lisa Young's husband, Arthur, had offered to help Levinson with the appeal, which might be why the District Attorney's Office was negotiating a plea deal. Ambler had never spoken to Young about his son, Johnny's father, whom Young had never laid eyes on. He helped John because of Johnny. Ambler's new hope would be that whatever weight Young had to throw around might influence the parole board, too. John had served enough time on a manslaughter conviction to be eligible for parole. The problem was, unlike time served, the outcome of a parole hearing was uncertain.

Still, it was good news. Also on the bright side, Johnny would be coming home from his spring-break trip that evening.

As thrilled as Ambler was, he worried if life among the patricians might have turned his grandson's head so he'd resent returning to his pauper life after his time as a prince.

With so much on his mind, he'd pretty much forgotten about Will Ford until he got another phone call in the late afternoon from a nurse at Presbyterian Hospital in Upper Manhattan.

'Mr Ambler?' a woman's voice said. 'I'm calling from NewYork-Presbyterian Hospital on behalf of a patient we admitted last night through the Emergency Room.'

The patient was Ford. He'd been assaulted. The police picked him up on the street and brought him to the ER; he'd been admitted because he'd suffered a concussion. The hospital didn't want to release him unless he had somewhere to go and someone to look after him. Ford gave the woman on the phone a few names but she either couldn't reach the person or when she did reach someone they wouldn't take responsibility for him. Ambler was the last name on the list. She asked if he'd come and get Ford. She said this in such a way that he understood he'd be doing her and the hospital a favor if he would.

He wanted to say no; he'd had enough of Ford. But he felt responsible – after all he'd brought him to New York – so he said he'd come up when he finished work. With luck, he might get Ford on a plane and back to Texas before the reprobate brought the entire city to its knees.

The problem was he didn't want to take him to his apartment because Johnny was coming home. He certainly couldn't send him to stay with Adele. He had two thoughts: Cosgrove and McNulty. With Cosgrove, there was his daughter to consider – like putting the fox up for the night in the chicken coop. It was late enough in the afternoon, so he called McNulty.

'Why not?' said McNulty. 'I've got a fold-out couch that most of the no-accounts on the west side of Manhattan have flopped on at one time or another. One more no-account won't hurt it.'

Ford was subdued as Ambler made his way through the discharge paperwork and most likely signed his life away to get Ford released.

'It'll be OK,' he said while they waited for a cab in front of the hospital. 'I've got insurance. I gave them the card.'

Ambler wasn't so sure he wanted to know but when they got into the cab he asked anyway. 'What happened?'

'I was drunk. I went to a place a guy in a bar told me about, a massage parlor in Washington Heights.' He hung his head and held his hands folded in his lap as they headed down Broadway. He sounded apologetic. 'I used to know the neighborhood, St Nicholas Avenue near 181st Street. It's changed. The massage parlor was above a Dominican restaurant, really more like a bar. I stopped for a drink before I went upstairs. When I left the restaurant, someone jumped me.'

'Did you see who it was?'

'Only flashes. A baseball bat, I think. Dominicans, I guess.' He lifted his head to look at Ambler. 'Dominicans are really into baseball.'

Ambler laughed in spite of himself. 'Two?'

'I don't know. Could've been ten.'

'Do you know why?'

'You'd have to ask them.'

Ambler didn't entirely believe the story he was told. Ford sounded too off-handed. 'What were you doing in Washington Heights?'

'I told you . . . going to a massage parlor. Happy ending and all that. The guy told me the bordellos on Manhattan Avenue got driven out by gentrification and the hookers moved uptown to massage parlors.' He glanced at Ambler out of the side of his eyes. 'I told you I was drunk. I tried to relive my past.'

'Someone jumped you for no reason? . . . Not something from your past catching up with you?'

'I'm tired of talking about that.' Ford's glance was sharp and accusing. 'You're the one waking up sleeping monsters. I want to get out of this fucking city as soon as I can . . . and in one piece. You're no help.' He rethought that. 'Thanks for getting me out of the hospital.'

Ford's thinking was foggy. He was in trouble and Ambler almost felt sorry for him. 'You know if instead of taking this on by yourself you told me what was really going on and what really happened in the past, I might be able to help. At least you'd have two people on your side instead of just you against the world.'

The cab had stopped on Broadway at the corner of McNulty's street. 'I used to live a couple of blocks down Broadway on 104th Street,' Ford said when they got out of the cab. 'This is my old neighborhood.' He stood for a moment taking in his surroundings. 'I remember Tom's. It's good something is the same when everything else changes.'

'You can stay with McNulty for tonight, maybe one more night, not any longer than that. They said at the hospital you shouldn't fly. Can you take a train back to Texas?'

'I appreciate your help and the bartender's.' Ford's expression was mournful but determined. He continued to glance around him, a stranger in a strange land. 'I don't need a caretaker. You can leave me right here. I'll go back to my hotel.'

'Where is it?'

Ford glanced furtively around him. 'I don't know.'

'Stay with McNulty tonight. You can go to your hotel tomorrow when you remember where it is.'

McNulty's apartment was a decent-sized one-bedroom in a rent-stabilized, pre-war building on 111th Street between Broadway and Riverside. He'd lived there a long time while the neighborhood became upscale around him. The part-time doorman opened the door and told them McNulty was expecting them. His apartment was on the first floor. Ambler left Ford at the door to the apartment. But before he left, he asked McNulty to step out into the hallway.

'When I talked with Ford in your bar yesterday, he told me about a kingpin gangster in Northern Manhattan who might have had something to do with the Manhattan Avenue murders. Next thing you know he gets beat up in Northern Manhattan. Do you know your way around Washington Heights?'

McNulty shrugged. 'I have more than a tourist's knowledge of the area. I had a girlfriend once who worked in Washington Heights. I got to know some people. I also have Dominican friends who I've worked the stick with who work up there now. Good guys. Baseball fans.'

'Can you check out Ford's story – a quick once over? Ask him to tell you what happened and then check it out?'

'I could.' McNulty scrutinized Ambler's face. 'Should I sleep with one eye open?'

Ambler was puzzled. 'I don't think so. Why?'

'If this guy does know who killed those folks back in the day, there's one surefire way he'd know.'

Ambler nodded. 'He could have done it. I don't think so. Someone might have told him what happened; possibly the killer himself. It's also possible he was there, a witness, and lived to tell about it – or more accurately, not tell about it.'

Shortly after Ambler got home after leaving Ford with McNulty – not a match made in heaven – the doorbell rang and Johnny was home. Strangely, as soon as the bell rang, somnolent Lola went nuts. Through some sort of dog telepathy she knew it was Johnny.

This was the longest his grandson had been away from him since he first discovered he had a grandson three years before – and the longest Johnny had been away from Lola since she arrived a year or so ago. She stayed at the door barking and whimpering while he went to open the downstairs door.

The Youngs' driver carried Johnny's bag from the curb to the building entrance. Ambler came down to the door, even though Johnny had a key and only one bag so could easily have come up to the apartment himself. As he waited in the doorway, he felt tears building behind his eyes. Johnny watched him as he walked beside the driver to the door. The boy had a glowing tan and his hair was a couple of shades lighter.

'Hey,' Ambler said. 'I'm glad you're home. I missed you.'

'Hey,' said Johnny. He took the bag from the driver and thanked him.

The driver put his arm around Johnny's shoulder and gave him a little hug. 'Good kid,' he said, nodding at Ambler for longer than you'd think someone would nod. 'A real good boy.'

Ambler smiled.

'Should I take the bag?'

'No. I got it,' Johnny said.

'Put it down so I can hug you.'

Johnny put the bag down and allowed himself to be hugged.

When Ambler finally let go, Johnny picked up the bag. 'You should see the Youngs' digs in Florida,' he said. 'A house as big as an apartment building and a yard as big as Madison Square Park. They got the ocean a half a block from the house and they got a swimming pool. What kind of weird is that?'

He held the bag with both hands lugging it up the stairs. 'Here's where we need a swimming pool.' He let go of the bag with one hand to wave it at his surroundings. 'Can we have dinner with Adele? Chinese?'

Ambler wanted to help him with the bag but knew better than to try. 'Did you have fun?' He didn't know what he wanted the answer to his question to be.

Johnny wrinkled his nose. 'I guess. There weren't any other kids around. You get sort of bored sitting by the pool. We went to Disneyland one day and Sea World another day. Those were fun. Mostly I liked to sit on the beach. Pelicans flew right over your head and I saw manatees . . . I forgot. One time we went to where you could swim with dolphins. That was sort of cool, but I felt like the dolphins were being exploited.'

'Exploited'? 'Digs'? This was vocabulary he learned from Uncle Brian McNulty.

'I'll call Adele and tell her you're home and see if she wants to have dinner.'

'Did you see her while I was away?'

Ambler blushed and stammered before he said, 'Of course. I see her all the time. We work together.'

'That's not what I meant.' Johnny looked at him significantly, as if he were the adult. Ambler felt uneasy under the scrutiny. Could Johnny have thought Adele and he . . . while he was gone? No. Johnny was too young to think about that. Wasn't he?

Lola danced and whirled and jumped on Johnny as soon as Ambler opened the apartment door, knocking him and the suitcase over, wagging her stub of a tail, wriggling and dancing and licking his cheeks while he laughed and tried to push her away.

Ambler did call Adele, with an unfamiliar nervousness, and she did want to have dinner. The nervousness was because he didn't know what seeing her would be like after the night before, especially since it would be with Johnny. Would she be different? Would she expect him to be different? Did she regret what happened?

When he and Johnny met her in front of the restaurant – the Szechuan place on Third Avenue where the waiter knew them by name – Mr Ambler and Miss Adele – and remembered Johnny liked cold sesame noodles – everything felt the same. Johnny ran to hug her and started telling her a half-dozen things about his trip to Palm Beach. She smiled at Ambler over the top of Johnny's head.

The restaurant was never really busy and it was never really not busy. The waiter met them at the door and led them to a table near the window. 'Long time,' he said.

Johnny told him he'd been in Florida.

'Florida.' The waiter smiled and nodded rapidly. 'Cold noodles?'

Johnny said yes and laughed.

Ambler met Adele's glance three or four times and each time glanced away. She didn't; she kept her eyes on him, smiling dreamily. He didn't know what to say. Certainly, he shouldn't mention . . . Should he say thank you or 'it was fun' or . . . Instead, he told her he had to get Will Ford from the hospital that afternoon and what had happened to him.

'He got beat up again?' Adele said. 'That's three times in one week. McNulty, you, and whoever got him last night.'

Johnny was all ears. 'You and Uncle McNulty beat somebody up?' He bounced in his seat and pouted. 'I miss everything.'

'Stop,' Ambler said. 'We didn't beat anyone up. Adele's exaggerating. But Mr Ford did get hurt last night. He said someone hit him with a baseball bat.'

Johnny demanded to know what else happened while he was gone, so Ambler reluctantly told him the bare bones of the goings on.

'Can I read the story the guy wrote?'

'No. You don't need that kind of story; it's too grisly.'

'I watch grisly movies,' he said.

Adele and Ambler both jumped at him. 'Not when I'm around you don't,' Ambler said.

'Where did you see grisly movies?' Adele's admonishing tone sounded like he'd tortured a cat.

Johnny realized he'd made a strategic mistake and hung his head, a picture of the guilty accused.

'Well?' Adele asked. For some reason, Johnny was more contrite when she was mad at him than when Ambler was.

'I had my own room in the hotel when we went to Orlando, so I could download movies on the TV . . . The Youngs aren't so used to having a kid around. They don't know what I'm supposed to be able to do, so they ask me. They don't know what to talk to me about either, so mostly they ask what I've been doing. And I haven't been doing anything except sitting by the pool or on the beach. It's a good thing I like to read. They had lots of books in the house.

'I spent more time with the cook, and she let me help with the cooking.' He gave Ambler a sour look. 'Not just washing the dishes.'

In the middle of the afternoon the following day McNulty showed up in the crime fiction reading room on his way to work. He pulled up a chair across from Ambler at the library table that served as his desk. 'You were right that what Ford said happened wasn't what happened. I got a different story from a guy I know.

'He was my bar back at a hotel I worked at. Now he's a bartender at a neighborhood joint up there and knows pretty much everybody in the nightlife. He asked around for me.

'The guy who runs La Casa Grande, the place where Ford had a drink, said what happened to Ford was a hit, not something random. What he said is the guy waited for Ford outside. He must have followed him. No baseball bat. The guy hit him with a *cachiporra*, a sort of Dominican nightstick.'

'Who was the guy waiting for him?'

McNulty didn't like being prodded and gave Ambler the kind of glance a small-town librarian might use when she was shushing someone. 'I'm getting to that. The crime boss up there – the guy Ford told you about – is Nick Pappas, a Greek. They call him Big Nick. Everybody knows he runs the rackets in Upper Manhattan. But no one ever says that, especially not to him. He's a businessman. No one says out loud that he's anything else. Our pal went looking for him at a private club where Pappas likes to play *Tres y Dos*.

'As I said, Mr Pappas doesn't like to be noticed, especially doesn't like drunks coming by his private club throwing his name around.'

'You think Mr Pappas had Ford worked over?'

'It would not surprise me.'

When McNulty left for work, Ambler pulled out the file box from the Will Ford collection that contained the short story that caused all the trouble. He didn't want to read the story again but hoped to find something else in the box that might tell him more about the time the events of the story took place.

As soon as he opened the box, he saw with alarm that some of the files were gone. He felt a shock, the kind of otherworldliness you feel when something wildly unexpected happens. He had the same kind of shock once when he was young, in college, and the car he'd borrowed from a friend was stolen. He'd parked it in the alley outside the back door of his apartment. When he came out to get the car, it was gone. He stared unbelievingly at the empty space where the car had been an hour before. He kept staring at the empty space as if somehow the car was there and he couldn't see it. He couldn't imagine that it was gone. This was the feeling as he stared into the half-empty file box. What was happening couldn't be happening. How could half the files be missing? As with the missing car, it took him some few moments to figure out what to do next.

That time he called the owner, who called the police. What he should do this time was call security, but he hesitated. He might be in trouble. Was it his fault the files were missing? He'd had all sorts of people in the reading room. He decided to call Adele first. In addition to everything else she was to him – more than ever after the other night – she was the union steward for Manuscripts and Archives.

She was at her desk and picked up the phone right away.

'Something really weird happened.' His throat was so dry he croaked out the words. 'Some of the Ford files are missing.'

'I've got them,' she said calmly.

Once more, he wasn't sure he understood what had happened. She had the files? This also seemed not possible.

'I was going to read the story again but when I glanced through the box I saw he kept a kind of writer's journal, so I began reading that. It was interesting, so I took it with me. Did you know his mother deserted him when he was a baby? She came home after a year or two and then deserted him again for good when he was four.'

'No,' Ambler said. 'You have the files from the file box?'

'Yes . . . Sorry. I suppose I should have left you a note. I didn't expect you to go apeshit.'

He laughed. That was Adele. You could take the girl out of Brooklyn, but you couldn't take Brooklyn out of the girl. Her language at times would embarrass a sailor.

'Do you need them back right away?'

'No. I got worried when I saw they were gone.'

'I want to keep reading. He hated his mother . . . I mean really hated her. You should read what she did to him. No wonder he became a misogynist . . .' She paused. 'I guess it's better he took his hatred out in his writing than if he went around killing women . . . unless he's been doing that, too.'

'Did you come across anything about the Manhattan Avenue murders?'

She said she hadn't. What she was reading was about when he was young, a kind of disjointed memoir. She lowered her voice, a tone he hadn't heard before except for the other night; he'd have to say her tone was sultry. 'The other night was fun,' she whispered, 'more fun than I'd expected. I might want to do it again. How about you?'

He was dumbfounded. Speechless. Of course, he wanted to sleep with her again.

'Are you still there?' Her tone changed; she sounded worried. 'You're not mad, are you?'

'About the files?'

'Not about the files, you asshole!' she bellowed like a truck driver.

Ambler stared at his phone. She'd hung up.

TWELVE

McNulty finished cleaning and restocking the bar a little after midnight, checked the kitchen to make sure the garbage was out, all the burners turned off. On a normal night, he'd stop for a drink at Jimmy's Corner on 44th Street or one of the other late-night bars in midtown; other nights he might stop at a late-night bar uptown where the bartenders and waitstaff from the neighborhood hung out after work. This night, he wouldn't do either.

Will Ford had come in an hour before closing. That was strange enough. Even stranger was his request that McNulty go by the hotel he'd been staying at, pick up his suitcase that was mostly packed, not worry about leaving anything behind, and check him out. He didn't want to go himself because he thought his life might be in danger and that the hotel was being watched. He had one drink, paid his check, and gave McNulty the room key and a credit card. He didn't say who might be watching.

McNulty didn't ask him any questions. All his life for some reason he'd been a guy people asked favors of and he'd always felt obliged to do the favors. When he wondered at the reason for this, he thought it could be he might need a favor himself one day and was lining up folks he could lean on when that time came. At other times, he thought it was what you were supposed to do, a deal you made with your fellow man when you signed on for the trip.

This time he thought more about whether or not to do the favor before he agreed because Ford was such a strange duck. At times, he was inoffensive, polite, quiet as a mouse, keeping to himself. The next thing you knew he was stomping around like a bantam rooster, obnoxious, asking for a fight.

He'd seen men like Ford before. Something came over them; they had one drink too many, and a memory of a slight or an insult caught up with them, and they went off on some poor soul near them minding his own business. It was like in the horror movies. The guy's standing there and all of a sudden his teeth start growing; his ears get pointed; he growls instead of speaking. The guy who'd had one too many would come back the next day either contrite or acting like nothing happened. McNulty didn't hold a grudge; but he didn't forget how the guy had acted either. He wasn't joking when he told Ambler about sleeping with one eye open.

The hotel Ford stayed at was on Eighth Avenue a couple of blocks up from Port Authority, one of the second-tier hotels making a play for budget travelers, which meant a lot of Europeans. Nothing wrong with them or the tourists from Kansas or Arizona, it just made for an understaffed, hectic, and colorless lobby. Since he wasn't familiar with the hotel and didn't want to wander around the lobby looking for the elevator and attract attention, he found a chair and sat down to get his bearings. It didn't take long.

Unlike some hotels, in this one all of the elevators went to all of the floors, so he didn't need to sit long. He showed his key card to the security guard and took the first elevator that opened its doors to the ninth floor. No problem with the key for the door and no problem packing up everything that wasn't already in the suitcase. Ford, like McNulty himself when he had reason to travel, lived out of his suitcase instead of unpacking and using the drawers and closets. Ford's laundry was in a couple of the hotel-provided plastic bags; he had one suit in a garment bag hanging in the closet, a pair of shoes beneath it on the floor; everything else including his toiletry bag was in the suitcase.

The suitcase was good-sized, bigger than a carry-on, on wheels, but still awkward to maneuver while carrying the garment bag. He didn't like carrying things, especially on the subway, so he'd need to take a cab. To check out of the hotel, he had to stand in line. He thought it would be too complicated to check out over the phone. It bothered him that the patronizing desk clerk talked too loud, called him Mr Ford, and asked too many questions, but he let it go.

What he did do was find another chair and survey the lobby to see if he could spot anyone who might be watching for

Ford. He hadn't seen anyone in the hallway upstairs; he didn't see anyone in the lobby paying any attention to him when he first arrived, and he didn't see anyone who attracted his interest now.

The pompous desk clerk did bandy Ford's name about more than necessary and was still glancing over at him while he did his reconnoitering. Otherwise, the lobby was busy – folks coming, folks going, families huddled with their suitcases waiting for their rooms to be ready, small groups meeting up with other small groups. A security guard checked key cards near the elevator. Probably there was a hotel dick hiding in plain sight in the lobby. But that was it. He made his way out to the street and let the doorman hail him a cab.

When he got home, he found Ford at his dining room table with a bottle of Appleton rum in front of him. His eyes were heavy and he slumped in his chair more than sat in it. McNulty threw the bags on the couch across from the table – he called it his dining room table but he didn't really have a dining room, or else he didn't have a living room – poured himself a drink from Ford's bottle and sat down across from his unwelcome roommate. 'I don't normally drink rum, but you look like you need help. When'd you eat last?'

Ford shrugged.

McNulty went to the kitchen, took a couple of slices of pizza from his freezer and turned on his toaster oven. 'These are good slices; you can't heat them in a microwave,' he told Ford. They drank in silence until enough time had passed for McNulty to put the slices in the oven. While they heated, Ford told him he'd made a train reservation for the following morning.

'The last time I left this fucking city it was under a dark cloud also. I wasn't sure I'd make it out alive. And here I am again. I shouldn't have come back. I knew better. But I came anyway.'

McNulty nodded and drank.

Ford laughed, a raspy, self-mocking laugh. 'I was being honored. I thought it would be cool; I'd never been honored. Not much of an honor it turned out. A bunch of angry broads put the kibosh on it.'

McNulty went for the pizza slices. Ford looked distastefully at the slice in front of him.

'You want to make it back to Texas, you need to eat. If you stay drunk, they'll likely throw you off the train.'

Ford began eating. 'The city brings out a violent and angry part of me that I don't like. In the country, I'm a nice person. I hunt, fish, take care of my horses. I'm OK as long as I stay away from women. Just every once in a while I get an urge. Like the old-time cowboys, I go to town, get liquored up, shoot up the saloon, terrorize some woman, and wind up in the hoosegow.' He looked at the pizza slice he'd taken a few bites of while he talked. 'Thanks for this. It's good.'

'Not something you can get in Texas.' McNulty looked at the rum bottle. 'You gonna drink until you go to the station?'

'I can go now. I don't want to impose any more.'

'Most nights I'm up 'til four or five. We can have another drink and get breakfast at the all-night Greek diner down the street.'

'Why are you doing this?' Ford scrutinized him. 'You don't know me. What you do know of me you don't like much.'

McNulty didn't like the question because he didn't like the answer he might have to give. Most nights after work, he drank in a bar until closing time, not a lot, two or three beers, and then went to breakfast with whatever wino was left at the bar when the lights went up. What he'd have to tell Ford if he answered was he needed the company, which was another way of saying he was lonely. Late at night when the music stopped he didn't like being alone.

Instead of answering the question, he raised the stakes. 'Maybe, as long as you're leaving town and I've done you a solid, you'll own up to what you were doing in Washington Heights the other night and who you think it is that's out to get you.'

Ford shook his head. 'I'd like to tell you. I really would . . . I can't. Not telling anyone is the only chance I have.'

While they were finishing their drinks, McNulty put on a record; he had a small collection of vinyl jazz and country records, not according to any plan he had for collecting but because he'd accumulated them at some point years before and because he'd been in the same apartment for so many years so had they.

As they listened to 'He Stopped Loving Her Today', Ford said, 'I drank with George Jones one night at Threadgills, a music joint in Austin. He had a crew cut and wore a blue polyester suit. He was plastered.'

'The Possum fits in pretty good at this time of night,' McNulty said.

'I'm surprised you listen to country music.'

'I worked at the Lone Star back in the day. I used to smoke pot with Kinky Friedman.'

Ford chuckled. 'We're a good couple of name-droppers, ain't we?'

McNulty realized Ford had let down his guard – become a likable guy with an easy laugh, a friendly glimmer in his eyes – which meant Ford had been on his guard every time he'd seen the man since he'd been in the city, even when he was drunk.

McNulty made sure he met Ford's gaze. 'I'm not into judging people; I've got my own snakes to kill. But I'm leery of men who hurt women.'

No flare up. Instead, what McNulty took to be sadness darkened Ford's eyes. 'I don't like that part of me either; I try to keep a lid on it. It's why I don't like cities. Cities bring it out. It's why I live in a cabin on the hill. The angry broads were right to be angry. Honoring me wouldn't be right. My books are what's worthwhile. Not me.'

Ford was in his cups now, maudlin. McNulty was sorry he'd brought him to that. 'It's time to go to breakfast,' he said.

Ford went on as if he didn't hear him. 'I've never physically hurt a woman, and some women, at least one, I think I loved. Some women are, because of their own demons, susceptible to abuse. If you asked the abuser, he'd tell you they asked for it.' Ford was now deep into his soliloquy.

'One thing I'll tell you I probably shouldn't. During that time in New York, the way I got to know those folks who were killed that night and how I got myself into the mess I'm in now, I was a pimp. Not much of one, I was an apprentice to Annabelle Lee.' He returned from his reverie. 'Enough about that, before I'm hoisted on my own petard.' He laughed. 'Annabelle Lee was a reader, and might have become a writer if she hadn't been murdered. She talked to me about pimping. I talked to her about writing.' He raised his eyebrows. 'Her name wasn't an accident.'

McNulty waited for more but whatever spell had come over Ford was broken. 'I don't suppose this Greek diner has grits.' He shook his head. 'I want to get back to Texas and live long enough to die of old age.'

For a long time afterward, McNulty would remember with sorrow Ford saying that. They never made it to the Greek diner. Broadway was a lot safer than it once had been. His neighborhood had never felt unsafe to McNulty. But he always made himself aware of what was around him anyway, especially when he went out into the small hours of the morning.

A fruit stand above 110th Street was open all night; a pizza slice joint, a tiny deli, a donut shop were also open. A few taxis with their dome lights on made their way downtown after late-night fares to Upper Manhattan, a cop car was often stopped in front of the donut shop, so there was enough activity to discourage bandits from lurking in alleys and doorways. Even more so since the area had been reclaimed by the bourgeoisie, it felt safe.

Still, he glanced left and right when he came out of his apartment, up and down Broadway when he got to the corner. Ford walked beside him watching his feet. Crossing 109th Street against the light, McNulty watched an oncoming car crossing Broadway and didn't look west soon enough. He heard something, felt something wrong, and in a split second Ford wasn't next to him. A hand grabbed his belt from behind and something hard and cold, like the barrel of a snub-nosed revolver, pressed into his ribs.

The hand holding his belt propelled him into the dark of 109th Street and a man's voice said, 'Keep walking, walk fast, and don't look back if you don't want to die.'

Out of the corner of his eye, he watched Ford on his knees next to a car at the curb. The writer held one hand against his head, and reached for the car's fender with his other hand, more feebly waving at it than reaching for it.

The voice with the gun said, 'Run. Now.'

McNulty ran a few steps and reached into his pocket for his roll of quarters. As far as he could tell, it was only one man. He ran a few more steps and turned, his hand wrapped around the quarters, thinking he could take the guy who would be concentrating on Ford. As soon as he turned, he heard two shots and dropped to the sidewalk. When he looked up, no one was between him and Broadway. He pulled himself to his feet and froze when he saw a form on the ground, half on the sidewalk, half in the street, draped over the curb. The shots hadn't been for him. They were for Ford.

He walked to where the body lay and looked down. Ford lay with the side of his face on the sidewalk in a slowly forming pool of blood.

A man crossing 109th Street headed downtown on Broadway glanced down the street at them. McNulty didn't know if he was the killer. He hollered, 'A man's been shot.' The man crossing the street stopped. 'Call 911,' McNulty shouted. The man took out his cell phone. It was near three in the morning. A group of four or five young people walking up Broadway looked down 109th Street toward McNulty but kept walking.

The man with the cell phone yelled to McNulty that he'd called 911, took another long look down 109th Street at them, and moved on. McNulty watched the corner and every few seconds glanced at the body. He didn't know if Ford was dead or alive. But it didn't matter if he knew or not. What could he do to help him? If Ford was alive the cops or the medics would do something. He kept his eyes on the corner as if his watching would speed up whoever was coming.

A patrol car, lights flashing, its siren a low moan like a whimper, arrived first and another a few seconds behind it. The first cop drew his gun when he got out of the car and told McNulty to show his hands, which he did by extending his arms above his head like they did in the movies. The second cop came toward McNulty without a gun drawn and told him to put his hands on the roof of the parked car he stood next to and take a couple of steps backward.

'I want to search you,' he said. 'Will I find anything dangerous?'

'No,' McNulty said. He'd had enough encounters with cops over the years to know he should let them do whatever they had in mind to do before he tried to explain anything.

The cop pressed his hand against McNulty's thigh and felt the quarter roll in his pocket. 'What's this?' It was clear what he meant.

McNulty told him.

'Is it taped?'

'No.'

'A weapon?'

'No.'

'For the laundromat, I suppose.'

'It's not important. I didn't shoot the guy with it.'

'Did you shoot him?'

'No. I was with him. We were walking down the street.'

'Where were you going?'

'To the Greek diner.'

'Who is he?'

'Can I put my hands down?'

'Slowly and hand me that roll of quarters.'

THIRTEEN

Ambler made dinner that night for himself and Johnny. He was chopping onions for a simple marinara sauce when Johnny told him he was using the chef's knife wrong.

'You chop with the back of the knife. Want me to show you?' He did. 'The Youngs' cook showed me.'

'Back to school tomorrow,' Ambler said as they ate dinner.

'Yeh. I know.'

'Did you have any assignments for over the break?'

'A book to read. I have to write a report.'

'What's the book?'

'*A Wrinkle in Time*.' He paused for a moment. Ambler guessed he was remembering something about the book. Johnny liked to read so that part of school was never a problem. A streak of rebelliousness created a discipline issue now and again but so far nothing serious. 'It was weird, then it was really good, then it was really sad at the end.'

Ambler thought for a moment about what to say. 'Sad is part of life, so I guess it could be part of a good book.'

Johnny nodded solemnly. 'I feel sad sometimes when I think about my mom.'

Ambler nodded, too. 'I'm sure you do.'

'And my dad . . . Everybody thinks if someone's in prison he must be mean and nasty and bad. Dad isn't any of those things.' His eyes were liquid when he looked up. 'Are we going to see him soon?'

'Soon.' Ambler said. The pasta and sauce turned to dust in his mouth. He hated not telling the boy about his father's upcoming hearing. But he was afraid it might not happen. Something might go wrong. He couldn't say anything until they knew for sure John was going to have a release date. Getting Johnny's hopes up only to have them dashed would break the boy's heart.

They were quiet for a moment until Ambler said, 'I'll do the dishes tonight since you helped with the prep work and you have a paper to write.'

'OK.' He stopped on his way to his room. 'I could cook dinner some night. Mrs Scott taught me. She said I have the knack for it.' He wrinkled his brow. 'That's good, right, having a knack?'

Ambler's cell phone vibrating on the night table next to his bed woke him. He answered wide-awake with alarm. It was almost morning and it was McNulty's name that lit up the waning darkness. Something was terribly wrong.

'I figured you'd want to know,' McNulty said and told him what happened. 'It was my fault,' he said after a pause. 'Someone picked me up at his hotel and followed me to my apartment and waited for him to come out. Patient bastard. I was stupid to let them follow me. Ford told me they were watching the hotel. That's why he didn't want to go there and sent me. And I was stupid again not to know we were followed down Broadway. It's not like we were in Times Square. The sidewalks are mostly empty that time of night.'

Ambler tried to tell him it wasn't his fault. But McNulty prided himself on knowing his way around the city better than most people, like an animal in its natural habitat. He didn't get himself in situations where someone could get one over on him. He'd failed himself and no one could tell him different.

But Ambler knew if anyone was to blame for getting Ford killed it was him; he opened Pandora's Box – digging up bones, not letting bodies stay buried. He told McNulty this but it didn't help.

'He was coming around, maybe not such a bad guy after all. He was a couple of hours from getting on a train back to Texas where he planned to mind his own business.'

Ambler wanted to know if Ford had told McNulty anything new about the Manhattan Avenue murders. Asking him that now would be too callous. McNulty was having a hard enough time coming to grips with what had happened. A man he'd been talking with and walking with – who in his strange way he felt responsible for – had been murdered right alongside him.

'Where are you?' he asked instead.

'On my way home. The cops took me in but they finished up with me a little while ago. My guess is they think I was in on it.'

'Was Mike Cosgrove there? Did anyone call him?'

'If he was there, I didn't see him. If anyone called him, they didn't tell me about it.' McNulty was quiet for a moment. Ambler could hear him breathing as he walked. 'What happens now?' His tone suggested he didn't much care.

Ambler said he didn't know.

'I'm home,' McNulty said, and hung up.

Ambler, wide awake, stared at the ceiling. He'd caught McNulty's despair. His own was as bad or worse. He'd made a bad mistake and someone else paid for it. His curiosity led to Ford's death. If he'd left well enough alone, Ford would be alive. He could have read Ford's story and put it down like he'd done with a thousand other mysteries he'd read. Why didn't he? Why did he need to know Ford's secrets? What had all his snooping around accomplished?

In the morning, after he'd taken Johnny to school and arrived at work late for a staff meeting, which he sat through as blank as a wall, he caught up with Adele in the McGraw Rotunda and told her about Ford. She was shocked and saddened, sadder than he expected her to be.

'The more I read about his childhood, the more I felt sorry for him. It was so miserable.' Ambler watched her eyes redden and grow moist. 'What he wrote about his father was heart-breaking, so tender and loving. His mother ridiculed his father, too. She told the boy they were poor because his father was weak and stupid. The father he describes comes across as gentle and kind. His father was a truck driver but he read books. He took the boy to the library on Sundays when he was off work. It was because of his father Ford read and that led to his becoming a writer . . .'

Adele smiled through her tears. 'I can't believe I'm talking about him like this when two days ago I wanted to rip his eyeballs out.' They were standing in the McGraw Rotunda on the third floor. To avoid looking at Ambler, she turned to study the mural above the door that led to the Rose reading room.

After a minute, she said, 'You can't blame him for how he felt about his mother. He was a child. But once he grew up, he could have tried to understand why she was the way she was. She lashed out with all that hate against him and his father because, for some reason that wasn't her fault, she hated herself. She spent her life punishing herself. His father found her twice when she'd tried to kill herself and he had to call an ambulance. Doesn't that deserve sympathy, too?' Adele went back to studying the mural – one of a series of murals in the rotunda portraying the history of the written word – and wiping her tears.

Ambler didn't try to comfort her. He thought about his own son and what had gone wrong for him. John's mother, Ambler's ex-wife, neglected their son – not through malice; she couldn't help herself because she wasn't able to keep her own head above water. And he, the boy's ineffectual father, didn't protect his son; he left her, and left the boy with a mother who couldn't care for him.

When Mike Cosgrove called later and wanted to meet at the Library Tavern to talk, Ambler suggested the Oyster Bar instead. He didn't want to bring a reminder of Ford's murder to McNulty at work. The murder weighed heavily on Ambler's mind, too. He couldn't concentrate and couldn't bring himself to go through Ford's papers, so he spent most of the day browsing through book auction catalogs, drifting off every few minutes into thoughts, sorrows, and regrets, about Ford.

'The guy was asking for it,' Mike said when Ambler sat down across from him at a small table in the Canopy Bar. Ambler eyed the martini in a stem glass on the table. 'I'm off duty,' Mike said. 'It's not my case.'

'Because you're too close to it?'

Mike's eyebrows shot up. 'Who said I'm close to it?'

Ambler sighed. Were they going to dance around the elephant on the barstool? He ordered a glass of wine. 'Do the cops who got the case have any suspects?'

'No.' Mike spoke to his martini glass. 'It could have been a random, spur-of-the-moment robbery. It could be someone Ford had a run-in with that day or the day before saw him on the street and went off. Or some guy with a grudge from the past – Ford insulted his wife; fucked the guy's wife – recognized him and took revenge. A scorned woman from his past got someone to do it for her, hired a hitman.'

'That doesn't quite cover all the bases,' Ambler said. Mike knew as well as he did that he was dodging the issue, avoiding obvious possibilities because they were too close to home. The scorned woman option, though, reminded him of the woman who'd stabbed Ford years before when he was in New York the last time. She was one of the angry women who picketed the library the night of the reception. She could have hired a hitman. It was unlikely but not impossible.

'I know you don't jump to conclusions,' he said. 'You look at every possibility no matter how improbable. I'm OK with that. What I'm not OK with is you not looking at a possibility you don't like.'

Mike sipped his drink and glanced about the bustling restaurant rapidly filling with tourists and homeward-bound commuters.

Ambler kept at him. 'Ford was in a position to possibly blow the whistle on what might have been a police cover-up of a multiple murder.'

Mike's eyes widened in feigned amazement. 'That's not what I heard. What I heard him say is he didn't know anything about the murders.'

'He told me Sanchez knew Donovan was a plainclothes cop. It was no secret. He wasn't working undercover.'

Mike glanced at Ambler, glanced away, met his gaze, showed surprise, but not as much surprise as you'd expect. It was the feigned astonishment the beneficiary of a surprise party who knows what's coming puts on when everyone yells surprise. 'They found out Billy Donovan was a cop and killed him. Was Ford saying that didn't happen?'

'Chris Jackson lied when he accused Ford of blowing Donovan's cover. Everybody in the room knew he lied, except me.'

Mike stared at his now empty cocktail glass and then with an irritated expression gestured for the server. He glanced at Ambler's untouched wine. 'Ready for another?'

Ambler said, 'No,' sharply enough to be a rebuke. Mike was being evasive. That wasn't like him. Always before, if he didn't want to tell Ambler something, he said so. He held back information the police had that the public wasn't privy to. That was an understanding they had. Something was different this time. He held something back and wouldn't say that was what he was doing. He looked miserable.

Ambler sympathized but not enough to let up on him. 'What was Jackson covering up? Who's he protecting, himself or someone else?' Ambler paused; a small voice in the back of his mind told him to let up. But he went ahead. 'Are you protecting Jackson?' He realized he'd just accused Mike of covering up a crime – and regretted doing it as soon as the words were out of his mouth.

Mike didn't blow up. He didn't show disappointment either in what he might well see as Ambler's betrayal of their friendship. His gaze was level and his face held that expressionless expression cops develop, no judgment, not even expectation, a face like a blank wall.

After a moment, instead of looking at Ambler, he chose to watch impatiently for the server with his drink, a second martini, not something Mike ever did; he might have one drink before dinner, usually not; he preferred a glass or two of wine with dinner, a beer once in a while, a martini rarely, never two. Now he watched anxiously for his drink like the proverbial climber stranded on a wintry mountainside watches for the St Bernard with the cask of brandy around his neck.

When the drink arrived and he'd taken a sip, he cleared his throat. 'I've got a lot on my mind,' he said softly. 'I'd appreciate you not pressing me. If you don't know by now that I take any murder seriously, you don't know me after all.'

Ambler began to protest, apologize, explain – but stopped before he started because he saw that Mike wasn't finished and was deadly serious about what he was saying.

'The men working the Ford murder aren't reporting to me

and aren't asking me for advice. I'm willing to wait to see what they come up with. It looks like you're not. If you're planning your own investigation, I'd warn you against it.'

In the silence between them, Ambler took a long sip of his wine. 'I'm sorry I said what I said.'

Mike looked away. When he and Mike had once before uncovered wrongdoing by a cop, the discovery wasn't a triumphant moment for Mike. He did it because it was the right thing to do, even though it earned him a reputation among some of his fellow cops as a rat. He'd gotten threats. The ones that go like, now we know you don't have our backs, we may not have yours. It was undeserved. Mike was as loyal a cop as there was – and any cops that knew him knew that.

'The explanation for how Billy Donovan got killed doesn't hold up,' Ambler said. 'There's a lot I don't know about what happened. The fact is I don't know anything, except I have a strong hunch Will Ford knew what happened. Now he's dead. It might be his death has nothing to do with what he knew about those murders on Manhattan Avenue. It might also be that he died because of what he knew. And if that's true . . .' Ambler's voice trailed off. Mike knew what he'd say so why say it? He waited.

Mike watched his martini for a moment; distastefully, Ambler would have said. When he looked up, Ambler again faced his cop stare. 'Suppose you lay out for me what you know for sure. I've heard your fanciful ideas on what happened three or four times now. So here we go. Number one . . .'

'I said I don't know anything for sure. Now that Ford's dead, I may never know. And it doesn't look like you're about to tell me what you know.'

Mike swatted Ambler's comment aside. 'Let me ask you about something else. One thing I did find out was Ford had a run-in uptown a couple of nights ago and wound up in the hospital. He called you, I was told.'

Ambler told him what Ford had told him about Pappas, and about his own assumption that Big Nick might have been a silent partner in the criminal enterprises run by Gilberto Sanchez and Annabelle Lee. 'Ford was drunk and went looking for Big Nick. I think he wanted his help in getting the police off his back. But I don't know that. McNulty asked around and was told Pappas likes to keep a low profile and Ford was making too much noise, so he had someone slap him around.'

Mike listened with interest. 'McNulty knows about this?'

'Not more than I told you.'

'What you told me, you should tell the guys doing the investigation.'

Ambler said he would. 'But I don't see how it helps. If Pappas was going to have him killed, why wouldn't he have done it that night instead of having him worked over?'

'Maybe he remembered something. Maybe he found out something new about Ford that made him a problem. It may be improbable but it's not impossible.'

Ambler scrutinized his friend, whose expression was deadpan. 'OK. I'll tell them about it. There's another improbable possibility I should tell you about.' He told Mike about the woman who stabbed Ford years before and that Doris Wellington and the Women's Action Against Misogyny group resurrected her and brought her to the library protest against Ford.

'Tell them about that, too.' Mike was getting ready to leave, not showing any effects from his second martini, which he only drank half of.

Ambler held out his hand as if to stop him. 'Do they know about Ford's link to the murders of Billy Donovan and the others . . . and Chris Jackson's unwillingness to talk about what really happened?'

Mike let down his guard. His blank, noncommittal expression crumbled, and Ambler saw the deep creases of worry in his face. Mike caught himself, tightened his face muscles into a grimace but the worry stayed in his eyes. 'I've got things to do,' he said. He took out his notepad and wrote down the names of the homicide detectives handling Ford's murder and gave it to Ambler.

FOURTEEN

Mike Cosgrove left Grand Central Station, walking up the ramp from the lower level to the main level and then up another ramp to 42nd Street, braving the onrush of determined commuters heading for their trains. The martinis had given him a buzz. But they hadn't fortified him for what he had in front of him.

It wasn't hard to find Chris Jackson's address. He lived in Addisleigh Park, a largely Black area with tree-lined streets, stately single-family houses, and well-groomed yards, one of the nicest neighborhoods in Queens, the kind of place folks work hard to get to.

Driving through the peaceful neighborhood made Cosgrove feel worse than he already felt. Sometimes, you don't mind bringing bad news to someone. They're getting what they deserve; they're going to jail. Too many other times, you see the pain and despair in the guy's eyes when he opens the door and finds you on the stoop. He knows you being there means his life's going down the drain. Behind him, you see a couple of kids and a wife, the kids wide-eyed, the wife's face wrinkled into a grimace of fear.

He didn't know what he was bringing Chris except questions, ones Chris might have answers to that would explain away the bad things. The tightness in Cosgrove's chest was because he was afraid his old partner didn't have those answers.

He rang the doorbell. Chris opened the door, dressed in a two-tone brown leisurewear sweat suit. His eyes held the despair Cosgrove dreaded. He didn't say anything, didn't invite Cosgrove in, stood there watching him and waiting.

'You know about Will Ford getting whacked?'

Chris's expression didn't change. 'What about it?'

'I'm afraid to ask.'

'Did I kill him?'

'Did you?'

Chris hesitated a beat. 'No.'

'Know who did?'

Chris didn't hesitate. 'No. Do you?'

'I'm going to find out.' He heard the cacophony of kids' laughter and shrieks from somewhere deep in the house.

Chris shuffled his feet impatiently. 'You're not assigned the case.'

'You're keeping track?'

'There's dozens of murders out there, Mike. Find a high-profile one that'll get you a promotion. I'll get you assigned. You don't need this one.'

'Why don't you want me on it?'

Chris's eyes grew darker. 'I keep defending you, telling One PP you're a good cop. George is sticking his neck out for you, too.'

'George?'

'Kowalski.'

'Why would he do that?' Kowalski struck Cosgrove as someone who took pretty good care of his neck.

'On my say-so.'

'Why do I need defending?'

Chris glanced behind him, not that anyone was there, and lowered his voice. 'You didn't do anything wrong.' He lowered his voice another octave. 'You know how things are.'

Cosgrove felt a prickle at the back of his neck, something rising in his throat. 'No. I don't know how things are, Lieutenant. What things are we talking about?'

Chris's voice rose. 'We're talking about loyalty. We told you what happened with that case back in the 90s. A cop got in over his head. We looked out for his wife and kids. Not by the book, but no one got hurt. The lowlifes were dead. It looks like the writer . . .' He looked questioningly at Cosgrove.

'Will Ford.'

'Right. He knew the story we told to cover for Billy Donovan wasn't what happened. I don't know how he knew. But he let it go. I gave him a chance to cop to something that would get us off the hook and keep him out of it, that would satisfy your friend the nosy librarian. He took it. He could have shot it down. I thought we were all together. That's why I asked

George to tell you what actually happened, so you'd let sleeping dogs lie.

'George wasn't sure about you. I told him you were a good cop.' He stood taller. 'Don't make a liar out of me. I'm sorry the writer is dead. I want as much as you to lock up whoever killed him. Bringing up something that happened more than twenty years ago is going to screw some cops who don't deserve it, including me. You gonna keep after this? For what? Blow the whistle on a cover up. The press will love you. The cop-haters will love you. You'll be a hero who rooted out dirty cops – again. This year's Serpico. Make all cops look like shit.'

Cosgrove gave Chris a moment to rein in his high horse, waited for him to remember what he knew about Cosgrove. 'I liked the movie,' Cosgrove said. 'But I don't believe everything I see in the movies. I came here to ask you some questions, not to accuse you of anything. You have your reasons for getting your back up. But I was a cop before you were, and even if I didn't work my way up the ranks I know the difference between a good cop and one who isn't. I broke you in to be a good cop. I hope you still are.'

Jackson's expression softened. Cosgrove couldn't say what he saw there. Later when he looked back, he'd think what he saw was Chris asking for help; and he thought if they both had laid everything on the table that night, what happened next wouldn't have had to happen the way it did. At the moment though, he was on his own high horse. He didn't like what Chris said, the words themselves and what went on beneath the words, the accusation and threat, if you do this, you're not one of us any more.

'Ask your questions,' Jackson said, his tone weary.

'The task force you and Billy Donovan were on, guns and drugs off the street, on your own, the law west of the Pecos, no questions asked. Kowalski was in charge. Who else was on the task force and where are they now?'

'Jesus, Mike. I'm asking you to lay off this. Now you want me to name names?'

Cosgrove bore down. 'I can find out without you. It's easier if you tell me, and less likely to cause the kind of mess you're trying to avoid. Despite what you think, I'm not out to get you. I'm trying to rule some things out so I can get on with other things.'

Chris told him the names of the two other cops on the task force; he'd lost touch with them over the years and didn't know where they were stationed or even if they were still on the job. 'Like me, they lived in the shadows of George and Billy. We did what we were told. They were green, too, not as green as me. Both of them were city kids, from the Bronx; they knew the streets from before they became cops. They weren't crazy like Billy, but they were harder than he was. Billy had a soft side, not tenderhearted but he could sympathize. He could care sometimes when someone got hurt. Not Hector and Erik. Not an ounce of empathy in them.'

'Kowalski was your rabbi, right? He had a rabbi, too. His uncle was a captain or inspector or something. Did he know what Donovan was doing?'

Chris was calmer now. It was like what happened to a suspect after hours of listening to the evidence stacked against him, when he came to see no way out. He resigned himself to what was coming and answered the questions he was asked. Didn't volunteer anything, didn't explain, just answered what was asked.

'He knew. George handled getting the story of how Billy got killed through official channels to protect all of us.'

Cosgrove took a moment and softened his tone. 'This is the tough one, Chris. I hate to ask and I'm not judging. It's almost for sure that if Donovan was doin' doors, everyone else on the task force was doin' doors too—'

Jackson exploded at him. 'That's not true.' Then he too softened his tone. 'You had to be a team player; the guys on the task force had to trust you. I was Black; I didn't drink with the guys, didn't do the four-to-four; I went home after my shift. I was an oddball. George took me aside and told me I had to go along even if my heart wasn't in it. Only a couple of times to get my hands dirty, so I couldn't rat on them without going down myself.

'I did a couple of raids, got my share. Most of the time, we took the drugs and the money and let the perps go. If we didn't let them go, we turned over enough of the dope to make a charge stick and put on the report we picked them up on the street. A couple of times, Hector or Erik asked me to sell what they'd copped. They figured I was Black so it was easy for me to find dealers who would buy it. When that happened, I used my own money to pay for the dope and threw it down the sewer.

'When I got a split from a raid, I gave the money to the church. I only did a few raids, only enough so they trusted me. My hands were dirty, so I couldn't be an Internal Affairs plant. If they went down, I'd go down with them. Even with that, Billy Donovan never trusted me. He was the Lone Ranger. He did what he wanted. No one said anything to him. If he needed you for a bust or a raid, you went with him. No questions asked.'

Chris's voice was barely above a whisper. 'Finding myself in the middle of all that was a real shock after being with you. I knew it didn't have to be that way. But I'd gotten myself into it. I couldn't rat. Who was I going to go to? I didn't know anyone downtown. George did. I relied on him.'

'Was he doing doors?'

Chris hesitated. 'If he did, I didn't know about it. I didn't ask. He kept the crew in line, even Billy halfway in line. He knew I didn't like what was going on, especially what Billy was doing. But he made it clear, I couldn't come to him to complain. And for damn sure I couldn't go above him.'

'What did he say about the raids?'

'Nothing. He didn't want to hear about it. None of us knew what he knew. What we had to do was be loyal to him and the task force and the job. Him first. He knew I wasn't doing any raids if I could get out of it. He was OK with that after the guys on the task force trusted I wouldn't rat. He told me – or more like he showed me – I should be loyal to him. No matter what. If I was loyal to him, he'd be loyal to me. And he was. He brought me with him up the ranks.'

Cosgrove folded up his notebook. 'What do you think happened to Ford, Chris?'

Chris shook his head. 'I know as much about the guy as you do. There had to be more to his life than what we're talking about. I hear he ran with some bad people back in the day – hookers, gamblers, drug-dealers. He wanted the street cred so he could show off – a literary bad boy. Maybe he was spending time with the wrong kind of people this time, too.'

Chris had gotten his swagger back. 'The guys who caught the case will look into that. Why not give them a chance? Forget about the stuff that happened years ago. Looking into it can only cause trouble for everybody . . . even you. Think about it, Mike. We're on the same side.'

Later, on his drive home, Cosgrove wrestled with the questions his talk with Chris Jackson had left him with. When he first called Chris – what seemed like years ago – to ask about the stupid mystery story Ray had brought to him, he thought Chris might know about what crooked cops had been up to, but he never suspected Chris had been one of them. He was wrong.

Chris did what he did reluctantly. Cosgrove believed him. No matter who you were, if you found yourself part of an outlaw task force or on an outlaw team or you discovered the partner you got by the luck of the draw was a thief, you kept your mouth shut; you played along or you'd likely find yourself a dead cop in a bust gone wrong. For Chris, a young, green cop, and a Black cop at that, in a world of mostly white men whose experience with the world of Black folks was for the most part hostile and violent, it had to be worse.

The question for him now was whether the band had gotten back together to take care of Will Ford. Cosgrove didn't ask for this mess. He didn't want it. But here it was. So now what? Go to his captain and tell him he had a hunch he was looking into. The hunch? 'Well, this lieutenant and this deputy inspector might have something to do with that street murder on the Upper West Side the other night.'

'And your reason for thinking this?' the captain might ask. 'I imagine you have a truck full of evidence parked outside.'

So you tell him, 'Well, it's not really a question of evidence; it's this short story by a mystery writer. He was the victim the other night. Raymond Ambler, the librarian, told me about the story. You remember Ray, right, the librarian?'

'You're goddamn right I remember the son of a bitch,' the

captain might say, remembering the last time their paths crossed and what kind of grief that brought him.

Nope. There was nowhere to take this one, no one on the job to talk to about it. Already Chris would have let Kowalski know Cosgrove was nosing around again, digging up bones. Kowalski could get the department wheels turning and in a couple of days Cosgrove might be assigned a case that took him to Israel or South America or sent to stake out an empty warehouse in Staten Island. He'd be gone before anyone missed him.

He hadn't told Ray about Kowalski's and Jackson's cover-up of Billy Donovan's crimes, and he probably should. Ray already figured out there was a cover-up. He didn't know what was being covered up, and Cosgrove told himself maybe he should leave it at that.

In one way, nothing Chris or George Kowalski did was that terrible. They made it look like Donovan was on the job, so his wife and kids got the death benefits. Everyone who was going to get killed was already dead. The only one who might have an argument to make was Hernandez. And he'd be where he was for the other murder they got him on whether he killed anyone on Manhattan Avenue or not. The brass at One PP spent most of their time covering up one thing or another to keep the NYPD from looking bad in the press. At least what Chris and Kowalski did helped some innocents.

The real problem was Will Ford getting himself murdered. The son of a bitch should have gone back to Texas when he got his check and gotten himself murdered there, if that was what he was going to do. But he was murdered here in New York and Cosgrove being who he was and knowing what he knew needed to do something about it. If he was lucky, he'd prove himself wrong.

Too much thinking gives me a headache, Cosgrove told himself when he'd finally found a parking space a few blocks from his apartment. At the small house he once lived in with his wife and daughter he'd always found a parking space on his street, most of time less than a block from his house. Now the streets around his building, like his apartment, were cramped.

On the walk to his building, he noticed a few daffodils blooming on the side of a small embankment on the far side of the street. He couldn't really see the flowers, just a paleness swaying in the darkness that he took to be blooms. It was a sheltered area and sunny in the mornings. He'd been watching the daffodil shoots grow and then bud when he headed to work each morning.

The street he walked on was busier than the one his daughter Denise had grown up on. He noticed a squad car cruising the opposite side of the street and waved as it passed him. The cop inside looked at him blankly and didn't wave back. No reason why the guy would know Cosgrove was a cop, too. He felt foolish. Just before he reached the sidewalk that led to his low-rise apartment building, he saw Denise walking toward him from the subway stop in the opposite direction, so he stopped.

When he stopped, he heard something behind him, a sound riding on the chilly night wind. He heard shots and knew they weren't the ones that hit him. He felt searing burns in his back, and a sharp pain at the side of his head above his ear. He heard Denise's screams and he thought, 'You don't hear the bullet that gets you.'

FIFTEEN

Raymond Ambler walked home from the Oyster Bar mumbling to himself; he was worried and annoyed after leaving Mike. Worried because something weighed on his friend that he wouldn't talk about. Annoyed for the same reason. Mike knew something about Will Ford's murder that he was sitting on. Ambler suspected he'd been party to Mike's adaptation of the blue wall of silence.

He could be doing this for any number of reasons, but it most likely had to do with Chris Jackson. It was unlikely Jackson had anything to do with Ford's murder. But an investigation into the murder might have other consequences for Jackson that could ruin his career. Mike would be inclined to protect his ambitious protégé unless Jackson had done something seriously wrong, so he'd probably want to find out what was what before the investigation got too far along.

Ambler's cell phone buzzed as he turned the corner on to his street. Since he was already preoccupied with his detective friend, his first thought was it would be Mike. But it wasn't. It was David Levinson with good news.

David was wound up as usual, more energy than one man should be allowed to have. 'Justice is blind, they say. But not so blind she doesn't know who's on the Social Register.' Levinson liked to talk in riddles, commenting on the ironies of life and making fun of himself and his profession.

As usual, Ambler didn't follow. He waited.

'A white-collar criminal-defense attorney from a white-shoe law firm called me and said a partner asked him to act as co-counsel for John Ambler and would I mind if he sat in.' David chuckled. 'The name of the partner who made the request is Arthur Young. Does that ring a bell?'

Ambler said it did and held back from saying anything more lest he set the lawyer off on a tangent. Besides talking in riddles, David liked to embellish his stories. Ambler suspected he did this because at a hundred and fifty dollars an hour talking was a lucrative activity. Whatever the reason, Levinson liked to hear himself talk.

'I told my fellow attorney we'd pretty much settled and all that was left was to go before a judge and get the plea approved. He said he knew that and wanted to go with me before the judge.' David paused to chuckle again. 'Are you following me?'

'No,' Ambler said.

'We have a plea deal. The judge can approve it, alter it, or deny it. I'm not the brightest attorney in Manhattan . . . and my barber has better connections among the courthouse set around Center Street than I do. But I know when I've been offered a seat on a gravy train. This young whippersnapper, his Harvard law degree still in its wrapping paper, says his colleague, the partner, went to law school with Judge Moynihan. "What does this mean?" you ask.'

'OK. I'll ask.'

'It means they have lunch together now and again at the Yale Club and belong to the same branch of the Federalist Society. Blind justice may not see me but she sees him.'

Ambler's heart began to race. 'What are you getting at?'

'Harrison Worthington III will join John and I when we make our appearance before His Honor Frank Moynihan. My guess is the judge will tweak the settlement and much to the chagrin of the ADA with whom I made the deal your son will walk.'

Ambler was amazed. Thrilled. John would be sentenced to time served. The weight of the world lifted off his shoulders. Tears came to his eyes and he laughed through them. He walked double-time to his doorway and took the stairs two at a time. When he got to his apartment door, he stopped and composed himself. Nothing was certain until the cell door swung open. He couldn't tell Johnny because something could still go wrong at the last minute and lead to crushing disappointment.

They ate leftover stew that he'd made while Johnny was in Florida. The boy had taken the stew out of the freezer and heated it up while he'd waited for his grandfather to get home.

Mike's daughter Denise, his after-school tutor – they'd changed her title from nanny once she graduated from high school and began college – had supervised. She still picked Johnny up after school on most days and had been pretty much a big sister to him since he'd been with Ambler. 'He's the new celebrity chef,' she told Ambler before she left.

During dinner, Johnny asked about Ford's murder. He'd heard the phone ring the night before and knew it was McNulty. That morning while they ate breakfast he'd asked what the call was about and Ambler had to tell him about Ford's murder, telling him the bare minimum in an offhand way, hoping the boy wouldn't dwell on it. He hadn't asked anything more on the way to school, so Ambler hoped he'd moved on from it. But now over dinner he had enough questions for Ambler to believe he'd spent the day thinking about it.

Ambler told him he didn't know who had killed Ford or why.

'But you're going to find out, right? It's a mystery and you're going to solve it.'

'To tell you the truth, I hope someone else solves the mystery.' Ambler was trying to put the boy off. But what he said was true. He half-hoped Mike was right and Will Ford's murder came out of nowhere and his murderer was someone entirely unconnected to anyone or anything Ambler had been thinking about as possibilities.

'But you've solved lots of murder mysteries.' Johnny wasn't going to let go. He was entirely too interested in the homicide investigations Ambler had taken part in.

'I got lucky – if that's what you call it – a couple of times. Murder is a terrible thing. If I could have a wish come true it would be that Will Ford's death was the last murder that ever happened.'

Johnny solemnly considered this for a moment. 'But they do happen, so you have to solve the mystery to stop them. That's a good thing.'

'My second wish would be that if there have to be murders they stay far away from me. Mike Cosgrove's job is solving murder mysteries. My job is working in the library, taking care of books and things related to books. That's what I should be doing . . . and keeping you out of trouble as you grow into a man.'

'When I can start solving murder mysteries,' Johnny said brightly.

Ambler closed his eyes and whispered, 'What have I done?' To Johnny, he said, 'My wish now is that you go do your homework.'

He cleaned up and washed the dishes, reliving his conversation with David Levinson, elated and dying to tell Adele what the lawyer said. He couldn't call her now because Johnny would eavesdrop on the call like he usually did. So to calm and recenter himself he did his tai chi exercises, going through the solo form a couple of times very slowly, telling himself he'd been neglecting practice and would go to push hands on Saturday morning.

He was doing the form, concentrating on his breathing, when the phone rang, so Johnny answered. He heard a gasp and watched Johnny's eyes spring open and the rest of his face crumble.

Johnny waved to him, clutching the phone with his other hand. 'It's Denise. Hurry. She's crying . . . really crying.'

Through hiccups and sobs, Denise told him her dad had been shot. She stumbled through more words trying to tell him what happened, what was happening, what would happen. One thing she said clearly, 'He might be dying.' He had a bullet lodged next to his spine. 'Please, please don't let him die,' she said, choking on her anguish, pleading with Ambler as if he had the power to keep her father alive.

'Where are you?' He wanted to say more, to tell her everything would be all right. But he couldn't make himself say it. Nothing was all right when someone had a bullet next to their spine.

They were at Bellevue. Denise was studying to be a nurse and knew of Bellevue's world-class trauma surgery department, so she persuaded the patrol cops on the scene of her father's shooting to tell the EMT ambulance crew to take her father to Bellevue rather than one of the Queen's hospitals where they were supposed to take him.

'I'll be right over,' Ambler said. He turned to Johnny, who

watched him wide-eyed, his face pale, his fist to his mouth. Ambler couldn't bring him to the hospital and he couldn't leave him alone. The poor kid was shaking. He called Adele, told her what happened, and asked if she'd come and stay with Johnny.

He turned to the boy when he got off the phone. 'Denise's dad was shot tonight. He's in the hospital and he's hurt pretty badly.'

'Is he going to die?' Johnny's fist was still to his mouth.

'I hope not. Bellevue's a very good hospital. Denise did a good job getting him there. I'm worried about her so I'm going to go as soon as Adele gets here.' Ambler was afraid Johnny would ask to go with him. He was really closer to Denise than Ambler was. But he didn't ask.

Ambler knew he should tell Johnny to go back to his homework. But he couldn't bring himself to say it. Instead, he sat down at the kitchen table and Johnny sat across from him.

'Why did someone shoot Denise's dad?' Johnny asked after a moment of heavy silence.

Ambler put his elbows on the table and pressed his fingers against his forehead. 'I don't know what happened.' He hadn't asked Denise any questions; she was too upset to tell him very much. The shooting was in front of their apartment building. Mike hadn't said where he was going when he left the Oyster Bar. But enough time had passed that he'd gone somewhere, somewhere he hadn't wanted to tell Ambler about.

Mike getting shot put Will Ford's murder in a new light, or maybe caused the light it had been in all along to shine brighter. He had to believe both shootings had their beginnings in the long-ago murders on Manhattan Avenue. He'd started out foolishly trying to get to the bottom of something that happened years before. Now he was faced with a murder – and please God! not two murders – in the present.

When Adele rang, he buzzed her in, kissed Johnny on the forehead, and grabbed his jacket. He met her on the stairs and hugged her tightly enough to squeeze the breath out of her. She kissed him lightly on the lips and ran up the stairs. Neither spoke.

Denise called his cell phone before he reached the hospital

and told him to meet her outside the hospital's front door on First Avenue. Mike had gone through emergency surgery and was in the Surgical ICU. No one could visit him until at least tomorrow and probably tomorrow would be too soon. The surgeon told her he'd gotten the bullet. It was too early to tell how much damage had been done to the spinal cord. He'd know more tomorrow.

Ambler took Denise to an all-night diner on Second Avenue not far from the hospital. She'd pretty much cried herself out by the time they got to the restaurant. She didn't remember the last time she'd eaten, so he ordered her the hot roast turkey sandwich – a Greek diner staple.

While she looked at her cell phone, he took the shopping bag containing Mike's clothes she'd been carrying and asked if he could look through it for Mike's notebook. He gingerly handled the bloody jacket and shirt. The notebook was in one piece and it didn't take long to find what he was looking for. The latest entry was, as Ambler expected, from an interview Mike did with Chris Jackson that night.

He'd made notes on the interview but his notes were cryptic, a shorthand to himself no one else could easily decipher, something he did to make sure that if his notes were used in court he'd need to be there to interpret them. Sometimes lawyers would subpoena a cop's notebooks for a trial and he didn't want lawyers – prosecutors or defenders – to know anything he thought or found out that he wasn't willing to tell him.

One thing Ambler did make out was Mike talked to Jackson about the Manhattan Avenue murders and the anti-crime task force Chris and the murdered cop had been on at the time. Mike had written down a couple of names of other cops on the task force. He'd also circled a cryptic mention of 'doin' doors', which Ambler didn't get, and he'd circled 'you gotta be a team player.'

'What are you looking for?' Denise asked. She'd eaten most of her dinner and was on a second cup of coffee. Color had returned to her face and some brightness to her eyes.

Ambler didn't want to tell her but she knew enough about her dad's work to guess.

'Do you think someone he was investigating shot him?'

'I don't know.'

'Do you know what case he was working? Wouldn't the other homicide detectives know who to go after?'

That was a tough question. He knew one case Mike was working the other homicide detectives didn't know about. 'When a cop gets shot, the police swing into action. Dozens of detectives will be on it. Cops from all over the city will come in on their off time offering to help,' he said to avoid answering.

Denise scrutinized his face. 'Did my dad tell you what he'd been doing?'

Ambler was getting more uncomfortable. 'The whole NYPD will be looking for whoever shot your dad. He and I were kind of working on a murder from a long time ago. That's why I wanted to look at his notebook. It's not something you need to worry about now. I'll tell you about it when things calm down, when you've seen your dad . . .'

She seemed satisfied with his answer or to not have much interest, her mind elsewhere. Her eyes were red, her eyelids drooping. The poor kid was exhausted.

'I don't want to send you back to your dad's apartment tonight.' He called Adele and told her about Mike and that he was with Denise.

'The poor kid. Johnny's asleep,' she said. 'Denise can come home with me.'

Ambler walked Denise back to his apartment and put her and Adele in a cab. He slept fitfully and woke early the next morning. Deep in thought, he made coffee and breakfast for him and Johnny, forcing himself to eat a boiled egg and a piece of toast. Johnny was as solemn as he was and knew enough not to ask his grandfather too many questions.

He took Johnny to school on the subway. By the time he got to the library, he'd made up his mind. He called Lisa Young and arranged for Johnny to come early for his weekend and perhaps stay an extra day or two. He asked if Lola could come with him. The dog could come, she said, but she'd have to stay in the staff quarters. He then called Chris Jackson at the phone number he'd found in Mike's notebook.

SIXTEEN

On the phone, Jackson sounded like a man who'd been drugged. He spoke slowly, drawing out his sentences, talking about what a good guy Mike was, telling Ambler he was the best cop he knew, that it took a cowardly bastard to shoot him in the back, that no one in the department would rest until they got the bastard.

'Who shot him?' Ambler interrupted Jackson's rambling monologue.

Jackson's tone changed, sharper, more alert. 'Something he was working on, I guess. He got too close to someone without knowing how close he'd gotten. It could also have been someone out of his past with a grudge. Mike made a lot of collars in his time. He's been on the job long enough some of the perps have served their time by now. Someone could hold a grudge. Someone with a long memory.' Jackson hesitated. 'There's another angle. I'm not going to tell you because it's his personal life.'

Ambler knew what he was talking about. 'Anne Gannon's husband?'

'OK so you know.' Jackson didn't sound surprised; he sounded irritated. 'It's a delicate situation; her husband's a cop.'

Ambler knew as much as anyone about Mike's personal life. He'd spent any number of dinners commiserating with him as he worked his way through his divorce. He knew about Anne too, Mike's childhood sweetheart, though he'd never met her.

'Ex-husband,' Ambler said. 'They're divorcing or divorced. She has an order of protection on him. Did something come up that implicates Gannon?'

'I can't talk about that. I know Mike's your friend. He'd tell you, like I'm telling you, let the police handle this. I know you've made a hobby out of homicide investigations. On this one, you'll get in the way or get yourself in trouble. We're deadly serious when a cop's been shot.'

Ambler didn't trust Jackson or any of the police on this. Already, Jackson had left something out of his list of possible suspects. 'What about a connection to the Will Ford murder? Is anyone looking into that?'

Jackson took a long moment to answer. 'What connection? No one's looking at a connection. Why would we?'

'I think we should talk.'

'We're talking now.'

Ambler took a gamble. 'I have Mike's notebook . . .' He hadn't found anything incriminating about Jackson in the notebook, and he didn't know if Jackson remembered Mike's shorthand that no one could decipher but him. But the ploy worked.

'It's come to this,' he said, after another long pause. 'I don't want you to come to my house.' He gave Ambler directions to a parking lot near Rochdale Park, not far from where he lived in Addisleigh Park, and said to meet him there that afternoon at four.

Shortly after Ambler got off the phone, Adele came to the crime fiction reading room to tell him Denise had called her. 'She tried to reach you but you were on the phone. Mike is still unconscious and in critical condition. But the doctors are hopeful.' Adele studied Ambler's face for a moment. 'What's wrong? Who were you on the phone with?'

'Someone I last saw in the same room with Will Ford and Mike.'

Adele's eyes widened.

'I've got a lot to tell you.'

She pulled up a chair and sat down across from him.

'The good news first.' He told her what David Levinson had told him.

Adele cocked her head and raised her eyebrows. 'Lisa Young's husband can influence the judge? The Wall Street lawyer can fix the case so your son gets out of jail? Does that kind of thing really happen?'

He hadn't thought of it that way. 'I don't think they call it "fixing" the case at that level. A municipal court judge might fix a case for a bribe. This is too highbrow to be a fix. It's something else.'

'What else?' For all of her down-to-earth understanding of how the world worked, Adele had the innate sense of justice of an innocent. She believed in telling the truth and being fair and when that didn't happen she got her dander up.

'There are different kinds of corruption.' Ambler tried to explain something he didn't understand himself. 'McNulty can explain it better than I can.' The last thing they needed now was for Adele to go charging into the courthouse and accuse the judge and Arthur Young of trying to fix John's sentencing, piss off the judge, and get John remanded to the prison system for another ten years. He couldn't even get through the good news without a potential disaster.

'What else?' Adele's pretty eyes flashed danger signals.

He told her his thinking about Mike's shooting and its possible connection to Ford's murder. 'I don't have proof of this and I might easily be wrong. But I think both shootings go back to those murders Ford based his short story on. I'm pretty sure Mike thought the same thing.

'Ford knew about the murders, and I'm pretty sure Chris Jackson knows what Ford knew. Mike was trying to get Jackson to come clean that evening before he was shot. So I'm going to follow up and ask Chris Jackson what he and Ford knew.'

Adele's voice was shrill. 'And you think he'll tell you? If he killed Ford and tried to kill Mike, why wouldn't he kill you?'

Ambler shook his head. 'That's not it. For one thing, I don't think Jackson killed anyone. Mike would have handled this differently if he thought there was any chance of that. I do think Jackson knows what happened on Manhattan Avenue that night. And after what happened to Mike, he might tell me.' He told her about meeting Jackson later that afternoon.

Adele was skeptical. 'Why are you meeting this cop you think might be a murderer in some secluded place out in Queens, for God's sake?' Adele had the Brooklynite's disdain for Queens.

'Queens has been civilized for some time now,' he said. 'Jackson's not a murderer and I'm meeting him in a residential neighborhood in the middle of the day. He has a wife and kids, so he probably wants to keep what might be unpleasant business away from them.'

'Why couldn't you talk to him on the phone?'

'I did. People with something to hide are careful about what they say on the phone. They're concerned they might be overheard.'

'That may be. I still don't understand why you're doing this. You don't think the police will track down whoever shot Mike?'

'They'll look into other things. They're not going to look into what Mike and I were working on. No one in the department knows about it. If I tried to tell anyone now, they wouldn't pay any attention to me. The case was closed. The murders were more than twenty years ago. They'd say they have enough to do. They're not going to open a closed case based on nothing but hearsay from me.' He smiled, which may have been condescending and may have been a mistake. 'I appreciate that you're concerned about me. I'm meeting a lieutenant in the NYPD. That shouldn't be anything to worry about.'

Adele glared at him. 'Bullshit.'

He reached for his jacket.

'Where are you going?'

'To see Mike and Denise at the hospital and then to have a chat with Lieutenant Jackson. If he kills me, you can tell everyone so he gets caught.'

At the hospital Denise was sitting in the waiting room studying. She was worn out but calm. Mike was still unconscious, she told him. A uniformed hospital cop sat in a straight-backed metal chair next to the door to the Surgical ICU; everything was eerily quiet, except for ominous beeping that came from behind the door.

Ambler was glad the cop was there but his presence gave him an uneasy feeling, reminding him of scenes in movies or TV shows where someone – sometimes disguised in a police uniform – snuck into a hospital room to kill the patient they'd missed killing on the first try.

He made sure Denise was doing OK and walked to the garage on Lexington Avenue, where he'd rented cars before.

It was expensive, but having a car would give him more options if he didn't like how things looked when he met up with Jackson. He didn't suspect Jackson of being part of a murder plot. But he likely had been part of a plot to cover up a murder and there was no telling what that might lead to.

Once he got to Queens, he found the street and the parking lot without much trouble. A police-issue Chevy Impala was parked at the far corner of the lot facing out. Only a few cars were in the lot and none near where Jackson had parked. As he pulled in, he saw a figure behind the wheel of the Impala leaning against the driver's side window. If Jackson was calm enough to take a nap while he waited, you might think he had a clear conscience.

Ambler pulled into the spot alongside the Impala on the driver's side heading his car in the opposite direction. Before he shut off the motor he glanced at Jackson. He saw that his head was at a strange angle and the driver's side window was spattered and streaked with something . . . Looking again, he realized with horror that the spatters and streaks were blood and human tissue.

He began shaking and got out of his car without shutting off the motor. He knew better than to touch the door handle of the Impala, so he looked in through the windshield. Jackson's eyes were open, his face bloody. A gun was in his lap, blood and flesh and tissue were all over him and the ceiling and the window. Ambler turned from the window and vomited.

His hands shook; the parking lot in front of him shimmered; he felt faint as he dialed 911, so he leaned against his car. 'A man is dead,' he said. 'Shot. I was supposed to meet him . . . He asked me to come here to talk about this other murder . . .' Ambler knew he was babbling, his mouth running on its own, but he couldn't stop.

The dispatcher tried to speak calmly, told him to take it easy, take a breath, and tell her his location.

He couldn't remember where he was. 'A parking lot in Queens . . . Wait,' he said and found the location Jackson had given him on his phone's GPS. He told the dispatcher.

She was having a hard time staying calm herself when he

told her it was a cop. 'We'll send an ambulance. The police are on the way. Stay where you are.'

Ambler stood between his car and the black Impala. He couldn't bring himself to look at Jackson again. Beyond the parking lot was a park with baseball diamonds at either end. The infield and outfield grass was brown with a faint shadow of green, and the dirt of the infield was a different shade of brown, almost golden.

Farther away, a small field of daffodils swayed in the light breeze, only two or three had bloomed. The trees alongside the baseball field had a reddish tint to their branches. Alongside the parking lot cars passed by on the street he'd turned in off of, the drivers oblivious to the carnage they drove past. The faint sound of children's voices drifted on the wind from a playground blocks away.

It didn't help to not look at Jackson; he kept picturing the bloodbath he'd seen through the windshield. He'd seen death but never like this. Chris Jackson killed himself in a gruesome way and invited Ambler to the bloody aftermath. Why would he do that?

Another thought came to him. Could Jackson have been murdered and his death made to look like a suicide? Given what he saw, Ambler didn't think a faked suicide was possible. But he was no expert. The medical examiner would decide that.

If Jackson committed suicide, was Ambler supposed to find something at the scene? Had Jackson left an envelope with Ambler's name on it on the seat next to the body: a confession, admitting he killed a police officer and three criminals years ago and had killed Will Ford and tried to kill Mike Cosgrove to cover up the earlier murders? It was a stupid thought. And if he knew for sure an envelope addressed to him with a confession inside it was sitting on the front seat of that car, he couldn't bring himself to look through that windshield.

Then again if someone killed Jackson and faked his suicide, who? Did Big Nick give an order? Did Kowalski, Swensen, or Morales, or all three, decide Jackson could no longer be trusted to keep secret what happened that night on Manhattan Avenue?

Four or five patrol cars arrived within moments of one another and behind them an EMS ambulance and an NYFD ambulance, both with the same boxy structure built on to a pickup truck frame. The first few patrol cops to arrive looked into the Impala ahead of the EMS technicians, and the second cop to look through the windshield, like Ambler, turned and vomited. Another one of the cops recognized Jackson.

Word went around quickly, a murmur loud enough for Ambler to pick up that an NYPD lieutenant ate his gun. The sergeant who arrived after the ambulance herded the cops together. He sent a few poking around the parking lot. The rest stood around uneasily until a couple of black SUVs showed up a few moments ahead of the crime scene crew.

It wasn't until the crime scene investigators began their work that anyone thought to pay attention to Ambler. A tall officer wearing a blue uniform and a white shirt with a gold and blue badge walked over and asked Ambler if he was the person who'd called in the incident. Ambler said he was.

'Tell me everything that happened. Did you hear the gunshot?'

Ambler said no.

'How did you happen to look into the car? What were you doing in this parking lot?'

He told the lieutenant he'd had an appointment to meet Jackson.

'Here in the parking lot?'

Ambler said yes.

The lieutenant found this perplexing enough to call over a man wearing a blue overcoat and a brimmed hat with a gold badge.

The man in the overcoat introduced himself as Captain Andrews. He wasn't friendly but neither was he hostile. If anything, he and everyone else on the scene carried themselves with a kind of solemnity you'd expect at a funeral. The captain asked Ambler how well he knew Chris Jackson.

Ambler said he didn't know him at all. Jackson was a friend of Detective Mike Cosgrove and Mike was a friend of his.

'The cop that got shot last night?'

Ambler said yes.

The captain took off his hat and scratched his head. 'Lieutenant Jackson called you—'

'I called him.'

The captain had question marks in his eyes.

Ambler told him why he'd called Jackson but didn't tell him Jackson agreed to meet him when he said he had Mike's notebook.

'You wanted to find out what Lieutenant Jackson could tell you about Detective Cosgrove being shot and your friend killed. What were you going to do with any information the lieutenant gave you?' The captain didn't wait for an answer. 'Which he undoubtedly wasn't going to do, even if he had information.'

Ambler didn't want to explain. He wasn't sure he could for one thing. For another, this captain – who watched him with an unforgiving, accusing stare cops must pass on from generation to generation – would find his explanation – that he wanted to ask Chris Jackson if the cover-up of a multiple murder more than a quarter century ago was tied to Will Ford's murder and the shooting of Mike Cosgrove – preposterous. The only cop in New York who'd understand was Mike. And Mike was lying in a hospital bed near death.

Because he had to say something, he said, 'I don't know what he might have told me. He was a friend of Mike's. I thought he might have told me what he knew about the shooting.' He paused for a moment. 'Are you sure it's a suicide?'

For a moment, Ambler thought the captain was going to pop him one. Instead, he started to ask a question and then stopped. 'You ask a lot of strange questions. I'd like to know who the fuck you are.' He looked Ambler up and down. 'Maybe it's you watch too much TV.' He seemed to soften toward Ambler for a moment. 'That's a suicide, my friend. You can't fake that. He used a fucking cannon. I'm sorry to say I've seen it before. Cops make a mess when they do themselves in.'

After another moment, his brow wrinkled and his eyes narrowed. 'So I ask again, what would you do with any information the lieutenant gave you?' The captain didn't appear angry. He was a big man, a bit overweight, a large-boned man with a massive chest, hard as a brick wall, who, it was clear, wasn't averse to throwing his weight around. His question had undertones of an accusation.

'Mike's my friend. I wanted to know what was being done.'

'You thought the police might need help with the investigation?'

Ambler saw where this was going. 'No. I wanted to know what was happening, what was going to happen.'

The captain scrutinized Ambler's face for a long moment. 'I don't know why you were meeting Lieutenant Jackson. I don't for a minute think you're telling the truth, and I'm for god damn sure not finished with you.'

He asked Ambler for his identification and spent a long time examining his library I.D. card. When he handed it back, he told Ambler he could leave. 'I'm tired of looking at you,' he said.

Ambler drove back to the parking garage in Manhattan in a state of shock. Over and over, he asked himself why Jackson killed himself. Sometimes, it's despair, depression. Often, the victim is despondent. It can be shame or guilt. Was there something in Mike's notebook, or something he was afraid was in Mike's notebook? If that was it, Jackson acted too soon. Ambler hadn't found anything in Mike's notes. And if Jackson was worried about the notebook why not kill Ambler and take the notebook?

Ambler was halfway home on the walk from the rental car garage when he turned left instead of right and took himself to the Library Tavern. It was early in the cocktail hour, so the corner barstool was vacant. He ordered a double shot of Irish whiskey.

McNulty waited after he poured the shot. 'Is this something that might require me to have a shot along with you?'

Ambler gulped down a large swallow of the whiskey. When the burning in his throat wore off, he said, 'I saw a man who killed himself this afternoon. Put a gun in his mouth and pulled the trigger. I was the first one there. I can't stop seeing him . . .'

'God rest his soul.' McNulty shook his head. 'You never

know what torments a man is facing such as he judges them to be worse than death.'

Ambler described what happened. He needed to tell someone and the warmth from the whiskey made it easier to talk. He talked and McNulty listened until his cell phone rang. It was Adele.

'Well,' she said. 'Thanks for calling. What happened?'

'Chris Jackson killed himself. I found his body in his car when I went to meet him.'

'Oh my God! Where are you?'

He told her.

'Where's Johnny?'

'He's staying at his grandmother's for a few days.'

'Stay where you are. I'll be right over.' She hung up.

Fifteen minutes later, she was beside him. Leaning close, she took his hand in both of hers. 'How awful that must have been. I'm so sorry for you.' She looked at the empty rocks glass in front of him. 'You don't need whiskey. You need dinner and you need to be where it's calm and safe. I'm taking you home with me.'

Ambler stopped her. He was bothered again by the nagging thought that bothered him in the hospital. Jackson's death had set his imagination running wild. Suppose that captain was wrong, and Jackson was murdered. Mike might not be safe. His bizarre suspicion that someone might try to kill Mike could be right. He told this to Adele.

She took hold of his arm with both hands. 'What can we do? Should we take turns standing guard outside his room?'

Ambler had thought about that. Suppose the cop guarding Mike's room was one of the ones who thought he was a rat. Not all of the cops in New York were out to get Mike. A dozen or more of them had worked with him, knew what he was like, and would stand by him. He needed to find one of them. Denise would know her father's friends. He told Adele they needed to go to the hospital to talk with her.

Walking was faster than a cab at that time of day, so they walked – Adele trotting at times to keep up with him – over to First Avenue and the entrance to Bellevue. They found Denise sitting on a plastic chair in a different small waiting room outside the surgical step-down unit, her eyes closed, a book in her lap.

Mike had not come around; the doctors were keeping him heavily sedated. They didn't want him to move yet because the area around his spine needed to heal.

Ambler didn't want to tell Denise he thought her father was in danger. The kid had too much to handle already, so he asked if any of Mike's friends stopped by. She told him one of his former partners, Frank Elliot, had that afternoon and then went out and brought her back lunch.

Ambler remembered Elliot from an encounter a few years back. He was a hard-ass cop and didn't like Ambler butting into police business. But he was loyal to Mike.

'He gave me his card.' She fished around in her bag until she found it.

When Ambler called the number on the card, it took a few moments for Elliot to catch up with who he was and his connection to Mike.

'I remember now,' he said, a chill in his tone.

'I'm worried about Mike—'

'We all are.' His tone was brusque.

Ambler was afraid the guy would hang up on him, so he spoke quickly. 'Look. I have something to tell you, something Mike would want you to know. I don't want to do it over the phone. Can I meet you to talk for just a few minutes . . .'

'Sorry, Mr Ambler. I'm busy. And I don't keep secrets from the police department. You got me mixed up with someone else.'

Ambler was desperate. 'Can you come to the hospital? I'm here with Denise and don't want to leave her alone.'

'I was just there. I know Mike thinks you're OK. I don't. It happens Mike and I disagree sometimes.'

'I don't care what you think about me . . . Mike might be in danger.'

'He is in danger. He got a bullet in his back.'

'Not just that. What if they try again . . . here in the hospital?'

'There's a hospital police officer outside the door to his room. Tell him if you're worried. He can get backup if he needs it.'

'Mike needs someone protecting him that he trusts.'

Elliot lowered his voice. 'What are you getting at? You got something to say, say it.'

'You know some cops don't care a whole lot what happens to him.'

Sometimes you're right for the wrong reasons. You say something another person misunderstands in such a way that it ends up better than if he had understood.

'I get that . . .' Elliot hesitated. 'I don't know what you know about anything. If you've got information, give it to the homicide guys from the one-one-three who caught the case.'

Ambler tried again. 'This is more complicated than you think—'

Elliot interrupted him. 'I know Mike's not the most popular guy on the job. If I remember right, you had something to do with that—'

'But—'

'But nothing.' He paused for a long moment and when he spoke again his tone had changed. 'You may be right. I didn't think about that. What I'm gonna do is get some guys that know Mike to cover the shifts at the hospital for a day or two until we know who we're looking for on this . . . They'll do it on their own time, so no one that doesn't need to know will know about it.'

'Great.' Ambler had what he'd wanted, and he didn't have to try to explain who he thought might be out to get Mike. Elliot assumed he meant Gary Gannon, Anne's embittered ex-husband. For a moment, he started to correct Elliot but realized it was better to let it go.

He told Adele about the call and the extra protection.

'So what are you going to do now?'

'Wait for Mike to regain consciousness. I'm not doing anything else without him. I've already made enough of a mess of things. Even with him, I don't know what we're going to do.'

SEVENTEEN

Late the next morning, as a still-shaken Ambler worked on a funding proposal and tried to put a sense of normalcy back into his life, he had a visitor. The man standing in the doorway was thick and broad-shouldered, built like a linebacker. He wore a suit and because he wore glasses, had a somewhat bushy mustache, and dimples when he smiled, which he did as he handed Ambler his card, he appeared good-natured and unassuming, until the ice-like hardness in his eyes told Ambler he was a cop.

Sure enough, the card he handed Ambler was an NYPD business card embossed with a gold shield that read City of New York City Police on top and Deputy Inspector underneath what looked like a coat of arms. The name on the card was George Kowalski.

Ambler glanced up after reading it.

'Do you know who I am?' Kowalski's gaze was direct but not threatening.

'Should I?'

He studied Ambler's face for a moment. 'It's not important. I thought you might.' He studied Ambler again, as if he might discover something about Ambler's thinking from his face. After a moment, he gave up. 'I understand you found Lieutenant Chris Jackson's body.' He waited for an acknowledgment.

Ambler nodded.

'Chris was a friend of mine for nearly thirty years.' His grim expression told Ambler of his sorrow. 'You know he had four kids? How does a mother explain to them what happened to their father?'

Ambler stood as still as a statue while Kowalski talked, lectured might be a better description. He had no idea what the man wanted. 'I'm sorry for your loss,' he said.

Kowalski wasn't finished. 'A cop commits suicide. It happens too often. And it happens because the job gets to him.' He glared at Ambler. 'Everybody who knows anything about police work knows that. So the guy's family should get line-of-duty death benefits. But you know what? They don't. The job kills their father, their husband. They get nothing from the job.'

Ambler felt as if he were being blamed.

After a moment of angry silence, which Ambler felt was directed at him, Kowalski cleared his throat. His tone was formal. 'You told Captain Peterson you had an appointment to meet Lieutenant Jackson. Were you meeting him in connection with a case he was working?'

Ambler thought quickly about what he should say and decided on the truth, though he had no idea how the deputy inspector would take it; he'd never spoken to such a high-ranking police officer before and didn't understand why he was talking to one now. Before answering the question, he tried one of his own, an innocent enough one, perhaps a stupid one. 'Are you investigating Lieutenant Jackson's suicide?'

Kowalski had an expressive face, not the kind that gave away his thinking, more like he controlled his expressions for his purposes. He tilted his head like he might not have heard Ambler correctly. 'I'm going to assume you heard my question and you're stalling.' His tone was that of a stern uncle to an impertinent nephew. 'I asked you why you were meeting Lieutenant Jackson. I might have phrased it badly. But I'm told you're a smart guy . . .' He waved an arm to take in the bookshelves around them. 'An expert on police procedure, homicide investigation to be precise. I thought you'd catch on without a lot of unnecessary explanation, in other words that we could dispense with the bullshit.'

What Ambler caught on to was the deputy inspector had done some background checking – likely a great deal – before he came to visit and that the visit had a purpose that Ambler didn't know. Kowalski likely already knew the answer to his question and anything else Ambler could tell him. So if the deputy inspector most likely knew the truth already, it made sense for Ambler to tell the truth.

'I wanted to ask Lieutenant Jackson about Mike Cosgrove's shooting and the murder the day before of Will Ford. I thought the two shootings might be connected.' He watched Kowalski for a reaction and got a blank stare. 'If you want to know why I thought that, I'll tell you.'

Kowalski opened his arms like a preacher might. In his case it was to express astonishment. 'I know why you think they're connected. Because they're connected to you.' His formidable chest heaved and his voice rose. 'Why in God's name are you snooping around a homicide case from decades ago that has nothing to do with you? What do you get out of it?'

Ambler sat down in the chair on his side of the library table he'd been standing behind. It was the first time he'd moved since he stood up when Kowalski appeared in his doorway. He gestured to a chair on Kowalski's side of the table but Kowalski stayed standing.

The question, really an accusation, hit a nerve. The correct answer was he wanted to find out if a cop had committed a murder and gotten away with it, as happened in Will Ford's short story. It was a simple answer. But he had a hard time saying it.

He met Kowalski's accusing glare and told him about the short story. 'I wanted to find out if what Ford wrote actually happened. I'm sure you'd want to know if one of your officers murdered someone, even if it was a long time ago.'

Kowalski gave him a look of disgust – the look he might give to a lowlife grifter he'd collared. 'All the fucking evil that goes on in the world and assholes like you go nuts when a poor bastard cop makes a split-second decision to shoot at a scumbag he thinks will kill him if he doesn't shoot first. If it turns out he was wrong, the lowlife didn't have a gun, what no one says is if the bastard did have a gun he sure as hell would have used it on the officer.'

'That's not what happened. It was—'

Kowalski's eyes blazed. 'How the fuck would you know what happened?'

The certainty in Kowalski's tone stopped Ambler. His visit began to make sense. 'Do you know what happened? Do you know the murders I'm talking about?'

Kowalski continued to glower at him, and he sensed in a way he hadn't up until that point that the man was extraordinarily powerful, like you might find yourself confronted by a large muscular man who could break you in two if he wanted. Kowalski wasn't powerful like that; rather, he burned with a kind of explosive energy of purpose that would crush the will of anyone who crossed him. Ambler thought about tai chi and wondered if he could muster the softness to turn that energy against the man across the table from him who seethed with controlled rage.

Kowalski put both his hands on the library table and leaned toward Ambler. 'You sent your detective friend on a wild-goose chase, digging up a case put to bed years ago, and got him shot for his trouble. You're damn right I know the murders you're talking about. I told Detective Cosgrove all about the case you dug up. I thought he might have told you, that he might have called you off.' He straightened up and scrutinized Ambler in the way he'd done earlier, as if he might know what was in Ambler's mind by studying his face.

'He didn't tell me.'

'What I told him is Chris did something to protect a cop who was killed in a gaming joint on Manhattan Avenue many years ago. The cop made a mistake – let's say he wasn't on the job when he was killed – and because of that his widow and kids wouldn't get his line-of-duty death benefits. Chris fixed it so the family did get the benefits. Any decent cop would've done the same thing. Even so, if what he did became known, even now, the department would have to come down on him.

'His career would be ruined. He'd be disgraced. Chris was a proud man. He couldn't handle disgrace. When Detective Cosgrove started nosing around, Chris panicked because he saw what he'd done getting exposed if Cosgrove kept at it. He told me. I talked to Cosgrove and asked him to drop his investigation. That was a big chance I took. I did it because Chris said the guy was a good cop. Some people had doubts.

'Cosgrove got what I was telling him. But there was another problem for Chris. The writer. Mr Ford knew what happened that night. He knew the cop who was killed, Billy Donovan. He didn't know what Chris had done. But he knew what came out in the press wasn't what happened. For years the writer kept quiet about what he knew. He had no reason to ruin things for Billy's family. It wouldn't help anyone.

'So that was that. He kept quiet and tended to his own business. Until you came along, brought him back to New York, and stirred everything up. The writer was a drunk. Now that he was back in the city, Chris couldn't be sure he'd keep his mouth shut. Cosgrove wasn't the only problem. Chris was in a box.

'Knowing Chris, I'd bet he talked to the writer, tried to straighten the guy out. Chris would give him every chance. I don't know what the writer said. Like I told you, he had a big mouth. When it came to where Chris thought he had no choice, he took the dumb bastard out.

'Chris panicked. He didn't think straight. He should've come to me. But he didn't. He went after the writer and then he went after Cosgrove because he knew what Cosgrove would think, what he'd figure out.' Kowalski paused, and again searched Ambler's face, maybe to see if he was getting through to him. 'You don't know what happened there . . . I know because I put it together after I talked to the Cosgrove girl. I wanted to know if she'd seen the shooter. She hadn't. After the first shots, she threw herself on top of her father. Chris needed one more shot but he'd have to shoot her to finish off Cosgrove. He didn't do it.

'Then there's you. My guess is he thought he needed to take you out, too. That's why he met you where he did. No one around. And when it came down to doing it, while he waited for you in that parking lot, he realized it was over. He'd do you. He'd have to go back for Cosgrove. Maybe he'd have to kill me. Where would it stop? He had nowhere to go, no way out, so he ate his gun.'

Kowalski's last few words caught in his throat. He took his eyes off Ambler, closed them for a moment. When he spoke again it was haltingly. 'You know what he did right before? He stopped at the middle school near the parking lot where his kids go to school to say goodbye, to tell them he loved them and they needed to promise to always listen to their mom if something bad happened to him.'

Ambler looked away as Kowalski composed himself in the

ringing silence that filled the reading room. When he'd arranged to meet Jackson, he hadn't ruled out the possibility Jackson had killed Will Ford and shot Mike, though he thought it unlikely. Nothing Mike said in the past and nothing he wrote in his notebook hinted he suspected Jackson killed Ford.

After listening to Kowalski, Ambler still wasn't convinced. He should be, and he couldn't put his finger on why he wasn't. What Kowalski said about Jackson's actions and motive rang true, yet he couldn't get beyond thinking the deputy inspector's presentation was for his benefit, designed specifically for him. What he said may or may not have been the truth. But why would Kowalski take the trouble to tell him this personally?

He had another question, the one he'd asked all along, the question raised by Ford's story. When some time had passed and it didn't look like Kowalski was going to say anything else, Ambler said, 'I'm sorry about Chris Jackson's death and especially sorry if I did something that might have contributed to it. I had questions for him. I didn't have accusations. I didn't think he killed anyone.

'That night, a few hours before he got shot, Mike told me the detectives investigating Will Ford's murder didn't have any suspects. But I was told by someone else there is a suspect in Mike's shooting, a cop with a grudge against him, a domestic thing, a divorce—'

Kowalski looked like he was about to snarl and snap his teeth. 'You think I'd tell you what I told you if I wasn't sure? You think this is easy?'

Ambler held up his hands in a placating apology. 'I'm sure it's not easy for you. I'm not arguing; I'm confused. Do you mind if I ask what the cop who was killed did that Lieutenant Jackson covered up? And if a cop walked away from the murders?'

Kowalski gave up his effort at control. His eyes grew enormous behind his glasses. He sputtered. Spittle sprayed from his mouth. 'What? . . . Walked away from the murders?' He swallowed a couple of times before something flickered in his eyes, a light dawned. 'You're talking about that goddamn story again? That isn't what happened. It's bullshit.'

'Were you at the crime scene? Was Will Ford at the crime scene?'

Kowalski glanced at the chair Ambler had gestured him toward earlier and sat down. He glared at Ambler as if he might wither him with his stare and then his glare wavered; he rubbed his temples like a man with a headache. After closing his eyes for a moment, he glanced at Ambler again; this time, his expression was calm, weary, perhaps sad. He spoke softly. 'You're stubborn, like a bulldog. You shoulda been a cop.'

Ambler shook his head. 'I don't think so.' He wasn't sure he should go on, but he did.

'I know enough about what cops do – the unpleasant things the rest of us don't want to do – to know I wouldn't be very good at it. I asked the questions because I'm trying to make sense of what you told me weighed against what I know myself. That's not doubting you. It's as much questioning me.'

Kowalski's gaze wandered about the reading room as if he tried to absorb some meaning from the thousands of books. 'You read all these?'

Ambler followed his gaze, feeling both protective and proud of the collection. 'Not by a long shot. Some are first editions that are artifacts rather than for reading. Others aren't the kinds of mysteries I like. A lot I'd like to read I haven't gotten to yet and may never get to.'

Kowalski didn't seem to hear or if he did not to care about Ambler's answer. 'You think if someone read enough of them they'd understand where evil comes from? Understand how people do things to one another you'd think wouldn't be possible – kill their children, kill their friends; kill a mass of people they don't know?'

Kowalski didn't want an answer to this question either, so Ambler didn't try. Maybe he was trying to tell him something.

'Some men are hard when they become cops. Most men aren't. Being a cop makes them hard.' He spoke softly, glancing at Ambler now and again; most of the time gazing past him. 'You remember the crack cocaine years – the '80s, the early '90s?

'Outlaws ran the streets. You arrested a drug-slinger and the next afternoon you'd see him on the street corner a block from where you locked him up. Cops were pushed out on the streets with a system that didn't back them up. The punks laughed at us until we got tough and scared the shit out of them.'

He studied Ambler like a judge might stare down a defendant before sentencing him. 'Solid citizens pretended they were horrified when they found out some of the things cops did to stop punks terrorizing the streets. The system wouldn't stop them. Cops had to stop them. The system wouldn't punish them, so we punished them.

'In a perverted way, trying to stop them, you were in danger of becoming like them. You lie down with dogs, you get fleas. That happened to Chris.' Kowalski sat with slumped shoulders, as if he'd exhausted himself in telling Ambler what he told him.

Ambler didn't know what to make of Kowalski, didn't know why he'd come to the library, didn't know what he was asking for or if he was asking for anything, didn't know what he was holding back, didn't know if everything he said was true or nothing he said was true.

After a few moments, Kowalski pushed back his chair and stood. When he did, Ambler noticed his left leg didn't bend when he moved it. 'I hope Cosgrove makes it. I like the guy. I'm told he's in bad shape.' His shoulders still slumped, he rubbed his temples again, a man who carried a problem that was too big for him for too long and was weary of it.

'It didn't have to end like this. Chris shoulda come to me. He always did before. I coulda fixed things. But you know you do one thing and it leads to another thing and then what happens next is out of your hands; you don't control what you do any more. What you already did decided what you have to do next. I'm not gonna ask you to understand Chris. What he did was crazy. That's what the job did to him.'

He turned back as he headed for the door and met Ambler's gaze one last time with a hard stare. 'What I told you, you need to keep to yourself. It's not for public consumption. I told you what I told you to keep you quiet until we see what happens with Detective Cosgrove. I need to handle this carefully. If he pulls through, that means one way. If he doesn't make it, we may need to go a different way.'

EIGHTEEN

When Kowalski left the reading room, Ambler tried without success to make sense of the deputy inspector's strange visit. While he was lost in his thoughts, a library clerk delivered a file box a researcher who was due later that day had requested.

Half-daydreaming, he picked through the box until some notebooks the writer had entitled 'Story Journal' caught his attention. The author, all but forgotten, was a short-story writer who'd published a story in almost every issue of *Ellery Queen* from the end of World War II until 1955 when he died. In the story journals, he wrote what might be called treatments or rough outlines of stories he planned to write.

Glancing through them reminded him that Adele had been reading through Will Ford's journals, which got him to thinking. She'd told him some of what she'd found, mostly about his mother. So far, she hadn't been looking through them with any real purpose, so he thought he might suggest one.

He went looking for her and when he found her at her cubicle behind the information desk he told her about his visit from Kowalski.

'Did you believe him?' She asked this in a tone that meant if he did he shouldn't have.

'What he told me was believable. Yet I'm not sure I believe him. He said Chris Jackson made up a story to protect the reputation of the cop who was killed in that Manhattan Avenue gambling den. What he didn't tell me was what the dead cop had done that needed covering up – obviously something he wasn't supposed to do. Nor did he tell if a cop had walked away from the murders, as happened in Ford's story.

'You'd want to believe Kowalski is on the up and up. But Mike told me the main job of the high-ranking brass is to sweep things under the rug, so Kowalski might still be trying to cover something up. In Ford's story, Cisco Garcia, the private eye, is in the room when the murders happen. I think now Will Ford must have been at the actual crime scene.'

Adele's eyes sprang open. 'Will Ford witnessed the murders?'

'How else would he have known?'

'Someone might have told him.'

'That's possible. But the more I think about it, the more I believe the short story was based on something Ford experienced, not something he was told about.'

Either way it didn't change what Ambler wanted to ask Adele to do. He told her about the story journals he'd come across, and that Ford might have kept the same kind of journal of ideas for stories and background material. 'He might have written notes for "The Unrepentant Killer" at some point between when the murders happened and when he wrote the story. It's a long shot but it's worth trying.'

As Adele listened, her forehead wrinkled. 'And what will you be doing while I'm doing this?'

'I found a couple of names in Mike's notebook, two cops who were on a task force with Chris Jackson and Billy Donovan. I'm pretty sure Mike was going to interview them but he never got the chance. I've tracked one of them down and I'm going to find out what he knows about the Manhattan Avenue murders. It's possible but unlikely Jackson talked to him after Mike interviewed him. Billy Donovan might not have acted alone the night he was killed. One of the task-force cops in Mike's notebook might have been with him. Jackson could have warned him that Mike was reopening the case. If that's what happened, he, and not Chris Jackson, might have killed Ford and shot Mike.'

'So Jackson killed himself because he felt guilty for turning this killer, whoever he is, loose on Mike?'

'I don't know that's what happened but it's possible. It's also possible he knows what happened and might confirm what Kowalski told me. His name is Hector Morales, and he works for Big Nick Pappas, driving a liquor truck.' He told Adele the connection between Big Nick and Gilberto Sanchez that Will Ford had told him about.

'Driving a truck?'

'Liquor distributor drivers are salesmen as well as delivery men. It pays good money, especially if you have an exclusive area and work for someone with a lot of muscle. It's a legitimate job with a legitimate business, backed up by gangsters. Will Ford went looking for Big Nick a couple of nights before he was murdered. There's some reason to think that might be why he got murdered.'

The furrows on Adele's brow deepened. 'You didn't get yourself killed going to meet someone who might be a murderer in a vacant lot out in Queens, so now you're going to try your luck smoking out gangsters in the Bronx and see if one of them will kill you.'

Ambler chuckled. 'For one thing it was a parking lot in a family neighborhood in Queens, not a vacant lot. For another, Washington Heights isn't the Bronx, and for a last thing, I'm taking McNulty with me. We'll use a ruse to make discreet inquiries. We're not going to confront gangsters about anything.'

That evening after work Ambler took the A Train to the 181st Street station and met McNulty at a bar on St Nicholas Avenue. The place was loud with salsa music and a hum of what seemed like excited conversation in Spanish. The tables across from the bar were mostly unoccupied. All the stools at the bar were taken except for an empty stool next to where McNulty sat sipping a beer.

Ambler pointed to the beer taps and asked for a beer. '*Cerveza.*'

When the bartender brought it, McNulty introduced him to Ambler. 'This is Ray, the guy I told you about. Ray, Alberto.' They shook hands.

'Alberto knows Hector Morales. They went to grade school together.'

'We played baseball together, too,' Alberto said. 'He comes in a lot. Mostly, he deals with the boss over the liquor order. We get along. But we're not good friends any more. He does his thing. I don't ask what it is.'

'Does Big Nick Pappas come in?' Ambler asked.

Alberto froze. Ambler might have turned him to stone with the question.

McNulty gave Ambler a look. 'Don't mind him,' he said to Alberto. 'We want to talk to Hector. Nobody's looking for Mr Pappas.'

'I told Hector,' Alberto said. 'Let me tell you. You don't want to get on the wrong side of Hector. He got a mean streak.' He shot Ambler a withering glance. 'I wouldn't go asking him about Mr Pappas either. That's his boss.' He then had a short, whispered conversation with McNulty, using the ear on the side opposite Ambler and shooting a sidelong glance at Ambler as he spoke.

'What was that?' Ambler asked when Alberto had moved down the bar.

'He's worried you'll get him in trouble with Morales. I told him you'd keep your mouth shut and I'd do the talking.'

Ambler turned to McNulty. 'You're going to do that?'

McNulty hunched over his beer glass, scanning the bar through the mirror behind the rows of bottles on the back bar, meeting Ambler's gaze through the mirror. 'No. But you could use a censor. We'll sit at a table when he gets here. Don't ask about Big Nick unless he brings it up. If he doesn't want to talk about something, don't press him. You don't want to be accusing him of anything. Let him know anything he does or has done is fine with you. You're finding out about someone else.'

'What if—'

'No what-ifs. If he's the guy who did in Ford, he'll recognize me. If that happens, we're up Shit's Creek. But we pretend we don't care he whacked Ford or took a whack at Cosgrove. I didn't see the guy that night. Or I don't think I did. If it happens I recognize him, I won't let on. We only care about what happened years ago.'

'You think he'll fall for that?'

McNulty turned to face Ambler. 'If we pretend, he may believe us; or if he doesn't believe us he might pretend too, and we'll get out of here alive tonight.'

Hector Morales, a thick-chested, pudgy man, barreled into the bar like he owned it. Everything about him was pudgy, his neck, his arms, his fingers, even his head. He took up a lot of space and surveyed his surroundings, letting everyone in the place know he was ready to take on anyone who wanted a piece of him. He saw right away who was out of place and came up on Ambler and McNulty.

'Youse the guys who want to see me? Who told you to talk to me?'

The correct answer was, 'No one.' Ambler didn't think that would fly, so he said, 'Chris Jackson.'

Morales glared into his eyes for a long moment, as if deciding if he should break him in two.

'Let's get a table,' said McNulty.

Morales turned on him. 'Do I know you?'

'I doubt it,' McNulty said. 'I never saw you before.'

Morales continued to appraise him. 'You look like I seen you before.'

The goon's scrutiny made Ambler nervous but didn't seem to bother McNulty, who rubbed his chin. 'Maybe it'll come to you. I get around. I've worked in a lot of bars.'

Morales shrugged and turned to Ambler. 'That's too bad about Chris. He wasn't a bad guy. A fucking Boy Scout, but you could trust him to do the right thing.'

Ambler had concocted a story for how he came to talk to Morales. He didn't expect the guy to incriminate himself. But he might let something slip. The story was that the father of Dominique, the prostitute who was murdered along with Billy Donovan and the others, was a friend of his and had asked him to find out more about her death.

'Chris couldn't tell me much about her. He said you could tell me more. He was going to let you know I was OK. But . . . well, you know what happened. Whatever you tell me will stay with me. I don't need to tell the girl's father where I get what I tell him.'

'How do you know Chris?'

Ambler wasn't ready for the question and stumbled for an answer.

McNulty, quick on his feet as usual, gave him a shove in the right direction. 'It's OK to tell Mr Morales about your son.'

Ambler caught his drift. 'My son is doing time. It's a bum rap—'

Morales laughed. 'It's always a bum rap.' He shot a piercing glance at Ambler. But something changed in his expression, as if he felt easier, lowered his guard a little bit.

'I met Chris when I was trying to find the cops who busted my son. He listened. He was helpful. I found him a stand-up guy. When my friend asked me to find out about his daughter, I first was told to talk to Deputy Inspector Kowalski, who was—'

'I know who the prick is. He was our sergeant.'

This was interesting. Kowalski didn't mention the task force and his name wasn't in Mike's notes. It was also interesting Morales considered Kowalski a prick. There might be something to find out here if he didn't screw it up. 'He was no help. He didn't want to talk about what happened. But I found out Chris Jackson worked with the cop who was killed, so I called him. He told me about you, so here we are.'

'What's this father want to know for? It happened years ago. His daughter was a whore. He know that?'

McNulty interrupted. 'You got any kids?'

Morales turned on him. 'What if I do? What's it to you?'

McNulty spoke softly. 'The three of us got kids. Something happens to your kid, you want to know. You want to know anything you can find out because you miss a kid that dies young; it's different than how you miss someone else.'

McNulty got through to Morales. He had a way of getting through to almost anyone. Ambler didn't know how he did it. Like he did with Will Ford, McNulty found a way to connect with the most unlikely people.

'My kids are in the Dominican Republic. I don't want them here. Too easy for kids to get in trouble. I take care of them. They live in the country, in a nice house. They go to school. They play baseball. I got a good job. I provide for them. I don't want them here, not even to visit.'

Ambler spoke softly also. 'My friend knows his daughter was a prostitute. That came out when she was murdered. He started thinking about her again because the guy who's in prison for her murder wrote him a letter, told him nice things about her – and said that he didn't kill her.'

'Who's the guy in prison?'

'Felix Hernandez.'

Morales nodded slowly as if searching back into his memory. 'If I remember right, we had him on another murder and he copped to the girl and Billy Donovan for a lighter sentence, murder two instead of murder one. He's where he belongs. If he didn't kill her – and I don't know if he did or not – he did plenty of others. He's trying to worm his way out of what he copped to.'

'So he might not have killed her?'

'Dominique, the whore? I don't know why anyone would kill her. She probably got in the way. Wrong place at the wrong time.'

'Do you know who killed her?'

Morales shrugged. 'They got Hernandez for it. You ask Kowalski?'

'He said officially an undercover cop blew his cover and that led to a shoot-out. He also said Donovan had made a mistake and done something wrong that Chris Jackson covered up. So he didn't tell me what happened. But I understood him to say the official report was not what really happened.'

'That's George. He's got a cover story for everything. Did you ask him if he was on the pad?'

Ambler was finding out more than he'd expected to find out. 'Was he?'

'It wouldn't do any good asking him anyway. He'd lie. Billy Donovan was crazy. The joint he hit was protected. No reason Billy should go there.' He stopped and looked from Ambler to McNulty and back again at Ambler.

'There's no statute of limitations on murder, so what happened that night ain't somethin' I'm gonna talk about. I have my own ideas on what went down. Those ideas I keep to myself. Ask me what you want about the girl.'

'One other person I want to ask you about, a writer named Will Ford. Does that name sound familiar?' Ambler glanced at McNulty to make sure he hadn't gone too far. McNulty was stone-faced.

Morales folded his hands on the table. He had a tattoo of a dagger piercing a heart on the back of his left hand and the Dominican coat of arms on the back of his right hand. 'I remember a guy, a writer. I don't remember his name. He was a wannabe, a hanger on, a gopher for Annabelle Lee.'

'Was he involved with Dominique?'

'He wanted to be. I remember him because I was goin' to lock him up one night. But Annabelle Lee said to let it go. I had a kind of understanding with her. Let's say, I helped her out when she needed it. She helped me out when I needed it.' He glanced at Ambler and then at McNulty. 'If you know what I mean.

'The writer got into a fight with another patron. The fight was over Dominique. The writer guy thought he wanted to be a pimp. Pimps don't fall in love with their whores. He wanted to save the girl from the life. She didn't want to be saved, at least not by him. He was jealous.

'That night he got in the way. Got in some guy's face who wanted Dominique. He didn't understand. She liked what she did. No one hurt her. Annabelle Lee watched out for her girls. Anybody got tough with one of the girls, she made sure the guy got back twice what he did.'

'You said the writer you're talking about was a gopher.'

'Annabelle let him hang around the whorehouse, do errands, help out the girls. She thought she was an intellectual. She liked he was some sort of a professor. She pretended she had a high-class operation, like the Park Avenue call girls, when what she did was run a whorehouse on Manhattan Avenue. She and the writer guy were quite a pair. They'd take some of the girls to Lincoln Center to the opera or a symphony concert or they'd go to a play down on Broadway. They were a trip.'

'Could he have been at the gambling parlor the night of the murders?'

'The gambling was in a basement apartment under Annabelle Lee's operation. He coulda been there.'

Ambler took a chance, pushed his luck. 'If I were to think George Kowalski was on the pad, who would I guess was paying him, Gilberto Sanchez?'

Morales shook his head.

'Could it have been—' Ambler felt a sharp pain in his leg. McNulty had kicked him in the shin under the table. He winced and bent toward his leg.

Morales watched him. 'You all right?'

'A pain I get sometimes. I'm OK. I didn't know about cops on the pad. Was Chris Jackson?'

Morales shook his head. 'We made sure he wasn't Internal Affairs, but he wasn't into it. I told you he was a Boy Scout. He was sort of Kowalski's pet. But he kept his mouth shut.

'Kowalski turned out to be a bastard. He made me and a couple of other guys quit the force, take early retirement. He moved up in the department and didn't want anybody around with dirt on him.' Morales pushed his chair back and put his hand in the side pocket of his jacket. 'I'm telling you this stuff. I won't testify to any of it. I'll deny everything.

'We're gonna leave together, out the side door behind you. It goes to an alley. I'm gonna search you. If you're wearing a wire, I'm gonna leave your body in that alley.' He took a small revolver out of his jacket pocket and showed it to Ambler.

'You got nothing to worry about,' McNulty said. 'No one's wearing a wire. This conversation never happened. You asked Alberto about me, right? I told him I wouldn't do anything to embarrass him.'

'Your friend is nosy.'

'He doesn't know any better. He's a librarian. He reads about things in books.'

Ambler watched the two men talk about him like he wasn't there. He waited until he was sure they were finished to try to get his story straightened out. 'Could this writer have killed Dominique?'

Morales sounded skeptical. 'You wanted to know about the girl. Why all the other questions?'

Ambler met his gaze. 'Because Kowalski didn't want me to know what happened. Because the guy in prison told Dominique's father he didn't do it. Kowalski was hiding something, so I wanted to know what he was hiding.'

'You think you're gonna bring down George?'

'I didn't think that was what I was doing. Let me ask you this. Is there anyone else I can talk to who knows what happened that night?'

Morales considered this. 'You can ask that writer guy if

you think he was there. If you think he did it, you might want to be careful how you ask.'

Ambler watched Morales's face as he said this. If he was lying, he was good at it. 'The writer guy is dead. He was murdered a couple of days ago.'

This did cause a reaction. Morales blinked a couple of times, the kind of internal double-take you do when what you heard doesn't fit with what you know. He didn't say anything for a moment. 'What did this writer guy look like? Cowboy hat?'

This time, Ambler did the internal double-take. 'Yes.' He took a stab at describing Ford.

'A loudmouth drunk?'

'You could say that. Why do you ask?'

Morales took a moment too long to answer. 'I was trying to remember him.'

Ambler waited a moment. 'Anyone else?'

Morales shrugged. 'You're better off not knowing. Tell your friend everybody liked Dominique. The winos loved her. She was happy any time I saw her. She made plenty of money.' He paused. 'You might not want to tell him about the horse habit.'

'If I found out who was paying off Kowalski, would that help me find who killed Dominique?'

Morales watched Ambler for a moment, pushed back his chair, stood, and put his hand in his jacket pocket. 'Let's go check you for a wire.' He nodded toward McNulty. 'You come, too.'

'I need to settle up,' McNulty said. He walked over and laid two twenties in front of Alberto. 'No one's upset. Thanks for your help.'

In the alley, Morales held the gun on McNulty while he patted Ambler down, opened his jacket and shirt and told him to drop his pants. As Ambler put himself back together, Morales nodded toward McNulty, 'You, too.'

McNulty followed the drill.

In the cab, on the way downtown, Ambler watched the city slip by. He didn't think, only watched: tall pre-war apartment buildings on his side of the street, every few blocks a strip of storefronts, liquor stores, bodegas, a chicken shack, a Greek diner, cleaners, nail salons, storefront law office.

McNulty interrupted his trance. 'Did we find out anything?'

'Nothing about Big Nick Pappas, that's for sure.'

'I'll tell you what I found out. Morales didn't kill Will Ford.'

'Where did you get that?'

McNulty took a quick look at the cab driver, who was speaking on the phone in a language Ambler took to be Arabic. 'He got rattled when you told him Ford was dead. What confused him was he'd beaten a guy up a couple of nights before and now the guy was dead.'

Ambler had noticed Morales's reaction, too. But he wasn't sure. 'Can you find out if Morales was one of the thugs who beat up Ford?'

'I already pretty much know and what difference does it make? The guy didn't know Ford was dead.'

'He thought he recognized you.'

'If he recognized me from the night Ford was killed, he wouldn't have had any doubt about it. So what now? Big Nick didn't have Ford killed.'

'I'm not so sure. Big Nick has other people working for him.'

'We talked to the guy who had a reason to kill Ford and Cosgrove. This Kowalski guy, the police department mucky-muck, he knows where the bodies are buried and who put them there. What about him?'

Kowalski was smart and carried himself with authority, coming across as you might expect a high-ranking police officer to come across. Morales's accusation that he was on the pad, meaning he was taking bribes, came as a surprise. 'He may know everything there is to know. But he's not going to tell me anything he doesn't want to tell me. How do I get him to tell me if he doesn't want to? Go to the Chief? Go to the Commissioner?'

'Why would they listen to you?'

'They wouldn't.'

'You have to trick him.'

'Trick him?'

'Set a trap?'

Ambler stared at his friend. 'Where did that come from?'

'Nero Wolfe and Archie . . .'

NINETEEN

Early the next morning, Ambler's cell phone rang. Denise's name came up on the screen and his heart stopped. A few seconds later, his dread gave way to a feeling of relief such that he had to sit down to finish the call. Mike was going to make it.

He called the library and took the morning off and was at the hospital by 9:30. The waiting room where he normally found Denise was empty. Mike had been moved to a private room. When Ambler found the room, he also found a guy outside the door to the room. The sentry wore casual street clothes but was unmistakably a cop. He stopped Ambler before he got to the door, telling him politely he couldn't go in.

Ambler said he was Mike's friend and Mike would want to see him.

'I don't care if you're the Prince of the Archangels, you're not going in there.' The cop puffed out his chest. He was broad-shouldered, thick-necked, ruddy complexioned, and red-headed. His bearing said he'd mop the floor with Ambler without breaking a sweat.

Ambler tried telling the cop he could ask Frank Elliot for a reference. This news brought back the cop's polite manner but didn't get Ambler into Mike's room, so he went back to the waiting room and called Denise. Before he'd finished telling her what was happening, she came out of her father's room and waved to him. The cop watched him like a cat watches a canary but didn't say anything as Denise walked with him into the hospital room.

Mike followed Ambler with his eyes but didn't say anything.

Ambler fumbled for words. 'You look good,' was what he came up with.

'You come to make sure I'm alive or see if I was dead?'

Conversation was awkward. They talked about how long he'd been in the hospital, how soon he might go home, not about what had happened to him. Mike put up a good front but couldn't hide how depressed and angry he was. Without him saying as much, it was clear he'd rather be left alone. He made the effort to talk because that was expected of him. Every few moments he drifted off as if he were alone as he'd been for the last few days and Ambler got the feeling he preferred that.

When Ambler had been there for ten minutes or so, two detectives from the one hundred and thirteenth precinct in Queens arrived. They said they needed a few minutes alone with Mike and promised the visit would be short. Ambler went with Denise to the waiting room.

'He seems so sad,' she said.

'He wasn't really up to talking. I don't blame him. Did he talk with you before I got there?'

'He wanted to remember what happened and wanted to know what I saw.'

Ambler watched her, this girl who'd become a young woman, transformed from a cute, pouting, mercurial teenager to a strong-willed, determined woman, who at the moment was so worn out by her vigil she could have fallen asleep standing up. He met her gaze. 'I bet you didn't tell him you saved his life by risking yours.'

She blushed and looked away. 'The police said that. I didn't know. I didn't think about anything only to help my dad.'

'What did you see?'

She took a deep breath as if to steel herself against the memory. 'Nothing really. I heard the shots. I saw Dad fall. I screamed and ran to him. A man was back by the curb. He watched me run to Dad and then he must have left. He wasn't there when I looked up. No one was on the street. I called 911.' She took another deep breath. 'I remembered something I'd heard from my dad. I said, "10-13 . . . A police officer's been shot," and told them our address. The cops got there in no time. They were great. Them and the EMTs, they're the ones who saved his life.'

'Did you see the man who shot him? Was it the man on the sidewalk?'

'I saw someone. I didn't see what he looked like. He was

a shape, not anything more. I wouldn't recognize him if he was standing in front of me.'

'Could you tell if he was Black?'

She froze and glared at Ambler as if he'd slapped her. 'I swear I didn't expect that from you.' Her voice rose. 'You just assume the gunman was Black? Are you kidding me?'

Ambler felt a flush of embarrassment and instinctively looked around to see if anyone had heard her call him a racist. He held his hands out to quiet her. 'It's not like that. Listen for a minute.' He told her what Kowalski had told him about Chris Jackson.

'The man who shot my dad killed himself?'

'That's what he told me.'

'A detective who came to the hospital that night after my dad was admitted asked me if the gunman was Black. That's why I got mad at you, I guess. I sort of expected that from the cops, even though my dad told me most cops weren't like that so much any more because there's so many Black cops now.'

'What did the detective ask you exactly?'

She took a moment before she answered. 'He asked me to tell him everything I saw, everything I remembered. So I told him. He asked if Dad saw who shot him and he asked if Dad said anything to me. After all that, he said, "Could you tell if the man who shot your father was Black?"'

'After you'd already told him what you saw? What did you tell him?'

'What I told you; I didn't see who shot my dad.'

'Did your dad say anything about the shooting since he woke up? Did he see who shot him?'

She shook her head. 'I don't think so. I didn't ask. I suppose the detectives with him now will ask.'

Ambler realized Mike wouldn't know Chris Jackson was dead. He didn't want to be the one to break the news and hoped the detectives in with him now would tell him. Then again, Mike might not be ready for it. He might not be ready to hear what Kowalski had to say either. But Ambler figured he should tell him.

When the detectives came out of the hospital room, they

were close-mouthed about their interview, as Ambler expected them to be. One of them said, 'I think he's falling asleep.'

Ambler told Denise to go home and get some rest; he'd keep watch over Mike. He called Adele at the library and asked her to bring over some work for him to do while he waited. She arrived an hour later with his laptop, a folder of book auction catalogs . . . and sandwiches and coffee from a deli on Second Avenue so they could have lunch together.

'I don't think you should tell him unless he asks,' she said, as they finished their coffee. 'You can stay here and just be around. Let him decide if he wants to talk and what he wants to talk about. I can pick up Johnny today.'

'He's been going to his grandmother's after school since Denise has been at the hospital.' He had a sudden thought. 'God. I hope Lisa didn't tell him about his father's hearing.'

Adele lowered her coffee container. 'I don't think it would be so bad if she tells him.' She laughed. 'It's a chance for her side to take credit, so I imagine she will. It won't be so bad.'

When Adele left, Ambler walked into Mike's room. This time, the cop at the door nodded, so Ambler stopped. 'You're a friend of Mike's?'

The cop eyed him suspiciously.

'I just want to thank you for what you're doing.'

The cop spoke grumpily, as if talking to Ambler was an imposition. 'Some guys hear shit and make judgments without knowing the guy. Anybody knows Mike knows he's always done things the right way.'

Ambler spent the rest of the day with Mike, sitting in a stiff Naugahyde armchair, working through some book auction catalogs. Mike slept a lot of the time and when he was awake they didn't talk much. Every now and again, he would ask a question – where was Denise; tell her she should be in school; how was Adele – and now and again he'd tell Ambler to go back to the library; he didn't need to be sitting there.

After his second nap, this one undisturbed for a couple of hours until the dietary aide brought his dinner – soup that he ate through a straw the aide held for him – he was alert and wanted to talk.

'A helluva friend you are,' he said, after a moment of gazing intently at Ambler. 'Why aren't you looking for the bastard who shot me? You only interested in that if they kill me?'

'I'd think the entire NYPD is out looking for whoever shot you. Isn't that what they do when a cop gets shot?'

'You'd think that, wouldn't you.' Mike's short laugh was mirthless. 'They got two guys, both of them waiting for their retirement papers to come through, working the case. The rest of the department couldn't be bothered; some of them think I had it coming.'

It was easier talking now. Mike was more like his old self. He was tired; sometimes his voice would trail off, his eyes would close. A couple of times, Ambler suggested he should rest. But he wanted to talk. When he finally got around to asking what was new on the Ford shooting, Ambler decided it was time to break the news. He didn't know if Kowalski's edict on not making what he'd been told public included telling Mike but decided it didn't.

'I've got bad news,' he said.

Mike didn't really move but it seemed to Ambler like he was bracing himself. 'I knew you were getting up your nerve to tell me something bad. No sense putting it off. I'm not going to feel any worse than I already feel.'

In truth, Mike looked as downcast as if he'd already heard the bad news, so Ambler straight out told him. 'Chris Jackson is dead. He killed himself.' That part was hard; the next part would be harder.

He gave Mike some time to come to terms with the death of his friend, a moment of silence so he might go back through some memories. Whatever it was he did, he closed his eyes and looked inward.

A disembodied voice came from the collection of bedclothes and tubes and wires. 'A rotten shame.'

'I've got more to tell you.' Ambler lowered his gaze. He didn't want to look at Mike. 'I found his body. He was in his car in a parking lot near where he lived in Queens. I was supposed to meet him there.'

He took a deep breath. 'I took your notebook from among your things the hospital gave Denise to take home. So I knew you talked with Jackson right before you were shot.' Ambler paused to gather up his will. 'I told him I had your notebook. That was why he agreed to meet me.'

Surprisingly, Mike didn't sound angry. 'The notebook wouldn't have told you much unless you can read my mind. Actually, I'm glad you took it. I'd rather you have it than the department get hold of it right now. You said you found his body?'

Ambler described what he'd seen.

'No note?'

'None that I know of. But there's more . . .'

Mike didn't say anything so Ambler told him what Kowalski had told him in almost the same terms Kowalski used. Mike was silent when he finished, silent for so long Ambler thought he might have fallen asleep. Leaving Mike to his thoughts or dreams, Ambler went and stood by the window, catching a glimpse of a barge and its tugboats on the East River.

'Chris didn't shoot me,' Mike said quietly behind him. 'I don't know what Kowalski was up to with telling you that.'

Ambler waited for an explanation but didn't ask. Mike had kept his thoughts to himself since Ambler first brought Will Ford's story to him. Maybe he'd continue to do that. Ambler wasn't going to tell him he couldn't.

But he didn't stay quiet. He wanted to keep talking. 'So you found my notes from when I talked to Chris that night. You must be a code-breaker. Brilliant attorneys have tried to decipher my notes and failed.'

'I knew you'd talked with Chris Jackson. That was about all, except for the names of cops who were on the task force with him at the time of those murders. I spoke with one of them, Morales.'

'Did you take a shower afterward?'

'He told me Kowalski ran the task force with Jackson and the others – something Kowalski didn't tell me – and that he was on the pad during that time. Should I not have believed him?'

Mike didn't show any surprise. 'Even liars tell the truth if it's in their interest.'

'Was Chris Jackson a dirty cop?'

Mike's tone turned stern. 'You want to be careful throwing

that term around . . . with me anyway. You know what they say about walking a mile in a man's shoes before you judge him?'

'Does that go for Deputy Inspector Kowalski, too?'

'It goes for any of us.' Mike's tone softened. 'The two guys who interviewed me just now wanted to know about Gary Gannon. I don't remember if I told you Anne was getting a divorce.'

'You told me.'

'What happened between her and Gary had nothing to do with me. I didn't see her when she was married. Or not in a romantic way. Denise and Anne's daughter are the same age, went to the same schools, ran with the same crowd. So as parents we'd see one another.

'We didn't socialize; I didn't like Gary. I never liked him. We grew up in the same neighborhood, Anne too. He had a cruel streak when he was a kid. Bully younger kids; torture alley cats. His father was a miserable bastard, too. Most everyone in the neighborhood was leery of the Gannon family. But they were Catholic, Irish, and old man Gannon was a cop, so they were part of the neighborhood. It was like an extended family.

'Anne shouldn't have married him. She should have married me. But I was too dumb to know that at the time. She thought she was supposed to marry a cop because her old man was a cop and his old man had been a cop. Growing up where we did, a daughter marrying a cop was almost as good as a boy becoming a priest.'

Mike was off on a tangent. Ambler thought he'd lost the train of their conversation, probably because of the painkillers. 'Did Gannon shoot you?'

'I don't know who shot me,' Mike said wearily. 'He certainly wouldn't lose any sleep over my being shot.

'When I blew the whistle on those intelligence guys – I should say "we blew the whistle" – Gannon led the charge to paint me as a rat. He didn't know anything about the case. It was a chance to ruin my reputation and he took it. Because of that, a lot of cops wouldn't care that I got shot. Maybe some of them wouldn't mind shooting me.'

'Do you know it was a cop who shot you?'

Mike was suddenly alert. 'I didn't say that. I don't know

who shot me. Anyway, I did talk to Chris that night. He told me some things.'

'Kowalski said he told you a while back the truth about the Manhattan Avenue murders.'

Mike closed his eyes. After a moment, without opening his eyes, he said, 'Sit back down, Ray. You look like the Grim Reaper looming over me.'

Ambler sat. When he did, he could no longer tell if Mike's eyes were open or closed and was afraid he was staying too long, causing his friend stress and maybe doing him harm. 'You need to rest,' he said after another moment. 'I should go and let you get some sleep.'

Mike ignored what he said. 'What Morales told you was part of the truth. I'm not going to try to tell you why things happened the way they did. I'm going to tell you what Chris told me.

'The cop who was killed, Billy Donovan, was holding up that gaming room – doin' doors on his own – when he got into a shoot-out. That's what got everyone killed – a holdup gone bad. That's what Chris and George Kowalski covered up. There's a guy in prison who confessed to killing Donovan and another one of the victims. Now, he says he didn't do the murders. But they all say they didn't do it if it looks like they can cry foul and get away with it.'

'"Doin' doors", so that's what it means?'

Mike made a sound, a grunt more than anything else. 'It's more complicated than that. I don't have the energy to explain it to you. In a strange way, by their own lights, some of the cops doin' doors thought they were enforcing the law.'

Ambler made something of a grunt himself. 'You're right. It wouldn't be easy to explain that to me. Why did you want to talk to Jackson after Will Ford was murdered?'

'I won't lie to you. I wanted to know if there was a connection.'

'And?'

'I don't know.'

'Did Chris Jackson kill Will Ford?'

'He said he didn't.'

'If you don't know who shot you, how do you know it wasn't him?'

'That's another one I don't have the energy to explain. But I'll give it a try. I worked with Chris. With cops you need to know that your partner will be there if you need him. And you need to find that out pretty fast and for sure. I knew that about Chris. Chris knew that about me, too. He knew that if I was going to turn him in for anything, it would have to be really serious, something I couldn't let go and live with myself. He'd also know that if I was going to do that, I'd tell him.

'I believe Chris might kill me if that was his only way out. And you're not going to get this and I don't care . . . But he wouldn't shoot me in the back.'

TWENTY

'What we're left with is the question we began with.' Ambler sat at Adele's kitchen table watching her make tuna salad for sandwiches. Johnny was in her bedroom watching television.

Adele spoke over her shoulder. 'Mike's friend, the police lieutenant, was a crooked cop and the cop who was killed a long time ago was a crooked cop? Who was the cop in Will Ford's story?'

'That's the question we began with and that we're left with.'

'I don't have any dill.'

'It could have been Morales. It could have been Chris Jackson. It might have been Kowalski, the deputy inspector. The one person left – that we know about – Erik Swensen from that ill-fated task force died three months ago.'

'You'll have to eat the sandwich without dill. What are you going to do next?'

'A tuna-fish sandwich is fine without dill.'

Adele handed him his plate. 'That's cute that you say tuna-fish sandwich. That's what we called it when I was a kid.' She called to Johnny and sat down across from Ambler.

He chomped down on his sandwich and finished the first bite. 'It's good,' he said. 'I'm thinking I might find Deputy Inspector Kowalski and ask him why he didn't tell me the cop who was killed was holding up the gambling joint.'

'So since the lieutenant you thought was a murderer didn't kill you, and the hoodlum from the Bronx didn't kill you, you're going to see if the deputy inspector who might be a murderer will do it.'

'I didn't say I thought he was a murderer. Actually, I didn't say I thought anyone was a murderer. And the hoodlum was in Washington Heights. But you were right about that one; I should've been more careful.'

Discovering that the police officer said to have been killed in the line of duty was actually killed during the commission of a crime didn't mean that Kowalski wasn't telling the truth that Chris Jackson covered up for the rogue cop, murdered Will Ford, and shot Mike Cosgrove. The only reasons Ambler had for not believing him were Mike said Chris didn't shoot him and Kowalski's account didn't square with Ford's short story.

There was, of course, plenty of reason to doubt a cop actually had walked away from a murder. Ford could have made that up, as he maintained he did. In both the story and in real life, as far as anyone knew, the only cop at the murder scene was the cop doing the holdup, Donovan. In Ford's story, Cisco Garcia was at the murder scene and got away. If Ford was at the scene of the murders, which Ambler believed he was, he walked away, too. It was curious that he wasn't murdered.

Johnny took his sandwich from the kitchen and went back to the bedroom, despite Ambler's disapproval.

'You're spoiling the kid,' he told Adele. 'Bad enough his grandmother spoils him. He's supposed to eat at the table.'

'I didn't want him to hear us talking about criminal cops and murders. He's supposed to know that he can go to a policeman if he's in trouble.'

Ambler needed to chew for a moment and swallow before he could reply. 'He knows that. Most people know that. Johnny doesn't live in a world where he's likely to get in trouble with the cops. He knows Denise. He knows Mike. He knows most cops want to help people.'

Adele watched him for a moment. She often surprised him by what she was thinking and did again now. 'I guess there are crooked librarians, too.'

'I guess,' Ambler said dubiously. 'Do you think Will Ford lied about everything and he was the actual murderer?'

Adele's eyes popped open. 'Well then who murdered him?'

'Big Nick Pappas had him killed because he knew too much and couldn't keep his mouth shut.'

'It's convenient to have a gangster handy to blame for everything, almost as good as having a dead guy. And who shot Mike Cosgrove after Will Ford was dead?'

Ambler didn't answer for a moment; he didn't have an

answer. 'Morales, the former cop McNulty and I talked to, said Kowalski took bribes.'

'From the gangster guy, Nick whatever?'

'I tried to ask Morales that but McNulty kicked me under the table.'

'I'm sure he wouldn't have told you anyway. So the big mucky-muck police guy is a crook, too?'

Ambler nodded. 'If we make a list of suspects, he should be one. For that matter, so should Chris Jackson. Mike could be wrong that Jackson wouldn't shoot him in the back. If I tell Kowalski now that I know the cop who was killed was robbing the place, he might come clean and tell me everything. If it turns out Chris Jackson or someone else from that task force was with Donovan on that gambling-den robbery and managed to avoid getting killed, that might point us to who killed Ford.'

'What if it was the big shot?'

'That's possible. Nothing at the moment points to him. Jackson told Mike that Kowalski stayed clear when the task force guys were doing their thing, which I've learned is called "doin' doors". He didn't take part, didn't want to know. He was the sergeant; maybe he got a cut. But according to what Jackson told Mike, Kowalski wasn't part of the gang robbing the drug-dealers. Morales was part of the gang "doin' doors". He said Kowalski took bribes. He didn't say he busted up and robbed drug-houses.'

They finished their sandwiches, and Ambler cleared the table and washed the few dishes they'd used.

'You're becoming domesticated,' Adele said. 'You might make a good husband yet.'

He stopped, startled. Did she mean for her?' He waited for her to say something else so he'd know what she meant. But she didn't.

Instead she said, 'I haven't found anything in Ford's journals that has anything to do with that short story you think is based on those murders. But there's no real way to look for anything. He didn't date his notebooks. Everything's mixed together. He'd be writing about a book he was working on and in the middle of a page he'd write a couple of paragraphs about an idea for a story he might write someday. And then he'd go back to making notes on the book or he might drift off into something else in his own life that might have happened that day, or happened years before, that didn't have anything to do with the story or the book he was working on . . . And there's a lot of them. Notebooks, I mean.'

Ambler had been through enough writers' notebooks to know they often didn't make sense. Journals didn't have a thread that tied their contents together like the thread that ties together a story or a novel. Most of the time they weren't meant to be read by anyone else. 'That's not so unusual,' he said.

'I know it's not. But it's frustrating. Not only because I can't find what we're looking for. But I'll get interested in something – like his wife caught him cheating, which happened more than once with more than one wife – but he wouldn't finish the story. He'd say the cops came and then nothing about what the cops did; if they took him off to jail – which they should have – or what happened.'

'Did anything you've seen so far make you think he could kill someone?'

Adele glanced toward the bedroom where Johnny was. Her apartment was small, so he wasn't far away, and she knew as well as Ambler did Johnny had a habit of eavesdropping. She spoke softly. 'He had a violent temper and sometimes his writing was filled with rage, especially at women he thought had insulted him or done him an injustice of some sort, and he kept going back to denouncing his mother.

'I thought it was a good thing he took out his rage in his writing, rather than aiming it at people in his life.' Her eyes widened with what might have been fear. 'He'd write something like "I should have murdered the bitch", or "she's lucky I didn't break her neck". I thought of them as expressions of his anger, not as something he'd do. Yet, if he were enraged at me, certainly when he was younger, I'd be afraid of him.'

The tuna sandwiches weren't much of a dinner so Ambler and Johnny stopped for a slice of pizza on the way home.

'Denise's dad's gonna be OK, right?' Johnny asked.

'It looks good. He's much better.'

'You're going to find the guy who shot him, right?'

'I hope the police will.'

'But it's personal with you.'

'I'd hope it is with them also.' It was a half-hearted answer. Johnny probably knew that but his grandson didn't press him, leaving him to his brooding thoughts. Because of how everything unfolded, because he and Mike and no one else knew what might have led to Mike's shooting, finding whoever shot Mike was up to Ambler in a way that finding a murderer never had been before.

In the morning, he took Johnny to school and went to the hospital. He was going to visit Mike for a few minutes and then go to work. But Mike was much improved, wide awake, and wound up. 'I don't remember much of what we talked about yesterday. I was kind of out of it. Tell me what I told you.'

Ambler told him and then said, 'You seem better today.'

'I am. I can't get out of bed. But I can move my arms so I'm going to do some work since no one else cares about finding the bastard who shot me.'

Ambler had been hesitant to disagree with Mike before, but he seemed feisty enough that he could take it now. 'You might be wrong about Chris Jackson. He was desperate enough to kill himself. Why wouldn't he be desperate enough to shoot you in the back?'

It took Mike a few minutes to get to it, but he did. 'I could be wrong. My hunches about people are good; they're not a hundred percent. You had a hunch about Morales.'

'Not a hunch. I made an observation. He was surprised when I told him Will Ford was dead. He might be a good actor. But I'd say the surprise was genuine.'

Mike was good even when he was drugged up. 'Chris could have called him after I left. So he'd know in advance you'd tell him something he should act surprised about, so he was ready for it and put on an act.'

Ambler hadn't considered that but he should have. 'OK. Morales is a suspect. I found out Erik Swensen died. Did you talk to anyone else after you talked to Jackson that night?'

Mike's eyes shifted around, so Ambler could tell he was uncomfortable. 'Something I didn't tell you.' He spoke gruffly, the way he did when he was embarrassed. 'I stopped and had a drink with Anne after I talked to Chris. She's staying at her sister's, so we had a drink at a place there in Woodside.'

'Would her ex-husband have found out?'

'It's possible. It's Woodside; still a lot of Irish. Everyone into everyone else's business. Someone could have seen us and told him. Even if he did find out,' Mike said dismissively, 'prick that he is, he'd confront me and not shoot me in the back.'

Ambler chuckled. 'It's good the men who want to kill you will all do it to your face, not behind your back.'

Mike snorted. 'The detectives who were here yesterday said they'd check his alibi. I'll wait for them to do that. Meanwhile, since I'm not supposed to move for a couple of days, you can do some things for me.'

'I need to take another day off from work?'

'I'm gonna level with you. I kept some things from you because we were dealing with what might be a police department matter. I don't like being known as a one-man Internal Affairs squad. I talked to Chris that night because I wanted to clear up a few things. I wanted to rule out him and anyone else in the department in the Ford shooting.

'The truth is Chris didn't rule out anyone. Kowalski was his rabbi going back to when he first went to the two-seven. Kowalski was his sergeant then but he was on his way up, the skids were greased; he had an uncle, an assistant chief. You already guessed Donovan was a dirty cop. They all were, the task force.

'You asked me about "doin' doors"? What happened was the task force would raid a drug location, like cops are supposed to do. Only instead of locking up the suspects and turning in the drugs and money they found, they kept it. Maybe they beat up the drug-slingers; maybe they threatened them. What are the drug-dealers going to do? Call the cops?

'So the task force was busting up places and robbing them. Everybody knew it was happening, even the brass. Honest cops kept their mouths shut because they knew what happened to rats. Later, the Mollen Commission came along. And the reforms. So things changed; everyone was more careful. Bygones were bygones. A few cops got busted. Some retired. They closed down the street crimes units, the kind of operation Kowalski's task force was.'

Mike closed his eyes, and made a sound somewhere between a moan and a roar. 'You can't imagine the anger I feel lying here like this, thinking it might have been a cop who put me here.' He paused and spoke more forcefully. 'Forget I said that. I don't know who put me here. Maybe the guys investigating will come up with something – some bonehead I put away years ago who kept a grudge. Maybe Morales was partners with Donovan and had more to do with what happened than anyone knows. Maybe Big Nick wanted me out of the way.'

A nurse came into the room with some pills and a glass of water. 'I'm getting painkillers through the IV. I don't know what these are. I've stopped asking.'

Whatever they were, the pills didn't slow him down. 'What I know now is that Kowalski's task force had a lot to cover up, a lot to hide. Morales saying Kowalski was on the pad changed how I see things. Chris didn't tell me that. I don't know that he knew. I don't know why Morales told you. He wants to bring Kowalski down?

'That story Kowalski and Chris told me about saving Donovan's benefits for the widow and orphans is a crock of shit. They made up the story to save their own asses. I believe Chris didn't buy into vigilante law enforcement – the task force's version of Robin Hood, stealing from the hoods to line their own pockets.

'He said he couldn't blow the whistle on the operation. No one would do anything. No one would care. He was probably right about that. So he didn't blow the whistle and because of that he became part of it; anything he said would be a confession as much as an exposé.

'After I talked with him, he knew I was going to dig up all the dirt, some he didn't even know about. So he needed to find out first, to protect himself. I did some checking earlier this morning.' Mike chuckled. 'You can't be a cop for going on thirty years and not have your own set of informants, even inside the job. They call it a back channel.

'Chris's phone was in an evidence locker in the precinct in Queens. They were able to unlock it and someone listened and made notes. Chris called Kowalski first. After that he called Morales. My guess is he discovered he'd covered up something much worse than what he'd thought he'd covered up at the time, something ugly enough he couldn't face it.

'His talking to Morales may have set me up for Morales and Pappas. If it did, I don't think he'd do it on purpose. It also means Morales knew Ford was dead when you talked to him, so he's a good actor. Guys like him get to be good liars.' Mike paused; the excitement went out of his voice. 'This is all guesswork I'm giving you. Something else might have happened. What I do know is Chris started a new investigation into what happened that night on Manhattan Avenue and then he killed himself.

'I don't like this. I hate doing it. But I can't take what I told you to anyone on the job. That means you and me are going to follow up on Chris's investigation – you until I can get out of this bed. Here's where we start.'

TWENTY-ONE

A couple of hours later, Ambler was on his way to Grand Central to catch a train to Beacon, New York. It was a trip he'd made many times to visit his son at a prison not so far from the prison he was about to visit to talk with Felix Hernandez. Mike gave him the phone number of Hernandez's attorney, who turned out to be David Levinson, his son John's attorney.

After Ambler's lengthy and convoluted answers to an interminable series of questions from the attorney – who remembered arranging the same sort of visit for Mike Cosgrove – as to what he was doing and why, Levinson set up the prison visit.

Before they hung up, Ambler said, 'I look forward to seeing you in court, soon, I hope.'

'Working on it, Mr Ambler. The wheels of justice turn slowly. Sometimes they don't turn at all. In your son's case, I'm pleased to report they've been well oiled.'

Levinson lowered his voice. 'One more thing . . . you realize, I hope, this guy you're going to see is nothing like your son. Some unfortunates are a menace to society and we're better off with them in prison.'

'I'm not trying to get him out,' Ambler said.

'I understand. I'm telling you this so you're aware that what he tells you will be what he thinks is best for him, especially if it's in aid of his getting out of prison.'

'I'm not sure I do understand.'

'Not to put too fine a point on it,' Levinson intoned in his attorney voice, 'he won't tell you the truth if something other than the truth would serve his purpose.'

'Gotcha.'

'I hope so. Desperate men develop a high level of cunning. This is to say, they're much better at lying than less desperate men – such as yourself – are at recognizing lies.'

Levinson's warning gave Ambler pause. The lawyer was smarter than he let on, and Ambler wasn't as smart as he sometimes thought he was; he hadn't been as wary as he should have been in dealing with ruthless men with a great deal on the line. So far he'd escaped any dire consequences, but it was time he learned to keep up his guard.

Levinson's advice turned out to be worthwhile because Felix Hernandez was nothing like he expected. Slight and wiry, with black hair, dark soulful eyes, and a smooth almost hairless face, he looked more like an altar boy than a convicted murderer. His voice was soft and slightly accented. His smile was gentle. He remembered Mike's visit and asked if Levinson was going to arrange for a new trial so he could recant his confession.

'I didn't kill no one. The cops framed me.'

'Which cops?'

He didn't know their names. 'The ones who arrested me and the ones who questioned me. They said they'd give me a deal. They couldn't have proved nothin'.'

'I was told they had evidence, the murder weapon in your apartment, your fingerprints at the murder scene.'

'You don't know how cops are, man. Someone like me that can't afford a real lawyer, the cops make shit up. Then the lawyer they give you tells you they got evidence, so you got to cop a plea.' The young man spoke calmly, not raising his voice, rattling off injustices like they were a run of bad luck. 'The lawyer – it ain't his fault; this guy Levinson is a right kind of guy.

'He was straight with me. He said, "I can't get rid of their evidence. We'd need a private investigator and it would be years before Legal Aid investigators could get to it. If you cop to the plea, it's murder two, so it's life, but you're up for parole in fifteen years. Otherwise, on murder one you're not up for parole until twenty-five years. Or it could be life without parole." So I took the plea.'

Ambler listened to this kid, who'd spent his life on the streets, spouting legalese like a Philadelphia lawyer. Mike had checked on him after he'd visited him. Hernandez was a suspect in at least three murders, not counting Billy Donovan and the prostitute, Dominique. The police had an iron-clad case for the murder he was picked up on – arrested a block from the scene within minutes of the murder, eyewitnesses, blood samples, the murder weapon.

Ambler stayed away from asking about the original murder Hernandez was arrested for. This didn't stop Hernandez. 'The cops almost never get caught making stuff up.' He chose his words carefully. 'You think you guys are gonna catch them on this? You know I'm innocent, right. You found the guy that did the murders, right? So it can't be me.'

Ambler didn't want to tell him they didn't have a suspect for the Manhattan Avenue murders, so he didn't agree or disagree.

Hernandez wasn't fooled. He waited a moment, his eyes registering his disappointment, but he went on. 'What happens is if the cops get caught making up stuff on this one, the judge got to throw out all the other convictions in case they made up evidence on those ones, too.' He looked at Ambler hopefully.

'I'm not a lawyer. You need to ask Mr Levinson about that. Can you tell me why the police found your fingerprints at the murder scene?'

He shook his head. 'It was a gambling place. I went there sometimes. I knew Gilberto. I didn't have nothin' to do with the whores, though.' He met Ambler's gaze with the haughty expression of the self-righteous.

'And the gun in your apartment?'

He shook his head. 'Not mine, man. You use a gun; you get rid of it. You don't keep it around. They planted it, like they plant drugs on you when they want to bust you.'

'Do you know who the cops were who searched your apartment?'

He shook his head. 'I remember the cops who questioned me.'

'Was one of them Black?'

He shook his head. 'One big guy with a mustache, the other guy Dominican. They showed me the piece. The big guy said, "Look what we found."

'I said, "That ain't mine."

'"We found it in your apartment," the Dominican guy said.

'I said, "That's a lie. I don't have no gun in my apartment."

'The big guy said, "Who's the judge gonna believe, you or us?"' The young prisoner spoke without animation, not with the indignation you'd expect; his hands folded on the table in front of him didn't move.

'The big guy, did you catch his name?'

He shook his head.

'The name Kowalski sound familiar?'

He shrugged.

'Glasses?'

He had to think about that. 'I think so.'

'Walk with a limp?'

Bullseye. 'Yeh. A limp. He sort of dragged one leg.'

IDing Morales was easy. Hernandez remembered the tattoo of a dagger piercing a heart on the back of his hand.

The trip back to the city was long and uncomfortable. The train swerved and jiggled and bounced as if it ran on a bumpy road instead of tracks. He didn't know if Hernandez told him the truth. It didn't seem likely he'd know to identify Kowalski and Morales if they weren't who had interrogated him. Yet Levinson said cons were cunning so he might have figured out what Ambler wanted to hear. Maybe Mike asked about them on his visit. Hernandez said he wouldn't keep a gun in his apartment that he used in a murder. The cops planted it. That was possible, too. But criminals had done stupider things.

He dozed fitfully on the train and was in a sour mood when he finally made his way to the hospital. Mike, on the other hand, had napped and was chipper again, listening without comment to Ambler's report.

'It's pretty much what I expected,' he said when Ambler finished. 'I didn't ask who the cops were when I interviewed him. I didn't know what I was looking for then. Chris told me he was part of the cover-up, but it looks like he wasn't part of framing Hernandez, if that's what happened.'

'How would Hernandez know to identify Morales and Kowalski if they didn't interrogate him?' It was eerie talking to Mike as he lay in a hospital bed with tubes snaking out from his arm, an oxygen apparatus hissing under his nose, and machines blinking and beeping by the side of the bed. The bed itself had raised bars on either side as if he were in some sort of jail cell.

Mike spoke without moving anything other than his mouth and his eyes. 'It could be they did interrogate him and did search his apartment and didn't plant the gun but found it there. For some reason when he got arrested, they wanted to talk to him. Something about him – where he was picked up, the circumstances of the murder he was charged with, what he'd been doing that led to the murder he committed – got them interested. It's not unusual for us on a hunch to want to talk to someone picked up on something unrelated to what we're working on.'

'There's also Hernandez's fingerprints at the crime scene,' Ambler said. Mike was making it seem plausible that Hernandez was lying – that Hernandez had bamboozled him; despite Levinson's cautions, the con conned him. 'He knew Sanchez. He'd been to Sanchez's gaming room. His fingerprints didn't need to be from the night of the murders.'

'It would be nice if his fingerprints were on the gun,' Mike said. 'But even a dummy would know to wipe the gun.'

Ambler was irritated. Mike needed to make up his mind. 'Well, is Hernandez lying or not? What did I go up there for?'

Mike sounded unconcerned. 'Everything we find points to the next thing until we have an answer. Or we get to the end of the line.'

'Maybe you could let me in on what we're investigating. I don't like being an errand boy when I don't know what the errands are in aid of.'

He saw the agitation in Mike's eyes and regretted upsetting him. It wouldn't be good at all for him to get pissed off and try to show Ambler a thing or two by getting out of bed. Mike was a do-it-himself guy. Not being able to do the investigation himself was driving him nuts. 'Sorry. Take it easy. I'll do whatever you want. We'll find out together what happened.'

Mike was quiet for a moment. 'Sometimes knowing too much is a worse problem than not knowing,' he said as if to himself. 'What I should be doing is talking to my boss or to the Chief of Detectives' office. I'm not. It's not because I don't trust them. I do. It's because I know what I tell them will get out, not out to the public. It will get out into One Police Plaza. Once that happens, the case will disappear.' He made a sound that might have been a chuckle. 'Or I'll disappear.

'You remember Stalin? One of the Politburo guys tells him some other Politburo guy is killing innocent people. The next thing you know, they have a quick trial. The loyal Politburo guy who blew the whistle, who fought in the Revolution, is off to the loony bin. You never hear of him again.

'My name comes up in a precinct somewhere, or, God help us, comes up at One PP, conversation stops; everyone listens for what will come next. Who's he gonna rat on now?

'If I went to my boss and told him I'm working a case that involves the brass at One PP – what's he say? "You gotta be fucking kidding me." Or maybe, "Get the fuck outa here." Or most likely, "Put in your retirement papers, Mike. I'll take it from here."'

'He'd let someone get away with murder because the suspect is a high-ranking officer?'

'That's not it. Or that's not only it. Who's he gotta tell? He can't keep it to himself that we got an investigation going that's gonna blow up the department. Whoever he tells got to tell someone, too. Until it gets to the captain or inspector or deputy inspector who throws a monkey wrench into the works, kills the investigation in its cradle. You're not going to chance bringing down someone with a lot of juice – who's done you favors, who can undo favors, who can have you walking a beat out in Far Rockaway when you thought you were golden for the captain's test.

'My boss is a good cop. High-ranking brass aren't my kind of people. Once you get past lieutenant or captain, you start breathing different air; you get a different take on life; you forget where you came from. Most of them care about the job. They want to do it right. But what they care about is different than what the cop on the street cares about. They gotta take care of what the politicians and the lawyers and Wall Street care about. They look at cops on the street as a problem that has to be handled.'

What Mike was saying sounded like resignation or surrender. You can't fight City Hall. 'So why are we doing this?' Ambler demanded. 'You want to forget about it? Who needs the grief?'

Mike took a long time to answer. 'Don't be so sure I wouldn't have let this go. I don't know that I would've taken Chris down. Whatever he did back then, he'd been a good cop since then. People make mistakes. If I'd done something wrong and he was the only one knew about it, I don't see him busting me. I mean that. Your partner has a problem, makes a mistake, you take care of him; you watch out for him. You help him straighten out. Like he was part of your family.'

'So what changed your mind?'

Mike sounded weary but not defeated. 'Chris is dead . . . Someone shot me.'

'And you know who it was?'

'I don't know. I *suspect*. I don't accuse until I know. Are you with me?'

Ambler knew. '"Suspect everyone. Accuse no one." Gotcha, Sergeant Cuff.'

'Someone from Central Records is bringing me copies of the DD5s and whatever else is in the file from the original investigation of those Manhattan Avenue murders. While I'm lying here, I can't do anything but think. So I figure I should make sure who actually shot who. Back when we – I should say, you – started this debacle, I spoke to one of the detectives who originally caught the case and was then taken off it by then Sergeant On-His-Way-Up Kowalski. He told me a lot. But there might be something in the report he didn't tell me.

'Then there's Morales. We don't want to rattle his cage until we know as much as we can about what happened. We'll need to pick out the truth from among his lies. With luck, we might find something we can use to flip him if that's in the cards.'

Before he left, Ambler told Mike that Adele was going through Will Ford's papers to see if he'd written about the Manhattan Avenue murders in his notebooks. 'A lot of writers keep journals, notes for stories they might write, conversations they overhear, something they see happen in a restaurant, stories people tell them, . . . maybe murders they witness.'

Mike was skeptical. 'You think he witnessed the murders? Why wouldn't he have been killed if he was there?'

Ambler didn't know.

Skeptical or not, Mike didn't leave stones unturned. He said when he got the file from his Central Records contact, he'd see if they ran all the prints they found at the murder scene. 'Ford was locked up enough times in his life, even if for drunk and disorderly, his prints must be on file somewhere.

'It's likely Donovan killed everyone in the apartment, except for him and the girl. The question is who killed him. The girl is a different question, unless she got it by accident. Hernandez took the fall. He's still a good bet, despite what he says. If he didn't do it, whoever framed him did a good job. You might say a professional job. You want to add the writer to the list? We can. If he did it, why did they frame Hernandez? Who got the murder weapon into Hernandez's apartment?'

'Ford was a mystery writer. He might have researched things like that.'

'Maybe to write about it. That's not the same as doing it.'

Ambler didn't have an answer to that. 'Was Morales working for Big Nick at the time?' Something in the back of his mind came to the front. 'Morales said Kowalski was on the pad. Suppose Big Nick was paying him – paid Kowalski to frame Hernandez.' He couldn't see why Big Nick would go out of his way to protect Will Ford. But he would to protect Morales.

Mike didn't show any surprise at any of this, leading Ambler to believe this was something he'd already thought of.

He kept going. 'Donovan robbed an establishment Big Nick was paying Kowalski to protect. So Pappas killed Donovan or had him killed.'

'Pappas was there?' Mike said. 'I don't think so.'

'Someone called him.'

'I suppose someone who's not been accounted for could have been in the room when the shit hit the fan. You say it was the writer. The record says it was Hernandez. Now you think it might have been Morales. So we need to find out who. Unless you think Miss Morgan can find out for us from those papers the writer donated to the library.'

'Don't be so sure she won't.' Ambler didn't like Mike making fun of his making use of the crime fiction collection. He'd found evidence in the collection in the past. On one case, Mike had assigned a crew of detectives to go through the crime fiction archives. 'It's happened before. You don't know what turns up in a collection. What people write about their lives lives on after them. Researchers have found deathbed revelations, deathbed confessions.'

As he said this, Ambler remembered something Will Ford had said the night he talked about Big Nick. If Ambler wanted to learn anything more about Nick Pappas,' Ford said, 'he'd have to read about it in his memoirs.'

TWENTY-TWO

Adele was at his apartment with Johnny when he got home. They'd walked Lola and gone to the store for groceries and made shepherd's pie – one of Johnny's favorites – for dinner. The dish was in the oven and she, Johnny, and the dog were on the couch reading, except for Lola, who was sleeping. The two persons glanced at him over their book covers and Lola opened one eye. No one, not even the dog, got up to greet him.

'I thought everyone ran to the door to welcome the breadwinner when he got home,' Ambler said.

'Adele makes just as much bread as you do,' Johnny said, and after a moment, 'My dad called.'

'Hm . . .' Ambler went on alert and waited to find out what his dad had told him.

'He's coming into town next week to go to court. He might get his sentence reduced.'

The cat was still partly in the bag or part of the cat was still in the bag. John knew enough about the capricious nature of courts and judges to not raise Johnny's hopes too soon.

'Can I go to court with you? He said to ask you.'

'You've got school.' Ambler didn't want this. He didn't want Johnny in the courtroom if something went wrong and the judge intoned, 'Plaintiff's petition is dismissed and the plaintiff is remanded to the custody of . . .'

'I can skip.'

'That might not look so good to the judge – your dad being the father to a truant.'

Johnny was quiet for a moment. 'I didn't think of that.'

Ambler was glad *he* had.

'What do you think?' Johnny turned his big round blue eyes on Adele.

'It's up to your grandfather. We'll have to see,' she said, in the tone mothers use to put an end to questioning.

Later, while Johnny did his homework in the bedroom, Ambler sat beside Adele on the couch.

'Johnny is really excited he might see his father.' She put her arm through Ambler's. 'It would be the first time he'd see him outside of a prison visiting room.'

'Suppose something goes wrong. He'd be heartbroken. If everything goes right, he'll see him outside prison for a long time.'

'He knows something out of the ordinary is happening. He's talked about his father every five minutes since the phone call. I doubt you've heard the last of it.'

She moved closer. 'You look exhausted. Is Mike Cosgrove OK?'

It was surprising how comforting it was sitting beside her. 'He's better. Alert and chomping at the bit to get moving. He sent me to visit a prison today . . . not the one John is in.' He told her about Felix Hernandez and about his talk with Mike. 'I remembered something when I was talking with him.

'It was that day in the Library Tavern when Will Ford tried to assault you, after that weird interview with Mike and confrontation with Chris Jackson.' Ambler stopped for a moment struck by the realization that two of the men he was talking about were dead and one had barely escaped death. Adele watched him with an odd, worried expression.

'Jackson accused Ford of exposing Billy Donovan as an undercover cop. Ford looked bewildered by the accusation but he didn't challenge it. Later, in the bar, he said Jackson was lying. Donovan wasn't working undercover. Everyone knew he was a cop.

'He also told me something I don't think anyone else knew. This underworld kingpin Big Nick Pappas was a silent partner in the gambling operation and the brothel. When I pressed him on that, he clammed up. He said if I wanted to find out about Pappas, I'd need to read his memoirs. That might have been just a turn of phrase to put me off. Or it might mean he had a memoir or notes for a memoir about the time in his life when the events that story was based on took place.'

Adele yawned. 'I hope you're not relying on what I find in Ford's papers to solve your mystery. I like looking through them, reading bits and pieces. I told you, trying to find something specific is a nightmare. They're a mess. There's no kind of order.

'How many boxes of his papers do we have? Six, seven?' Before Ambler answered, she went on, 'And the notebooks you want might not even be in the collection we have. They might be in that library in Texas with the rest of his papers. It would take forever to go through all of that.'

Ambler sighed. 'I suppose we'll have to wait and see what Mike has up his sleeve. He's got an under-the-table operation going on with his contacts at police headquarters.'

Adele brightened. 'Remember the time he assigned a half-dozen cops to go through your files looking for something? Maybe he could do something like that again. Anyway, I'll do what I can.'

She yawned again and looked at him with the kind of lopsided smile she must have had when she was a tired little girl. He was hypnotized by what he saw in her eyes, a kind of longing, and he knew without doubt what the longing was for, and he felt it also.

'I don't want you to leave,' he said.

'I know.' She stretched gracefully like a cat. 'It would be too confusing for Johnny. We don't even know what we want. And he's beside himself thinking about his father. He has enough on his mind – and so do you.' She scrutinized his face for a moment. 'What were you thinking about when you stopped in the middle of what you were saying a minute ago? You looked so sad.'

'About Will Ford and Chris Jackson being dead when they didn't need to be. It made me sad. I thought about . . . I wished I'd never started this.'

She stood and put her coat on. 'I don't suppose you can stop now. Is anybody else going to get killed?'

'I hope not.'

He put the leash on Lola and walked Adele home. The streets were quiet; the night chilly but not quite cold. She put her arm through his arm that wasn't holding the leash. Their pace was slow because he let Lola stop often to sniff.

'Mike said he might not have followed up the investigation after he spoke to Chris Jackson if someone hadn't shot him.'

'And he doesn't believe Jackson shot him, even though the bigwig cop says that's what happened?'

They walked another block in silence. Ambler was deep in thought and didn't realize she'd asked a question he didn't answer.

She went on anyway. 'Why did he commit suicide? Mike discovered he was into shady doings. His past got the best of him. He couldn't stand the shame. Why would the bigwig say he shot Mike if he didn't?'

Ambler thought about Adele's question but ran into a blank wall. The only answer he came up with was that Kowalski told the truth, and he didn't like that one.

To Adele, he said, 'Mike told me Jackson found out more was going on than he thought, that the cover-up wasn't to protect Donovan's wife and kids as much as it was to keep the task force's wrongdoing from being exposed.'

They'd stopped at a corner, waiting through the Walk light because Lola was sniffing a garbage can. As they both watched Lola, Adele said, 'Mr High and Mighty Police Chief is a crook, too, right?'

'He's a deputy inspector not a chief, though that's where he thinks he's headed – which is a reason not to have skeletons rattling around in his closets. Mike thinks Kowalski is wrong about who shot him, but he didn't accuse him of anything else.'

'What did he say about the mucky-muck taking bribes?'

'He didn't say anything about it.' They walked without speaking the last block to Adele's building before Ambler said, 'Mike hasn't told me everything he knows; he's protective of other cops, even when they've done something wrong.'

'And he's asking you to track people down and ask them questions without telling you why?'

Even though that wasn't exactly what was happening, Ambler didn't like how it sounded. 'Not exactly,' he said.

'I think it is exactly.' This should have sounded like criticism but her tone made it sound like caring. When she turned to face him, she was smiling. 'I'm the one who's supposed to lead you around by the nose.' She kissed him lightly on the lips and was gone.

In the morning when he got to work, the first thing was a staff meeting he'd forgotten about. As usual it was boring but it reminded him he'd also forgotten to do the budget projections for the crime fiction collection Harry had asked for.

When he finally got to his desk, he had a backlog of emails but among them was an invitation to speak at the New York Library Association conference and another invitation to be a panelist at a mystery conference in Indianapolis. The invitations brightened his spirits. He had a role in the world besides muddling through murder investigations. He made a promise to himself to pay more attention to that role once he extricated himself from the current mess he'd gotten into.

He added an hour of vacation time to his lunch break to go over to the hospital to check on Mike. As he often did, he walked out the front door of the library, down the marble steps past Patience and Fortitude, the lions guarding the library, and across Fifth Avenue to East 41st Street, named Library Way between Fifth Avenue and Park Avenue.

He liked to walk the two blocks of Library Way because of the bronze plaques embedded in the sidewalk containing literary quotes; he'd stop and read a few of the quotes most times even when he was in a hurry as he was this day. One of his favorites he caught up with was by Carson Kanin, a screenwriter: 'I want everybody to be smart, as smart as they can be. A world of ignorant people is too dangerous to live in.'

Mike was asleep, or at least his eyes were closed when Ambler entered the room but he opened them a few seconds later. 'I thought you'd be here this morning,' he said.

'I went to work,' Ambler said huffily. 'I have a job.' He was recalling Adele's remark about being an errand boy.

Mike muttered something and then said, 'I had a visitor anyway.'

Ambler waited.

'Deputy Inspector George Kowalski.'

'Did he tell you Chris Jackson shot you?'

'He did. When he couldn't convince me – you might say he leaned on me – he switched to talking about pension benefits. He said I might not be eligible for a full pension because the rules are stacked against us and the pension board is anti-cop. But he knows a lawyer I can talk to.

'I didn't know I was planning to retire. His message was, "We hate to see you go but don't let the door knob hit you in the ass on the way out."'

'He didn't convince you Jackson was the shooter?'

Mike had a way of changing his tone of voice and moving his eyes, so that what he said carried more meaning than was in the words alone. 'He said he understood how I felt. He didn't want to believe it either but the evidence was there—'

'Evidence?'

'My reaction, too. He didn't come up with any. Instead he went back to talking about benefits. Chris Jackson's line-of-duty death benefits, to be specific. This man has talked to me more about pension benefits in the two times I've met him than everyone else put together has since I've been on the job. A real crusader.'

'Chris Jackson getting line-of-duty benefits?'

'That was it.'

'After he shot you and murdered Will Ford? . . . Kowalski told me cops who commit suicide don't get line-of-duty benefits.'

'He's trying to change that. I told you he's a crusader. The stress of the job is why they commit suicide. The deaths should be seen as job-related.' Mike mulled that over. 'Actually, on that I think he's right.'

Ambler had been standing alongside the bed. Mike had a button next to his hand that he could push for the back of the bed to rise. After fumbling around for a moment, he did that and brought himself into something resembling a sitting position, so Ambler moved back and sat down next to the wall beside the window.

'The kicker is he put a lid on the investigation into my shooting. A cop gets shot it's supposed to be all hands on deck until we get the son of a bitch, except it doesn't work that way when it's me that gets shot. He wants to get things lined up as best he can for Chris before the news breaks.'

Ambler had an inkling Mike felt the same uneasiness about Kowalski as he did. 'He's got enough clout to keep an investigation under wraps? And why doesn't he want an investigation?' He waited a couple of beats. 'Because an investigation will come too close to him.'

He tried to meet Mike's gaze to cement his point. But Mike wasn't having it. So he said, 'Why can't you come out and say something's not right about Kowalski? Whatever happened in that Manhattan Avenue gambling den, Kowalski was involved in it up to his eyeteeth.'

Mike was quiet for so long Ambler thought he wouldn't say anything. When he did speak he sounded as if it was from far away. 'You're surprised I'm not bringing charges against a deputy inspector who has connections to the Commissioner, the DA's office, the Mayor's office, who the smart money says will become the next Chief of Detectives?

'You think I'd want to go down in NYPD folklore as the steadfast, determined Detective One who brought charges against a superior officer without a shred of evidence? . . . Go down in NYPD folklore as the biggest fool to ever put on a NYPD shield?'

They were quiet after that. Mike was right that he couldn't take on Kowalski. But Ambler was right, too, and was glad he'd spoken his suspicion out loud. Mike went to talk to Jackson the night he was shot, not because he suspected him but because he wanted Jackson to come clean about Donovan, Kowalski, Morales, and Swensen, his partners on the task force who were a gang of vigilantes. Jackson didn't come clean, but he told Mike enough for him to suspect Jackson didn't know who killed Donovan, but Kowalski did.

'Let me try this on you,' Ambler said. 'I don't know who killed whom, but whoever killed Donovan called Big Nick Pappas and told him about the trouble. Big Nick contacted his paid protector – Sergeant George Kowalski – and told him something along the lines of "I'm paying you to protect my investment and you let this cop come in and try to rob me. You shouldn't have let that happen and now you need to fix it."'

Ambler waited for Mike's reaction. He wasn't a hundred percent sure things happened the way he said. In truth, he wasn't sure at all. Even if he did know for sure things happened the way he said, he had no evidence. Neither of them was going to go anywhere with accusations without evidence.

Mike's reaction was subdued. 'You told me not so long ago Will Ford shot Donovan. You've changed your mind?'

'He was in the room. I doubt he killed anyone. Whoever killed Donovan let him go.'

'Why would he do that?'

'Let's say it was Morales. Will Ford knew Pappas. At that time, Pappas trusted him to keep his mouth shut. They had some sort of connection; I don't know what it was. Morales called Pappas. Pappas said Ford is OK. Let him go.'

'All right. That's what you say happened. You don't have any evidence. You could tell me the tooth fairy did it. How do you prove it?'

'I can't. I could tell it to Kowalski and see what he says. I could tell him I'm going to take it to his boss.' Ambler saw the problem with this as soon as he said it. 'Of course, his boss would want proof.'

'How about the mayor? Take it to the mayor. Oh . . .' Mike's tone was facetious. 'Might he, too, want proof?'

'I could go to the newspapers.'

'Who aren't going to want proof?'

'I give up. Tell me what I missed.'

'We'll see.'

The files from Mike's contact at Central Records had arrived that morning. He was going to finish going through them when Ambler left to go back to work, so Ambler said he'd come back that evening if Adele would stay with Johnny.

When he tracked her down that afternoon at the reference desk, she said she'd ask Lisa Young to have her driver drop Johnny at her apartment. She'd found a couple of notebooks in Will Ford's files that could have been written in the early '90s. She was having them copied and could take them home and read them while Johnny did his homework.

Later that afternoon, Adele stopped by the crime fiction

reading room to tell him she'd spoken to a librarian at the university in Texas that had Ford's papers. The woman she'd spoken to had written the finding aids for the collection and was a fan of Ford's, so she was helpful. 'She said she was sad he'd been murdered but not surprised because of the kind of life he led.'

The Texas librarian didn't remember coming across anything about New York in the notebooks in their collection. She also told Adele that at Ford's request the library had embargoed a small portion of the collection until after his death.

'I'm going to fax her a copy of his death certificate and she's going to figure out what she needs to do to get the embargo lifted.'

'That's something,' Ambler said. 'Given library bureaucracies, I wonder how long it will take to get the files open. Maybe Mike can help. Meanwhile, I feel bad dumping Johnny on you. He's becoming a latchkey kid. I should be getting him ready for his father's court date next week.'

She patted his hand and left.

Before going back to visit Mike after work, Ambler stopped for a beer and a burger at the Library Tavern, the first time he'd eaten since breakfast. He wanted to talk things over with McNulty because the bartender saw the world differently than most people did and often gave Ambler a unique perspective on whatever it was Ambler had on his mind.

'I wanted to ask you,' he said, when McNulty came to lean on the bar in front of him during a lull in the action, 'you remember when we talked about this deputy inspector who I thought knew more about those murders Will Ford wrote about than he was willing to let on?'

McNulty remembered.

'You said we should trick him . . . set a trap for him. I can't figure out how that would work. What kind of trap would get him to tell me what he doesn't want to tell me?'

The bartender did a quick survey of his domain. All was quiet. 'If he found out you knew some things he didn't want you to know – or better yet, if you were about to find out some things he didn't want you to know – he might do something to keep you from finding out.'

McNulty needed to make drinks for the two servers who'd appeared at the service bar, so he left Ambler to consider what he'd said. The only way Ambler could think of that he'd know something Kowalski didn't want him to know would be if he found something in Will Ford's papers – which was exactly what he and Adele were trying to do.

A few minutes later when McNulty stopped to check on him, Ambler rolled out his first ploy. 'Suppose I talk to Kowalski on some pretense and tell him a librarian at a university in Texas was sending me a file box with documents from Ford's time in New York relating to the Manhattan Avenue murders. He might try to intercept the mail or he might try to steal the files from the library.'

McNulty thought about that for a moment. 'He could bribe someone in the mailroom at the library to tell him when the stuff arrives.'

'He might not find someone to bribe.'

McNulty raised his eyebrows. 'This is New York. You can always find someone to bribe. That's one of the things you want to find out, right, if *he* was taking bribes?'

'I think he knows what happened the night of the murders on Manhattan Avenue. That's what I want to find out.'

'Maybe he did the murders.'

'He's in the running.'

McNulty switched gears. 'On second thought, if I was a cop like him what I'd do is tell the mailroom workers that it's official cop business and they need to tell him when anything arrives for you from Texas and they can't tell anyone what they're doing . . . If he did that, *you'd* need to find someone in the mailroom to bribe . . . You want another beer?'

'No thanks. I'm going to the hospital to talk with Mike. Why do I need to bribe someone? Nothing's coming for me in the mail from Texas any time soon.'

'Don't you know any librarians in Texas?'

'Adele does. I supposed we might arrange to have something sent.' Ambler didn't bother to explain about Ford's embargoed files. He wasn't sure McNulty's idea of a trap would get them anywhere. 'We'll have to go over this later,' he said. 'It doesn't make sense to me now.'

'Me neither. It's the best I can think of on the spur of the moment.'

Denise was with Mike when he got to the hospital. Another woman, older than Denise, was in the room with them, so Ambler sat in the small waiting room until they came out. When they did, Denise introduced the woman as Anne Gannon, a friend of her father's.

She was pretty in wistful way, dark-haired and sad-eyed with a weary expression and a city girl's complexion. She spoke like the outer-borough New Yorker she was – fast, so that there weren't always spaces between the words in her sentences, and when she used words like talk – as in it was great to talk to Mike – and coffee – as in I'm dying for a cup of coffee – it sounded like they had w's in the middle.

After they'd *tawked* for a minute or two, she put her hand on his arm and smiled into his eyes as if they'd been friends since childhood, as she and Mike had been.

'Isn't she a *dawl*,' she said when Denise ran off to get them some coffee.

'Sit down with me for a minute.' She sat down on a stiff fake-leather couch and patted the cushion next to her. 'Mike told me about you. You're his good friend the librarian. Lucky for him. Cops don't have many friends who aren't cops.' She talked a mile a minute, and didn't worry about keeping secrets.

'I'm sure you know I'm getting divorced. Everybody else in the city knows; I don't know why you shouldn't. It's no scandal. Neither of us was screwing someone else – or each other, for that matter. I'm going to guess you know about the rumors, too. Gary, that's my ex, Gary Gannon, thought that it was Mike's fault I divorced him. He's too thick and full of himself to understand it was because of himself I divorced him. Men!

'Gary thinks I wanted a divorce to be with Mike. It's a long story. I could use a cigarette, too.' She looked around her. 'But not in here, I guess.' She leaned closer. 'I worked in Flushing

Hospital, in the records room, when I was a kid just out of high school and we all used to smoke in the cafeteria. No more. You smoke anywhere, you're a pariah . . . or however you say it.'

She gave him a small punch in the arm. 'There I go. Give me a chance and I'll talk your arm off. What was I saying? Gary blames Mike. He won't blame himself for anything. We were all kids together. I loved Mike then. In a way, I've never stopped loving him. Like an idiot, I married Gary. I was headstrong and didn't want to wait for Mike to come around.' She met Ambler's gaze; hers was earnest. 'It was tough being a girl back then. You know that song about how city girls find out too early . . .'

She got flustered, her cheeks reddened. Ambler was embarrassed for her and looked away. 'Well, that's enough of that. What I started to tell you was Gary threatened Mike. Mike wasn't worried Gary threatened him. He threatened me, too, and I was worried, so I got a restraining order on him and that really pissed him off. I don't care. I don't want him near me.

'The thing is I know he didn't shoot Mike. He's jealous but not like you'd think. Everything's all about him. He's not an "I love you and can't live without you" kind of guy. He's a year or so from retiring and we bought a condo in West Palm. He can have it. He doesn't care enough about me to give up the good life he thinks he's headed for in Florida. It's his pride why he cares. He's embarrassed I left him . . . And he doesn't want Mike to get one over on him. He might punch Mike out if he got the chance to show off. He's a big tough guy. But that would be it.'

Denise came back with the coffee and the three of them sat together and talked about Mike, whom it was clear Anne cared a great deal about, but no more about her ex-husband. She said he didn't shoot Mike. But as in everything connected to Mike's shooting and everything else that had happened, she didn't have any evidence.

Ambler liked her. If Mike was lucky and got through this, and she was lucky and her ex-husband retired and went off to Florida and didn't kill them, she and Mike might make a life together. As she and Denise walked out, she put her arm around Denise's waist and Denise leaned her head against Anne's shoulder.

So, Ambler told himself, you could think there might be a happy end to all this . . . if it weren't for a passel of unsolved murders hanging over their heads. He went in to talk to Mike.

TWENTY-THREE

Again, Mike was lying with his eyes closed. The tubes from his arm stretched up to an IV pole, an oxygen tube hung beneath his nose like a mustache, a monitor flashed a small white light and a small green light and beeped every few seconds. His skin was gray and stretched tightly across his face; his hair was disheveled and lifeless like straw. His expression wasn't serene as you might expect on a person lying with his eyes closed; he looked to be in pain.

Ambler watched him for a moment, realizing his friend was in bad shape. The alertness he'd showed the last couple of times Ambler was there he forced because of his iron will to do what he thought he was supposed to do, like a wounded dog keeps fighting because he knows by instinct no outside force will help him.

Mike opened his eyes and watched him for a moment as he watched Mike. 'Getting shot sucks. You might think you know what it feels like, but you don't. It's worse. No one knows if I'll walk again until I try. Right now, I don't want to try.'

'Can I do anything?' Ambler's mouth had gone dry so he barely got the words out.

Mike's eyes twinkled, a flash of the old brightness. 'If this was the movies and you were John Wayne, I'd tell you to go get the son of a bitch who did this. And you'd swear you would and you'd ride off on your white horse.' The twinkling stopped.

'Those heroics were bullshit. I suspected it when I was a kid. In the war, I knew for sure. You know what I did going into every situation – any situation, not only a firefight, but especially a firefight? I figured out what I needed to do to get out alive – the best place to stand, the best cover, the best direction out of wherever we were. I didn't give a shit if we won the war or lost as long as I got out alive.

'I'm not going to feel any triumph when we get the bastard this time – if we get him. I'll feel relief, he won't get to me again. Worse than what he did to me, I want to get him for what he did to Chris.'

Ambler felt a rush of excitement. He was sure Mike had found something that told him what happened to him and what had happened on Manhattan Avenue years before. 'You went through the files and you found what Chris found.'

Mike's tone didn't change; it stayed flat; he could have been reciting a grocery list. 'It's not something I can prove. I don't make accusations I can't prove.'

'Tell me what you've found. I'll make the accusation.'

People say a lot with movements of their eyes, changes of facial expression, hand gestures, body movement. Mike didn't have all of that to work with; he had his eyes and his facial muscles to give added meaning to his words. What Ambler saw there might have been a hint of shame.

'Billy Donovan's gun killed Gilberto Sanchez and the woman who went by the name Annabelle Lee. Donovan and the hooker Dominique were killed with the gun found in Felix Hernandez's apartment. The crime scene techs did find unidentified prints. We might still find a match with Will Ford, though I don't think it's important one way or the other.

'They found Hernandez's prints.' A movement of Mike's eyes caught Ambler's attention, as if he'd said out loud, *Pay attention; this is important.* 'Three or four sets, a couple of sets on portable objects, a drinking glass, a beer bottle.'

'Portable?' Ambler asked.

'I'm getting to that. The objects with Hernandez's prints were in the evidence locker. I'm not saying this is true. But the objects could have been taken from someplace else and added to the locker after the fact. I know the detective who did the initial DD5 and have a call in to him. He might or might not remember. The items I mentioned weren't in any of the crime-scene photos. That doesn't mean they weren't there. But they don't prove they were there. And Hernandez's prints might have been there anyway on a table, a doorknob, whatever.

'Here's another thing. You should understand I'm not making

an accusation. I'm telling you some things that happened and some things that might have happened. Putting them together leads to possibilities. It doesn't lead to a conclusion.

'For reasons of their own, the crime lab did a ballistics analysis of the gun used to kill Billy Donovan; this would be the gun found in Hernandez's apartment. That is, they tested it against bullets found at other crime scenes where there was a fatal shooting. They found the gun had been used in another shooting about three months before Donovan was killed that had nothing to do with Hernandez. What happened in that shooting was that two assailants killed each other.

'Only one gun was recovered at the scene. It didn't make a lot of difference since both assailants were dead. What's significant is Kowalski's task force was the first police presence on the scene of that shooting.'

Mike closed his eyes for a moment and lay back against his pillow. His face was still grayish, no serenity. Ambler had watched the thought process Mike went through when he was making a case, and this was what he was doing now. What that case was remained a mystery for the moment.

'I'm going to lay out for you more cop dirty laundry.' Mike spoke without moving his head or opening his eyes. 'Back in the day, some cops would pick up weapons off perps, especially dead ones who couldn't complain about it. We called the guns throwaways. These cops liked to have a throwaway handy in case they wanted to plant it on someone so they could lock him up. In a rare case, they might need to plant a gun on someone they shot who they thought was armed but wasn't. Again this worked best when the subject was dead.

'Someone could have come along and picked up this particular gun at the crime scene and sold it to Hernandez, or Hernandez might have happened by the scene himself and picked it up. What's of interest to us is if someone from the task force picked up the gun. It might have been Billy Donovan, and Hernandez took it off him and shot him with it. That's unlikely because if Donovan had a throwaway gun he would have used it for the stickup. That leaves Kowalski or Morales—'

Ambler followed his friend's thinking to a point. What Mike had determined – the unsayable – was that Donovan's killer might have been another cop. Will Ford's story of a cop walking away from a cold-blooded murder might yet prove to be what happened. Ambler didn't know which cop walked away. He thought Mike did know, or had a pretty good idea, but didn't have proof.

'I think I know what happened that night,' Mike said after a long silence. 'I don't know for sure, and it's likely we'll never know for sure.'

Ambler ventured a guess. 'Chris Jackson knew Donovan was killed robbing the place, but he agreed to help Kowalski alter the crime scene and make up a story to protect Donovan's service record and help out his widow and his kids. What Jackson didn't know, and discovered shortly before his death, was that he helped cover up that Kowalski was being paid to protect the place Billy Donovan robbed—'

Mike interrupted. 'That's my guess, too, but still a guess. If it is what happened, that's what would have gotten to Chris. He wasn't an outlaw. He didn't like what the outlaw cops on the task force were doing, but he wouldn't rat on another cop. He thought Kowalski was like him. He didn't know Kowalski was on the pad and he didn't know Kowalski had a beef with Donovan—'

A beef with Donovan? This was news to Ambler. 'You're saying—'

Mike's voice took on some of its former timbre. 'I'll decide what I'm saying.'

Ambler called Adele from the hospital and she said she'd bring Johnny over and meet him at his apartment. They arrived at the apartment a few minutes after he did. She'd fed the boy and he'd done his homework so he went to play video games on the computer in the bedroom.

'Did you decide if he's going to his father's hearing?' she asked as he poured her a glass of wine.

'I asked Levinson and he said it would be a good idea if Johnny did come, so I'm going to bring him.'

He told her about his latest talk with Mike. 'I think he's figured things out.' Adele's face lit up as he said this, but he stopped her before she said anything. 'This means he knows who shot him and killed Will Ford.' She watched him with a perplexed expression. 'The problem is he doesn't think he can prove what he knows. Because Kowalski is involved, there's no way of opening an investigation without him finding out and squashing it. You can't bring in a deputy inspector and grill him.'

'He thinks the deputy inspector is the killer?'

'He's a suspect. There are at least three. What I meant is he's the person with the answers. But there's no way to get him to talk.'

Adele looked at him curiously. 'You said he was the sergeant who headed that task force. Wasn't there something about a sergeant in Ford's story?'

Ambler stared at her. 'I don't remember that. Are you sure?'

She said she was.

'I need to read the story again.' He made like he was going to leave.

'You can read it tomorrow.'

In the morning when he got to work, he pulled Will Ford's story from the file box and read it again. Reading it after all that had happened since he'd first read it, he noticed a few things that hadn't stayed in his memory. Ford had fictionalized the murders and disguised other incidents and happenings, so Ambler couldn't tell who all of the characters were based on.

Something else made the story's connection to the actual events murky: the murderer in the story was an undercover cop – as in the cover-up story Chris Jackson and Kowalski made up – not a rogue plainclothes cop like Donovan. Something else Ambler hadn't remembered accurately. The killer cop and Dominique were alive when Cisco Garcia left the apartment and the story ended.

The sergeant, Adele remembered, was a minor character, not involved in the action of the story. He came up when the gangster running the gambling operation told the killer cop he had an in with the cop's boss, Sergeant Wilson. The cop said, 'Well, you're not going to get the chance to use it,' and shot him in the head.

Cisco survived the massacre because he'd pulled a .32 from

an ankle holster. He didn't shoot and the cop, whom Cisco knew, didn't shoot. A standoff. 'We can both die right here tonight,' Cisco said. 'Or I walk out that door, head back to Texas, and disappear.' For most of the story Cisco had been wooing Dominique and he expected her to leave with him. When she told him she wanted to stay with the cop, he slunk away brokenhearted. Rereading the story refreshed Ambler's memory. What it didn't do was get him any closer to what really happened. Mike might be right that they'd never know for sure.

Around five, he gathered up Adele and they went to the Library Tavern. Johnny was at his grandmother's again, so Ambler had some time and was hoping McNulty might have come up with a plan for tricking Kowalski into revealing what he knew. Ambler certainly hadn't come up with anything.

Business at the bar was steady but not busy, so McNulty could spare a few minutes. 'Our friend the detective knows who we're after but he won't tell you?'

'Mike doesn't make accusations without proof.'

'And cops don't rat on other cops,' McNulty said.

Ambler took a long sip of beer. That hit close to home. Even with Mike's open-mindedness, his gourmet tastes in food, his penchant for reading, he was a cop down to his toes. And this was a difference between them. Still, Ambler felt protective. 'I don't think that applies here. We're talking about someone who shot him.'

'You don't think it was his girlfriend's husband?'

McNulty was getting on his nerves. 'She's not Mike's girlfriend and both she and Mike said her *ex*-husband didn't do it.'

McNulty nodded toward a couple of regulars who were leaving, and they stopped to lean on the bar for a brief chat with him about opening day at the stadium, something McNulty had done for going on thirty years.

Back to the subject at hand, McNulty said, 'So we're looking at a situation where either a cop killed another cop or someone who did the killing was a big enough deal or paid a big enough nut to have his name kept out of it. That you might guess would be Big Nick.'

'It might be Morales did the killing on Big Nick's behalf.'

Adele, who'd been doing something on her cell phone while Ambler and McNulty talked, looked up. 'Or the killer might be the deputy inspector who keeps trying to cover everything up.'

McNulty brightened. 'The guy Morales talked about? The guy on the pad? Why not him?'

Ambler shrugged. 'He's on the list. Since we don't have proof of anything, why not?'

McNulty hung on like a bulldog. 'You need to lean on your detective pal. He needs to tell you who he's protecting.'

'He's protecting that deputy inspector,' Adele said.

Ambler was still playing defense. 'Who said he's protecting anyone?' After another moment, he said, 'We should do our own quasi-background check on Kowalski and Morales – and Chris Jackson. We should've done it before. They've been cops for a long time. We should find something about them in the newspaper databases.'

Ambler and Adele finished their beers and went back to the library. It was one of the nights it was open until 8:00. Most sections were open but some of the reading rooms, including the crime fiction reading room, closed at 6:00.

Adele knew her way around the indexes and databases they could use and had access to all of them from her desk in her module behind the information desk. Ambler probably had access from his computer, too. But unlike Adele, with her MLS, he was a curator not a librarian and didn't know how to search most of the databases or what was in them.

Some newspaper archives, like the *Daily News* and *The New York Times*, you can access from a home computer. But they can't be searched in the same way as ProQuest or some of the other databases search, by subject, name, keyword. Adele sat Ambler in front of one of the library's public computers, logged him into a database, and gave him an assignment like a teacher might give to a pupil.

She then went off to her own computer to whiz through a half-dozen databases while he stumbled through *Newspaper Archives* and ProQuest. An hour and a half later, she came to retrieve him. Despite his clumsiness with the search engine, he'd found a number of articles, most of them featuring George Kowalski, only a couple on Morales or Jackson. Adele had found a good deal more.

She printed out everything they'd found and they went to his apartment to go over their findings, which were sobering. George Kowalski killed his first victim when he was a rookie cop working undercover. It was a drug sting gone bad. The man he killed was a drug-dealer who killed Kowalski's partner and wounded him. It was pretty clearly a life-or-death situation, and it was where his limp came from. Difficult to think of as not being justified. Despite that harrowing experience, he went back to undercover work.

Three years later he shot another man to death. The circumstances this time were murkier. Only Kowalski and the man he shot were involved. He'd stopped a car in a drug area in the Coney Island section of Brooklyn. Kowalski's gun was the only weapon fired. But the victim had a handgun on his person. Kowalski said the man had the gun in his hand when he got out of the car. The shooting was found to be justified.

His third victim, he and two other officers beat to death. This time, there was an outcry in the neighborhood in Harlem where the beating took place. The department held an excessive use of force hearing. Kowalski and the other officers were exonerated. But the city paid a hefty settlement of a wrongful death suit to the family of the victim.

Adele found a later story from the *Amsterdam News* from 2009 when Kowalski was again charged with use of excessive force and was again exonerated. This time, he was a captain and led the clearing of a homeless encampment, again in Harlem. A number of homeless men were hospitalized and two died of their injuries.

The *Amsterdam News* story recapped Kowalski's career, listing nine times he'd been accused of using excessive force and nine times he'd been exonerated. He'd received one reprimand early in his career for throwing a man down a flight of stairs. In at least three of the incidents, the city settled with the families of the victims for significant amounts. The newspaper calculated that over the years the city had paid out in excess of a million dollars on Kowalski's behalf.

'The man is a monster,' Adele said. 'How did he get to be a high-ranking police official?'

Ambler gestured with the stack of papers he held. 'If you go by what's here, he has an unblemished record. He volunteered for dangerous assignments. He's got buckets of commendations and citations. All of the people he killed or injured were criminals. On paper, he looks like a hero.'

Adele waved the *Amsterdam News* story at him. 'A lot of people don't think he's a hero.' She looked up. 'Something's wrong with a man who's responsible for that much violence. Does Mike Cosgrove know about all of this?'

'He will tomorrow.'

Adele watched Ambler for a long minute. Her eyes were red-rimmed, her eyelids drooping. 'I want to spend the night,' she said, her voice heavy with sorrow. 'But I don't want you to touch me. Reading about this man has made me so disgusted I'd scream if you touched me.'

In the morning Ambler brought the copies of the news stories to Mike, who glanced at most of them but took his time reading the *Amsterdam News*. When he finished he was thoughtful but didn't say anything.

Ambler waited a moment and then spoke for him. 'You don't want to believe one dirty cop killed another dirty cop, and I don't blame you. Those guys are supposed to be your brothers. You'd never have to look behind you; they'd always be there. But that's not who they are. They gave up any claim they had to your loyalty. They were criminals. . . . Either Morales or Kowalski killed Donovan. Rats turning on rats.' He stopped and waited.

'Don't lecture me. You can tell me about librarians. Don't try to tell me about cops.' Mike raised his eyebrows. 'And the prosecution exhibit one is?'

This of course was the problem all along. 'You didn't find anything in the files we could use?'

Mike didn't bother to answer.

'One of the victims in Will Ford's story said he had an in with a sergeant.'

Mike smirked. 'That'll go a long way toward convincing a

jury. I thought about calling in a favor and having someone lean on Morales. Flip on Kowalski or take the rap himself.'

'You think it's Kowalski? Why not do that?'

'It doesn't work unless you really do have something on them. With no evidence, it's Morales's word against Kowalski's. Anyone with any sense wouldn't believe either of them. But Kowalski would win if it came to that. I'll keep sifting through the evidence from the original investigation. But I doubt anything useful will turn up. Someone sanitized the files pretty good.'

Mike was quiet for a long moment. 'I got other cases I can drive myself crazy with. I don't need the impossible.' He took a quick look at Ambler out of the corner of his eye. 'This won't be the first one I had to let go of. It eats at you to let someone walk away you know is guilty.'

He lay straight back, staring at the ceiling. 'That's not really true. The fact is if you can't prove it, you don't know they're guilty. In some cases, you might have inadmissible evidence or a witness backs out; then, you can say you know. Otherwise, you don't know; a lot of things pointing to it ain't enough. A reasonable doubt is a real thing.'

In his condition, it wasn't surprising Mike would feel defeated. The fact was you could make the argument they were defeated. Ambler was out of ideas, too. His sensible self agreed with Mike. They didn't have proof, so how could he be sure he was right? He didn't even know whether it was Morales or Kowalski he was sure was a killer. Still, he had to do something. He pulled out the only idea he had, half-assed though it might be.

'I have an idea. You're not going to like it.' He paced the few feet of floor space at the foot of the bed between the door to the room and the window. He didn't look at Mike. 'You're going to say I've gone John Wayne on you again. But you'll have to listen to me because you can't go anywhere and you can't close your ears.'

He laid out McNulty's plan to trap the killer by tricking him into believing Ambler had – or would soon have – incriminating evidence in his files at the library and would soon know who really committed the murders on Manhattan Avenue decades before.

Mike surprised him. 'Letting a suspect think we have evidence we don't have is as old as the hills.' His eyes lit up. 'Half the time it doesn't work, and it probably won't work this time since both our pigeons have used it a dozen times themselves over the years . . . Even so, what do we have to lose if we give it a try?

'But not at the library. I can't put two civilians in harm's way, even if one of them is that pain-in-the-ass bartender. We'll do it here in my hospital room.'

They argued for a few minutes. Ambler said the library was the only place anyone would believe that kind of incriminating evidence would be found. 'A librarian in Texas would have discovered a journal Will Ford kept,' he said more than once.

Mike's plan was to let word leak out that he'd pulled the files on the Manhattan Avenue murders. 'I'd let someone in Records know I'd found something that would blow the lid off the department. It will seep down to One PP in no time. You can bet your ass Kowalski has his sources in the Central Records, same as I do . . . You'll have to figure a way to get the word to Morales. It shouldn't be hard.'

'You'd be putting yourself in danger. How would you protect yourself?' Ambler tried again. 'You can't move.'

'I'll have Denise rig up my service revolver by wiring it to the top of the IV stand with a string tied to the trigger that I can pull with my teeth.'

Ambler stared at him in amazement. 'You can't be serious.'

Mike snorted. 'Of course I'm not serious. But I can move my hands and arms and I can wiggle my toes. Still, the shape I'm in I don't trust myself with a weapon. They're moving me to the rehab hospital in a couple of days. The way I'll handle it is I got a couple of friends left on the job who'd give me a hand if they thought I was going to be murdered.'

Ambler hesitated a moment and then told Mike some of his pals were already on the job. 'I talked to Frank Elliot when you first got here because I thought you were in danger, and a regular cop might not care so much if you were protected.'

It took a lot to surprise Mike, but he'd done it.

'Elliot assumed I was talking about you being in danger from Anne Gannon's ex-husband, so I let him think that. I didn't think he'd believe me if I told him what I actually thought.'

'Frank isn't who I had in mind. But it's good to know he's willing to protect me. . . . I'll need guys in street clothes, maybe borrow hospital scrubs. They'd have to take shifts here when they're not on the clock.

'A lot of things could go wrong. If it's Kowalski we have to tiptoe. He might come in because he wants to talk about what he thinks I found out. He might be protecting Morales. He might be protecting me from something I don't know about. We can't have anyone jumping the gun. You stay the hell out of it.'

It was in Mike's hands now. Late that afternoon, Ambler stopped by the Library Tavern and told McNulty about the new plan.

'Better to let the professionals handle the rough stuff if it comes to that,' McNulty said. 'What are you going to do if you catch the culprit dead to rights, read to him?' He chuckled. 'Or if it's me catches him, what do I do, make him drink?' He chuckled some more.

When he'd done enough chuckling, he poured them both shots of Irish whiskey and agreed to drop a few hints with his friend Alberto the bartender in Washington Heights that the guy would pass on to Morales. That would be enough to get the word to Big Nick if Morales thought he needed to be in the know.

Still later when Ambler called Adele, he told her, 'We have no idea how fast things will happen. But if someone thinks there's evidence lying around that would convict them of murder, I doubt they'd wait long.'

'I'm worried about Mike.' The worry echoed in her voice. 'He's helpless lying in that bed. What if the killer sneaks in without Mike's cop friends seeing him?'

'If I thought I'd be any help, I'd go over there. But he told me to stay out of the way. And that's probably best. He knows how to handle violent situations, how to prepare, what to watch for. As McNulty pointed out, that's not something I know how to do.'

TWENTY-FOUR

Mike Cosgrove felt that rush of adrenaline that came before every major bust. When he was young, he didn't exactly relish an upcoming action that had the potential to turn ugly. But the heightened sense of adventure, the excitement, did produce a physical reaction that in a strange way was pleasurable, like the feeling after the first sips of a good wine. Not something he controlled, more something that controlled him, a strange eagerness.

As he got older, the feeling wasn't the same. It was there but muted. His conscious mind played more of a role. The adrenaline rush was tempered by recollections of the times things had gone bad. This was how he felt now, lying in the bed waiting. But something else was at work this time. Never before had he been a decoy, defenseless, dependent on someone else.

He'd put others in this kind of a situation, victims of a protection racket, junkies who wore a wire to trap a dealer. He hadn't done that kind of operation often. He didn't like them for this very reason, putting the hapless patsy in danger with no way to defend himself if something went wrong. He'd always felt responsible for the informant in those situations and one time barely missed getting killed when he jumped in to rescue a CI when things went bad.

Now he was the patsy, lying here waiting. He wasn't scared, though he should have been. He waited with a kind of resignation, maybe like the lamb waiting for the slaughter. At one time, he would have felt a supercharged excitement at the chance of bringing down a killer. Not this time. He wanted it to be over. He wanted to see his daughter. He wanted to get his legs under him and walk out of this goddamn hospital.

As the last light of day faded on the ceiling, he told himself he might die tonight. All his life he'd worked hard to keep himself alive. What he realized now was that in the end the effort was futile. He would die. If he got by tonight, that would be great. He might live long enough to have grandkids. But whatever happened, it wouldn't be all that long before he'd be dead. Like Chris Jackson, like Will Ford, like the brothel madam who read poetry, like the young whore everyone loved.

'Hey, soldier! How you feeling? They can't kill an old war horse that easy, can they?'

He recognized the voice: George Kowalski. Had Frank seen him come in? His heart pounded. A rush of adrenaline shot through him but it wasn't excitement; it was fear. He tried to calm himself so the fear wouldn't show in his eyes.

Kowalski moved quickly to the side of the bed and pulled the call button away, his eyes focused on the files from Central Records on the bed beside Cosgrove. He picked them up and tucked them under his arm. At the same time, he took a leather pouch from his suit jacket pocket and a syringe from the pouch. Cosgrove watched the pouch. It was like one his father used to use for his pipe tobacco. He shifted his eyes to the syringe.

'I'm going to juice up your morphine a bit.' Kowalski reached for the IV line. 'An accidental overdose, or another cop suicide with the help of a sympathetic hospital worker. You'll travel peacefully. That's the least I can do for a brother officer. Who wants to live knowing they'll never walk again?'

'Since you missed the first time,' Cosgrove said. His voice sounded like someone else's. He cleared his throat.

'I could've shot your daughter, and I didn't.' Kowalski's tone was softer. He had the forlorn expression of a man who'd been misunderstood.

It was now or never. Cosgrove took his shot. 'You're not going to find anything worth reading in those files. I didn't.'

Kowalski hesitated.

'It's a trap. You took the bait. A dozen people know about it.'

Kowalski shook his head as if to clear it, to understand what he'd heard. Cosgrove thought he might ask a question. The uncertainty lasted only a second. He took the cap off the syringe and opened a small valve on the IV tube. Cosgrove made ready to lunge for him though it would mean he'd be crippled for life.

A peaceful death or life as a cripple, what kind of choice was that?

In that split second the room exploded with sound, voices shouting, furniture scraping against the floor, something crashing to the ground. He heard, 'Freeze,' as darkness descended.

He opened his mouth to scream, 'Pull the IV out.' He didn't know if any words came out. He didn't hear them. He reached for the bandage where the IV went into his vein. He didn't know if he reached it.

He lay with his eyes closed listening to the voices, indistinct murmurs. One, two, three voices, he couldn't tell. He was alive. The inside of his head was thick. He knew what they meant by cobwebs, more like his head was filled with molasses. Why did he think of molasses? It took a moment. He was in bed. He was in the hospital. It was coming back. Kowalski. Frank saw him come in.

He opened his eyes. Ambler and his girlfriend Adele sat by the side of the bed. Denise sat at the foot of the bed.

'Just in time delivery, right?' he said. 'They got him. They waited a minute longer they could've gotten him for murder.'

'They almost did,' Ambler said.

'Naloxone,' Denise said. 'They got it into you in time. You hadn't even stopped breathing.' She sounded very professional, not quite through her first year of nursing school.

TWENTY-FIVE

A week after George Kowalski's arrest, a large envelope arrived at the 42nd Street Library addressed to Adele, from the Wittliff Southwestern Writers Collection at the Albert B. Alkek Library at Texas State University in San Marcos. The envelope contained pages copied from one of Will Ford's writer's journals.

I'm thinking about a story based on Dominique and the murders when I was in New York in the early '90s. The murders weigh heavily on my mind. How could they not? I have nightmares. I want to write about it. And I will, but I need to be careful. One of the killers is still around and he's not going anywhere.

When I write the story, I'll need to change a lot of things for sure to make him unrecognizable. It's unlikely he'd see the story. But he might get wind of it. The thing is if I get too far away from what actually happened, it won't be the story I want to write.

A New York City cop I got to know held up an illegal gambling operation and killed two people. That part I think I can do. His name was Billy Donovan and he was a plainclothes cop who worked on a task force that meted out vigilante justice in a kind of lawless neighborhood I lived in at the time. I'd want to base a character on him because I know him so well, and he was so central to what happened. I also knew the man and woman he killed, and of course, Dominique who was killed when he was killed. The whole episode was more gruesome and corrupt than the best I could make up.

Dominique and I were playing blackjack in a gaming room in the basement of a brownstone in Upper Manhattan. My Dominique. We'd made love in her room upstairs right before. Of course, she called it turning a trick, and I, of course, paid for it. The apartment above the gaming room was a brothel. I made the mistake of falling in love with Dominique.

Billy killed the man who ran the gambling operation and the woman who ran the brothel in the process of robbing them. He hadn't intended to, but they got in his way. You wouldn't think cops did things like that. But this was New York City when crack cocaine was king. Billy was crazy – well known for 'tuning up' street criminals, which meant beating the shit out of them, sometimes for no reason. That's not right. He had a reason. He was the good guy. They were the bad guys.

I expected him to kill me and Dominique because we were witnesses. Instead, he let me go and she stayed with him. To my regret, he was in love with her, too. Worse regret for me, she was in love with him. I could title the story, 'Don't fall in love with a whore . . . she'll betray you'. Given the opportunity all women will betray you. But that's another story.

When I left that apartment at 891 Manhattan Avenue for the last time, a man and a woman lay dead on the floor, murdered by Billy Donovan, who I suppose was a friend of mine. Billy and Dominique were alive. He was waiting for his sergeant. The next day I read in the paper four people were dead in a shoot-out on Manhattan Avenue.

What the hell happened? Billy had made a mistake. The Mobster behind the gambling operation and the whorehouse was paying Billy's sergeant for protection. Not aware of this, Billy had called to tell the sergeant he'd run into a problem with a side job he was doing and needed his help in covering it up. The sergeant covered it up all right, taking care of Billy and Dominique, and telling a story to the papers that was as made up as anything I ever wrote.

The sergeant never knew I'd been in the apartment. If Billy and Dominique had had a chance to betray me, they didn't. If the sergeant had known, he'd have found me wherever I went and killed me. So when I write this story, it's not going to look like what actually happened.

'What do we do with it?' Adele asked Ambler after they'd both read the journal entry.

'I'll ask Mike. But I think we give it to the D.A. If Ford had told me this, he might still be alive.'

'Will it convict the mucky-muck of murder?'

'I don't know. But I'd like to hear him try to explain it.'

On another Tuesday, the week after George Kowalski pleaded not guilty to attempted murder and a slew of other charges at his arraignment, Ambler and Adele had a busy day. In the morning, with Ambler's grandson Johnny wearing his first suit, they attended a hearing at the New York State Supreme Court at 100 Centre Street at which John Ambler was told he had fulfilled his sentence and would be released from prison. Ambler, Adele, and Johnny burst into tears, while John shook hands with his attorneys, David Levinson and another young man who looked to be closer in age to Johnny than he did to John.

In the afternoon, following an invitation from Denise, they watched as Mike Cosgrove took his first steps at Rusk Rehabilitation Center, just up First Avenue from Bellevue Hospital Center.

That evening, John and Johnny had dinner with the Youngs, and Ambler went to dinner at Adele's apartment, a romantic dinner with candles and roses on the small dining nook table. There was a bottle of champagne, which Ambler drank quite a bit of because Adele took only a couple of small sips.

After the dinner, Ambler sat on the couch to finish his champagne and Adele came and sat on his lap. She kissed him. 'I've got something to tell you.' Her eyes sparkled as if she'd drunk all that champagne. 'I'm going to have a baby.'